AGAINST THE CURRANT

AGAINST THE CURRANT

Olivia Matthews

St. Martin's Paperbacks

This is a work of fiction. All of the characters, organizations, and events portrayed in this novel are either products of the author's imagination or are used fictitiously.

Published in the United States by St. Martin's Paperbacks, an imprint of St. Martin's Publishing Group.

AGAINST THE CURRANT

Copyright © 2023 by Patricia Sargeant-Matthews.

For information, address St. Martin's Publishing Group, 120 Broadway, New York, NY 10271.

www.stmartins.com

ISBN: 978-1-250-83904-6

Our books may be purchased in bulk for promotional, educational, or business use. Please contact your local bookseller or the Macmillan Corporate and Premium Sales Department at 1-800-221-7945, ext. 5442, or by email at MacmillanSpecialMarkets@macmillan.com.

Printed in the United States of America

St. Martin's Paperbacks edition / February 2023

10 9 8 7 6 5 4 3 2 1

To My Dream Team:

- My sister, Bernadette, for giving me the dream.
- My husband, Michael, for supporting the dream.
- My brother, Richard, for believing in the dream.
- My brother, Gideon, for encouraging the dream.
  - And to Mom and Dad always, with love.

CHAPTER 1

"He's back." My maternal grandmother, Genevieve Bain, spoke as though she'd swallowed something distasteful. Like bad fish or lukewarm tea.

I knew right away who she meant. Claudio Fabrizi, the owner of Claudio's Baked Goods.

Not again.

Dropping my head between my shoulders, I fisted my hands to keep from ripping out my hair by its roots. I didn't have time for this. It was early Friday morning. Still there was so much to do before tomorrow's soft launch of our family-owned West Indian bakery in Little Caribbean, the heart of our adopted Brooklyn, New York, neighborhood. Spice Isle Bakery was the realization of my childhood dream. Claudio, the pesky pastry chef, was single-handedly sucking the joy from the experience. Seriously, how many times were we going to have the same conversation?

I lifted my head, squared my shoulders, and gritted my teeth. After taking a moment or eleven to mentally prepare for yet another exchange with the bothersome baker, I straightened to my feet. Raising my eyes to the left-side front picture window, I met Claudio's glare. The stocky middle-aged man was of average height—perhaps five inches taller than me—and looked like a petulant rooster.

From the dining section on the other side of our customer service area, Granny kissed her teeth. She stood among the small, square tables, holding one of the dark yellow wall hangings she'd crocheted for the shop. The décor was coming together under her hands. My eyes swept the window valances and tablecloths that repeated the colors of the Grenadian flag: yellow, green, and red.

"Doesn't he have anything better to do than to stand there, eyeing us?" Her Caribbean cadence released her words in waves.

Urgh! I hated conflicts. This would be our third. *Oh, brother.*

Stepping away from the baked goods display I'd been dusting, cleaning, and arranging, I circled the silver granite counter. "I'll talk with him." *Again.*

"That one there?" Granny harrumphed. "There's no talking to him, *oui.*"

She wasn't lying. During our second exchange, he'd been more annoying and pedantic than the first. No doubt this third time would be even less constructive than the other two. We kept repeating the same arguments in defense of our opposing sides. There wasn't anything left to say.

"I have to try, Granny." *Didn't I?*

"Lynds." The concern in her voice halted my steps. Her long silver hair was pulled back into a tidy bun that emphasized her wide, worried dark brown eyes. "Should you get your father?"

I won't lie. A part of me wanted to take the out she'd offered me and run to Daddy. Have I mentioned I hate conflicts? I actively tried to avoid them. And my parents were just in the kitchen behind us, preparing the space for maximum efficiency. But if I wanted my parents to see me as their partner in this business venture—which I absolutely did—I had to stop hiding behind them. I had to project strength, confidence, and capability. I might as well start now.

I shook my head. "It's my shop. I'm the majority shareholder. It's my responsibility."

Straightening my spine, I drew a deep breath. It filled my senses with the light, fruity smell of the lemon-scented all-purpose cleaner I'd used on the store, including the blue-tiled flooring, sand-toned checkout surface, and glass product displays.

As I stepped outside, a brisk late-March breeze washed over me. It danced with my thin ebony braids before continuing on its way into the store. I pulled the door closed before facing Claudio. "Mr. Fabrizi, shouldn't you be taking care of the customers at your bakery?"

Claudio had opened his store in our Brooklyn neighborhood around the time I'd graduated from college five years ago. Since then, the community had learned all about him, including that he didn't live anywhere near us. In contrast, he'd shown little interest in the people who supported his business.

In my peripheral vision, I saw several pedestrians slow their steps and glance our way as they passed. Claudio was well-known and disliked in the area. I sensed their curiosity as though they were straining to catch even a few words of our conversation. I hated being the center of attention. It made me want to crawl into a hole.

Claudio waved a sheet of paper at me. "You've put these notices all over the place." In his thick fist, I recognized a copy of the sand-toned circular I'd designed to announce our soft launch, which was taking place Saturday and Sunday.

I'd delivered copies of the flyer to neighborhood homes. Several nearby businesses had agreed to carry a quantity to notify their customers. I was grateful for the cross promotion.

Annoyance stirred in me, prickling my skin in the cool late-winter weather. "You keep coming back here, saying the same thing: You don't want me to open my bakery. But I *am* opening it. Tomorrow. Nothing will change that."

Beneath my thin braids, the hair on the back of my neck stirred. Was Granny watching from the store? Of course she was. Please don't let her come out here. I didn't want my grandmother to be subjected to Claudio's hostility.

He shoved the flyer into his pocket and narrowed his eyes at me. "Open your bakery if you want, but don't do it in my market."

I frowned, searching his round, swarthy features. What was wrong with him? "Are you that concerned about competition? We aren't offering the same products. Our menu offers traditional West Indian pastries and entrées. You're offering cookies, cupcakes, and doughnuts."

"There's overlap."

"Very little. Your cinnamon rolls and our currant rolls are very different pastries."

"You'd better think twice before you open your place tomorrow." Claudio nodded toward my family's bakery. "If my business suffers because of you, you're going to wish you never had."

Was that a threat? It sounded like a threat. I couldn't let

that pass. I owed it to my family and myself to defend our business. We'd worked too hard for too long to allow anyone to jeopardize our goal.

"Don't threaten me." I was furious with myself when my voice wobbled. Fisting my hands, I continued. "Our bakery opens tomorrow. On schedule. If you don't like it, *you* move."

I turned on my heels. Every muscle in my body from head to toe was stiff with anger. I forced my legs forward, yanked open the bakery door, and marched inside.

Granny caught me in her arms. "Lynds! I'm so proud of you for standing up for yourself and the family like that."

I let her warm embrace soothe me. Several calming breaths drew in her scent, vanilla and wildflowers. "Thank you, Granny. But I'm not sure I can do anything like that again."

"Lynds?" My mother, Cedella Bain Murray, joined us. She sounded worried.

I looked toward the kitchen as she and my father, Jacob Murray, walked through the swinging door that connected the kitchen in the back of the shop to the customer service area.

Daddy's frown sharpened his spare, handsome features. "What happened?"

Keeping an arm around my waist, Granny turned to my parents with a proud grin. "Your daughter told Claudio Fabrizi that if he didn't want competition, he should move his bakery."

"Really?" Mommy's eyebrows flew up her forehead. "How'd he take that?"

"Not well." I walked past my elders, heading to the kitchen.

I needed a cup of tea. "But, please God, I hope we've heard the last of him."

"I can do more than mix cinnamon and sugar." My challenge was ignored by my crazy busy family early Saturday morning.

My older brother, Devon Murray, stood to my right at the top of the long center island, preparing coconut bread in our state-of-the-art commercial kitchen. His movements were natural and confident. It was as though he'd worked in a bakery all his life. He hadn't.

At thirty-two, Dev was the youngest junior partner of an international law firm headquartered in downtown Brooklyn. That's where he'd been yesterday while Granny, Mommy, Daddy, and I had been putting the final touches on the shop. Baking was more proof that he could do anything he set his mind to. In high school, he'd been captain of his track-and-field team, senior class president, and valedictorian. He was my hero. And he couldn't be more different from me.

Dev had always been big, strong, and self-assured. No one would ever think of picking on him. I'd been a quiet child who'd grown into a fearful adolescent and an insecure woman. My lack of confidence had been catnip to school bullies. The more they mocked me for being shy and awkward, the more I'd withdrawn into myself.

My parents fretted about my nonexistent social life. But I had my family. We'd get together with cousins, aunts, and uncles for holiday potlucks and picnics, trips to amusement parks and the beach, visits to relatives in Grenada and Canada. Otherwise, I preferred staying home, studying, reading, or daydreaming about my plans to open a family-owned West Indian bakery.

I looked at my father across from me, kneading dough for another batch of currant rolls. Beside him, my mother spread the spice filling over the pastry in progress. Last but far from least, Granny was beside me with a serrated bread knife, portioning the most recent batch of currant rolls pulled fresh from the industrial oven behind us. Each slice freed the pastries' warm, sweet, buttery aroma. Heaven on earth.

These three family elders were my role models, my rocks. I asked their advice before making big decisions. Those discussions sometimes crumbled into arguments with Granny stubbornly disagreeing with my parents. Their guidance came from a place of love and encouragement. They just had different ways of looking at things.

The air in our kitchen was swollen with nutmeg, cane sugar, coconut oil, and other herbs and fruits. The scents floated across the room and through the air vents in search of hungry pedestrians.

Along the way, it blew past me. My stomach hummed in recognition. Before I could reconsider, I pilfered a roll from the tray and bit into it. The warm, flaky pastry melted in my mouth. Sweet currants, cinnamon, and sugar kissed my taste buds. I closed my eyes in ecstasy.

"Stop eatin' the product." Granny slapped my arm.

My eyes popped open. "This is quality control." I spoke around a mouthful of deliciousness. "And since you hit me, you're going to have to change that glove."

Our antics caught my parents' and brother's attention. My father stopped singing along with the Bob Marley ballad flowing from the sound system. His duet was a sure sign he was nervous. Some people sing when they're happy. Others when they're sad. Daddy fed his every emotion with song, drifting further off-key with each verse. When he was especially anxious, he turned to Bob Marley.

To be fair, we were all on edge. In less than an hour, we were launching Spice Isle Bakery. Today was the realization of that childhood dream of opening a family-owned shop that sold pastries and entrées reflective of our West Indian heritage.

I closed my eyes as the enormity of the day washed over me again. My heart raced. My head spun. Inside my plastic disposable gloves, my palms sweated. I spun between *Hooray, the day's finally here!* and, *Oh, no, I need more time!*

But back to my complaining about being stuck mixing ingredients while everyone else did the real baking. I'm not going to lie. That irritated me. Also, I needed to distract my family before the kitchen imploded under our combined anxiety. Tension was building like water rising to its boiling point.

"Just because you *could* do more doesn't mean you *should*." Dev's amusement covered a thin layer of strain. His dark eyes, so like Daddy's, were warm with gratitude for my efforts to get their minds off the soft launch.

"Ouch." I smiled back.

My parents and Dev wore matching black chef's smocks and caps. Since most of my time would be spent behind the customer counter, I'd tucked my thin braids beneath my chef's cap. But instead of the smock, I'd draped a red apron over my tan khakis and a blue jersey with Spice Isle Bakery's yellow, red, and green logo. An image of Grenada was screened onto the lower-left corner of the apron.

Granny had agreed to the cap and apron for the sake of hygiene but had refused both the smock and the jersey. At eighty-one years young, she'd spent most of her life wearing the Grenville postal workers' uniform in her native Grenada. Now that she'd retired and was living her best life with us, she was all about fashion 24/7/365. For today's soft launch, she'd paired a cobalt blue, long-sleeved dress with matching low-heeled pumps, and her Larimar stone necklace and earrings set.

"Your baking isn't up to snuff." Granny continued cutting into the pastry's buttery sweetness. "It doesn't meet the quality and standards we want to offer in the bakery."

And there it was: brutal bluntness cushioned with love that was integral to the West Indian family. Imagine what she'd say and how she'd say it if she didn't love me. I shook my head with a smile and went back to measuring and mixing ingredients. Busywork. *Oh, brother.*

Spice Isle Bakery had been my dream since I was seven. When I was growing up, my family had been pulled in different directions. My parents were working. Dev was running track. And I was dodging bullies. In the evenings, though, we'd fix dinner together and the kitchen would come alive with laughter and stories of the past, present, and future. The day's sadness would disappear and I'd feel like myself.

My secret wish of opening a family-owned business had formed from those experiences. I could cook. Our menu included entrées and a few other dishes that would allow my talents to shine. Baking was a struggle for me, though. It seemed the harder I tried, the worse the results. Still I was determined to master the skill. Cooking was a pleasure, but baking—manipulating the dough, creating the batter—that brought me joy.

And it's the reason I decided to open a bakery instead of a restaurant. I wanted to sell West Indian pastries. I hoped that would keep us connected to our roots and let us share our culture with the greater community. We could've done that with a restaurant, but a bakery seemed more intimate. We'd connect more easily with our customers, exchanging stories with other immigrants and opening a dialogue with neighbors who were born and raised in the United States. It also would give me a space where I'd feel safe.

But there was a problem. Mommy and Daddy had wanted me to have a stable job like Dev, who'd always planned to study law. To invest in the shop, I'd saved every penny I could. When I was a child, those funds had come from my allowance, birthday money, and odd jobs. Later, it came from the stingy wages I'd earned working for a nightmare of a boss at a marketing firm. I didn't tell anyone my plans at the time, not even Dev. They'd only worry about the risk of going into business for myself.

I watched as Mommy arranged the raw currant roll loaf on a pan before turning to prepare another. She wielded the rolling pin before her fingers deftly manipulated the dough. Try as I might, that was a skill I couldn't master.

Unlike Dev, I hadn't inherited my parents' baking talents or engaging personality. Or height. I was the quiet one, sitting in a corner while Dev was in the center of the action. People couldn't believe I was his sister. I half expected them to ask for a DNA swab.

"You know, Lynds, if you spent as much time practicing your crusts as you spend on your kickboxing, your crusts would be even better than your father's." Mommy was reading my mind again.

"And your mother's." Daddy exchanged an adoring look with her. According to Granny, they'd been gazing at each other like that for the past fifty years. I admired their relationship even as I told myself I didn't have time for one. I was building a business.

When I was thirteen, my parents had enrolled me in kickboxing classes at the local gym to build my confidence after they'd learned I was being bullied. I loved the activity. At the gym, I felt strong and capable. I'd been taking lessons for fourteen years, getting up at 4:00 a.m. to work out before arriving at the bakery by six. The gym, the bakery, and church—not necessarily in that order—were the places I loved the most, and they were all within walking distance of my home.

"Don't mind the baking for now. You can cook, and you've done a great job with the publicity." A smile shaped Mommy's lips, but her brown eyes darkened with concern.

The same questions that had troubled my mind for months came screaming back. Had I done enough? Was this going to work? What if it didn't?

I'd put everything I'd learned from school and work into promoting our store. After earning a full scholarship to Brooklyn College, I'd graduated cum laude. My business degree had an emphasis in marketing. I'd then earned an MBA, all while working part-time for a doughnut franchise. After graduate school, I'd gotten a full-time job with the marketing firm. I'd learned a lot about promoting a business—and putting up with difficult personalities.

Our bakery had to work. I already had ideas about expanding into the currently empty upper floor to host events like anniversary celebrations, wedding receptions, and birthday parties. I shouldn't get ahead of myself, though. Focus on the launch. One thing at a time and do it well, as my parents and Granny always said.

Looking around the room, I felt both confidence and concern. Vivid splashes of color across the far wall rescued the space from the stark white, black, and silver colors of the shiny new equipment—emphasis on "new." The wall was my parents' homage to Caribbean music greats past and present. The top of the space displayed another of my mother's talents in her large, framed color renderings of soca star Buju Banton, the King of Calypso Harry Belafonte, and of course reggae pioneer Bob Marley.

The Grenadian flag was centered below their images. Its red border stood for courage. Yellow triangles denoted warmth and wisdom, while the green ones symbolized the island's vegetation. The nutmeg was its most famous produce. The large center star signaled its capital, St. George's, with six smaller ones representing each parish: Saint Mark, Saint Patrick, Saint Andrew, Saint John, Saint George, and Saint David.

These things represented our Caribbean heritage. We'd earned our U.S. citizenship and had made this country our home. But our roots were important to us. Our bakery would help to keep our traditions alive in us and in the community. The desire to share our culture with our adopted country motivated me to build Spice Isle Bakery into a household name.

It was hard to separate our dream from our debt, though. Every item in the shop and every inch of the building was the result of my family's savings. My parents and I were co-owners. Granny and Dev were our not-as-silent-as-I'd-like minority partners. Our local bank also had contributed in the form of a high-interest loan that would take a decade and a half to pay back. My throat dried. There was so much at stake. It was daunting, but I was determined to make this work. My resolve was another sign the bakery was changing me for the better. The old me would've shrunk from this hurdle, but the bakery's success meant too much to me. It forced me to develop a spine.

My loneliness had gotten worse when Dev had gone away to Harvard University. Cambridge, Massachusetts, was five and a half hours from Brooklyn by train, but it felt like the entire distance of the country. I didn't think I'd ever find my way out of my shell. My first year of college had been a nightmare. I'd been way out of my comfort zone, meeting new people, navigating new social settings. Several of my childhood tormentors had enrolled at Brooklyn College, too. *Oh, joy.* But working with my family over the past four years to plan the business had helped me see my worth. Granny in particular had encouraged me to discover my voice.

She'd come to live with us the summer before my sophomore year of college and had drawn me from my shell with a simple question: "What do you want for your life?"

No one had asked me that before. My parents had raised me to be practical. Study hard. Get a job. That was the example my mother had set. She was a talented cook and an amazing artist. But she'd become a math teacher. Being an artist was too risky. Whereas Mommy always played it safe, Granny had never met a risk she didn't want to take. She'd challenged me to follow my dreams.

Gathering my courage, I'd told my parents I wanted to open Spice Isle Bakery—and I wanted their help. They'd needed more than a little convincing, but in the end they'd agreed to take the leap of faith with me. Without Granny, Spice Isle Bakery wouldn't exist.

I checked my rose cell phone. "It's time to put the finishing touches on the display counter."

Sending up a brief prayer for success, I collected the tray

of currant rolls Granny had portioned and pushed through the door to the customer waiting area. Time to step out of my comfort zone again, this time to greet our guests.

My smile wouldn't be denied.

The customer order line stretched from the shiny new register in front of me to the entranceway across the blue-tiled lobby. Most patrons entered in groups of two, three, and four. A few arrived on their own. Their conversations twined with the classic Bob Marley hit "Could You Be Loved" bouncing from our sound system. Several customers' hips picked up the rhythm.

Our guests took in the décor as they formed the line. My family and I had rolled up our sleeves and gone through months of renovations. Now I took a mental step back to try to view the space through our customers' fresh eyes. The simple window valances, sturdy tablecloths, and delicate wall hangings reflected the bold green, yellow, and red of the Grenadian flag.

We were proud to showcase my mother's original artwork. She'd brought to life signature scenes from the island: Grand Anse Beach's blue-green bay and warm white sand, steel pan bands leading a parade of Samba dancers in jewel-toned costumes, and the Port of St. George's bordered by the azure waters of the Caribbean Sea and the grandeur of the emerald mountain range.

For those who'd been to Grenada, our little bakery would evoke memories. For those who'd yet to visit, perhaps the yearning would be planted.

"Morning, Tanya. You're out early this morning." Granny hailed our elderly neighbor.

She'd set up two chairs and a folding table against the wall to my right between the counter and the kitchen. The high-traffic area suited her need to be in the middle of the action at all times. Her latest crocheting project, a flower-patterned doily, provided cover to eavesdrop and observe.

"Good morning, Genevieve." Tanya Nevis smoothed her gray, chin-length hair before unbuttoning her spring coat. The small woman's dark eyes surveyed the crowded waiting area. "I'm out early and still find myself in a long line."

Conflicting waves of calming relief and exhilarating success swept over me. Were my feet on the floor or floating above?

I slipped off my sterling silver bracelet and tucked it beside the cash register. Its four charms—shaped to resemble a nutmeg, boxing gloves, a pair of jogging shoes, and a chef's hat—kept catching the cash register's keys, making it hard to type.

Claudio was next in line. A deep red flush darkened his round, dusky cheeks. His twentysomething-year-old son, Enzo, was with him. He'd brought reinforcements. This couldn't be good. Reluctant to make a scene in front of so many guests on the day of our soft launch, I forced a pleasant greeting. "Welcome to Spice Isle Bakery, Mr. Fabrizi. How can I help you?"

His stocky body trembled with anger. "I'm going to shut you down."

My smile drained. I drew a sharp breath, catching the scents of confectioners' sugar and baked fruits from assorted treats in the kitchen behind me. Claudio's fury was directed toward me, but his words threatened my loved ones. Big mistake. I couldn't—wouldn't—allow anyone or anything to harm them. I thought I'd made that clear the last three times we'd spoken. Granted, I still struggled to find the courage to defend myself. But my family was a different matter. I'd do anything to protect them. And my family and our bakery were one and the same. By targeting one, he was attacking both. I wasn't going to let anyone take this place from us.

"I won't help with that." My voice cooled as I returned his glare. If it was a battle he wanted, then bring it.

CHAPTER 2

Conversations ebbed beneath the music as friends and neighbors tuned into our exchange. The mood in the shop shifted from excitement to something somber.

Enzo stood silent beside him. His eyes avoided the question in mine. A tall, good-looking guy with dark wavy hair and kind black eyes, he must favor his mother, God rest her soul. What was it like to have the neighborhood bully for a father?

Claudio's beady brown eyes dismissed me. He craned his short, thick neck out of the collar of his shirt as though trying to see into the kitchen. "I'm done dealing with you. You're just a kid. Where're the owners? I wanna speak to them."

As the majority owner of the shop, I wouldn't let him dismiss me. I straightened to my full five-foot-three-inch height. "You have been dealing with one of the owners." Granny punctuated my statement with a curt harrumph. He was upsetting her. My muscles tightened. "You have to leave."

Claudio swung his arm toward the front of the bakery.

I pressed a fist to my chest as his wild gesture almost knocked over Ms. Nevis behind him.

"Watch it!" The older woman dodged the surprise assault with an agility that defied her age. The hot glare she delivered to the back of Claudio's head should've turned him into a pillar of salt. Enzo offered her an apologetic look. She rolled her eyes and turned away.

I took the belligerent baker to task. "You almost struck Ms. Nevis."

"Who?" Claudio scowled at me. "What're you talking about?"

"Ms. Nev—" Why bother? "Just leave."

"*My* shop is across the street." Claudio's lank brown hair strained away from his broad forehead as though it also took exception to his tone.

The picture window behind him framed early-morning pedestrians, shoppers, and joggers. The weather was warm for late March. We'd lucked into a beautiful day for our soft launch. But as for Claudio's point, his business wasn't as close as he implied.

I jerked my left thumb in the direction of his shop. "Your bakery is two blocks up and one block over. If you're so concerned about keeping it open, go back there and serve your customers."

Enzo's shoulders rose almost to his earlobes. His movements were jerky as he rested his hand on his father's arm. "Come on, Pop. Let's get you back to the store."

Claudio yanked free of his son's touch. His eyes widened as though my words had offended him. Seriously? "Of all the spaces in the borough, why'd you pick *this* one for your bakery?"

Customers began to grumble and shoot dark looks at my

harasser. Enzo shifted his feet, darting glances around him. His unease made me uncomfortable. I wondered again about his relationship with his father. It was one thing when parents embarrassed you by telling corny jokes, like mine did. But his father's dramatic performance in front of a crowd was taking parental humiliation to a whole other level.

I pressed my fingers into the cool sand-toned checkout counter. "My family has lived in this community for more than twenty years—"

"Not that it's any of your concern." Granny snapped her interruption.

"This is about more than having a business of our own. We know our customers. They're our neighbors. We know the people who own the nearby businesses and they know us." I gestured toward the pharmacy and fish market across the street, which I could see through our front window. The fresh produce store on the corner was just out of view. "Even more than this, we love this country we've adopted as our home. Sharing our culture and our customs is a way of expressing that love. It's our way of giving back." And as Granny had said, any insight beyond that wasn't his concern.

A murmur of agreement rolled across the waiting area. Enzo cut several quick looks at the patrons in front and behind him. His attention paused on a tall, curvy blonde in a navy skirt suit. His narrow shoulders lowered and his even features relaxed into a smile of recognition. She smiled back.

Claudio's face tightened. "You chose this place because you think you can steal my customers."

His claim made my skin burn. A red haze clouded my vision. This wasn't the first time he'd made that accusation. The fact he'd repeat it made it harder to hold on to my patience.

Stepping back, Enzo gripped his father's shoulder. "All right now, Pop. Let's go." His entreaty lacked conviction.

Claudio slapped his hand away. "We'll leave when I say it's time to leave and not before. I want to hear her admit she's trying to cut into my profits."

I'd had enough. I'd been dealing with bullies all my life. I wasn't about to be bullied in my own bakery. This was my space. No one could come here and treat me as though I didn't matter.

I stomped around the counter and stopped within an arm's length of my antagonist. "What're you afraid of, Claudio? There are plenty of customers in this neighborhood. Let them decide whether they can support two bakeries or if there's one they prefer."

A buzz of support swirled around me. My grandmother's hum of approval rose above the rest.

Claudio flushed almost as purple as a West Indian sunset. He opened and closed his mouth a couple of times before words emerged. "I'm going to make sure your bakery shuts down."

I squared my shoulders and matched him glower for glower. "I'd like to see you try."

Granny echoed my snort of disdain.

"You think I'm bluffing?" His voice was like gravel crunching beneath sandals.

It was well-known Claudio had identified as threats all the bakeries in the area that had come before ours and had harassed them into closing. It's how he'd kept his stranglehold on the baked goods monopoly in the neighborhood for so many years. With me, though, he was wasting his breath. I refused to be intimidated. I was going to protect my family's investment. We had too much to lose—and it wasn't only money.

"I've told you before your threats don't scare me, but you don't listen. Instead you've brought your ridiculous claims in front of my guests as though that's supposed to intimidate me. All you've done is embarrass yourself. Get out of my shop and don't ever come back."

"Lyndsay!" My mother's gasp cut off the pounding in my ears. She'd rushed out of the kitchen, my father and Dev in her wake. "Are you all right?" She placed her hands on my shoulders, shifting her body to protect mine and confronting my tormentor. "What are you doing here?"

The guests nearby cleared room for the cavalry while remaining close enough to follow this new development. Daddy and Dev wore matching scowls of anger and outrage. Their eyes frosted over as their attention shifted from me to Claudio.

"I'll tell you what happened." My grandmother's commanding voice cut across the thick and sudden silence. "My granddaughter once again defended our family and did a good job, *oui*."

A muscle flexed in my father's jaw. Tall and slim, he stood head and shoulders above the stockier trespasser. "My daughter told you to leave." His accent was taut as he chewed the words.

Claudio directed his scowl at Daddy. "You're her father? What the h—"

"Pop, let's go." Enzo's tone conveyed urgency this time. But he didn't wait for his father to hear him. He gripped Claudio's arms and half carried, half dragged him to the door.

"Take your son's advice. You're not welcome here."

Daddy's voice followed Claudio and Enzo to the door. "And don't speak to my daughter again unless it's to apologize."

The crowd parted like curtains in front of a stage as our guests witnessed the end of the performance.

"I don't have *nuthin'* to apologize for." Claudio spat the words as he struggled against Enzo's firm hold. "And even if I *wanted* to come back, your business won't be here in a week. Mark my words."

I planted my hands on the hips of my khakis. His temper tantrum didn't impress me. "If you dare to come back, your son'll be carrying you out."

Mommy turned from the wood-framed glass door as it closed behind father and son. Her eyes were wide. "Lynds, you did well, standing up for yourself. There was no reason for you to taunt the man, eh? It could get you in trouble."

I hadn't been standing up for myself. I'd been carried away by an urgent need to protect my family from all threats. For them, I had the confidence to do anything, including taking on the neighborhood bully. Hopefully, this would be the last time we'd have to deal with Claudio.

"Folks." Mommy raised her arms and voice to claim our guests' attention. It was a skill she'd perfected as a high school math teacher. "We apologize for the disturbance."

Laughter carried from the back of the group. "We should be thanking you. This was the best entertainment I've had since the last carnival."

More chuckles and cheeky quips followed. My mother lifted her hands to signal for calm. "Thanks for coming out and for your patience. My daughter will take your orders now."

"Dev, help your sister." Daddy inclined his head toward the guests who continued to chat and chortle. His expression eased. "It looks like we have a good turnout."

He gave me a final searching look. His eyes had darkened with concern. I offered him a smile to let him know I was OK. With a nod, he stepped aside to let Mommy lead him back into the kitchen. Dev took up a position in front of the register.

I smothered a sigh and faced our guests. "Everybody, I apologize for the scene." The sharp tearing sound of someone sucking her teeth drew my regard to my grandmother.

"What were you supposed to do, eh? The man came inside here vexed, causing all kinds of ruckus. Threatening this. Threatening that. You had a responsibility to stand up for yourself and for the family. You did well, love."

Granny's words soothed me. She understood me better than anyone else, perhaps because we were so alike in both personality and appearance. We were short in stature with full figures and heart-shaped faces.

Personality-wise, we were both quick to anger when faced with injustice, especially if that unfairness affected family and friends. I only wished I was as outgoing. And that I'd inherited her fashion sense.

Dev shook his head. "Don't encourage her, Granny. That kickboxing's gone to her head."

I scowled at Mr. Know-It-All. "You weren't even here, so don't pretend to know anything about anything."

"Your sister's right." Ms. Nevis gave Dev money for her currant roll and bush tea. The widow lived a few houses up from my family's home. "Claudio is a *nasty* man. He came looking for trouble, you hear? You should be proud of your baby sister for standing up to him. Who knew she had it in her?" The tiny but tough lady smiled at me as though dispensing a benediction.

"Thank you, Ms. Nevis." I returned her smile as I picked up the pad and pen before greeting our next customer. "What can I get for you, sir?"

The tall man appeared to be in his late twenties. Early weekday mornings, I often saw him standing at the bus stop in a suit and tie. Today, a long-sleeved gray jersey with the New York Knicks basketball team logo and worn dark blue jeans draped his athletic build.

He raised his voice with its thick Brooklyn accent and a five-dollar bill. "Where's your tip jar?"

My eyes dropped to his money, then lifted back to his face. "We don't have one."

Our checkout counter was crowded enough with the cash register, menu stand, order pad, and pens. Oh, and the two-gallon acrylic jug full of colorful tissue paper butterflies my grandmother insisted would bring us luck. I was reserving judgement on that. I'd always thought lucky butterflies were supposed to be alive, but she'd insisted these paper ones would do in a pinch.

"Really?" His expression was serious, but his dark eyes twinkled. "You should get one if you're going to offer live entertainment."

Other patrons erupted with laughter. Their hilarity was contagious. It was what I'd needed to dispel the last of my tension from the ugly morning scene. It reminded me of those magical evenings in the kitchen, cooking dinner with my family.

The good-natured ribbing continued as Dev and I filled their orders. With my brother and grandmother backing me up, I returned some of the teasing, matching wits and vol-leying jokes. Between the banter and reggae fusion music, it didn't take long to restore my good mood. Daddy had replaced Bob Marley with a playlist I recognized from our last family potluck. I glanced over my shoulder at the throughway to the kitchen. He must be feeling better. I breathed a sigh of relief.

Our next customer greeted me. "Thank you." The lilt of her native Haiti was in her voice.

"For what?" Puzzled, I considered the woman in front of me. Thick raven hair framed a pale brown face dominated by large ebony eyes. I'd never seen her before.

Her smile was mysterious. "Callaloo and dumplings, please."

I hesitated. She hadn't answered my question, which only increased my curiosity, but I didn't have time to pursue it. I'd already kept my guests waiting long enough during that ex-change with Claudio. I packaged her order while Dev pro-cessed the sale. There was a bounce in the long strides that carried her out our front door. Who was she and why had she thanked me?

A tall, attractive woman stepped to the counter. A pleas-ant expression warmed her smooth brown face. Joymarie Rodgers had been two grades ahead of me in high school. She reminded me of my cousin Serena Bain: cheerful and welcoming. I'd always liked her. And she'd always liked my brother.

Dev had inherited my father's good looks with his spare, warm sienna features. His wide brown eyes assessed the world around him with patience and humor. Given my im-patience and skepticism, we didn't always see eye to eye.

Joymarie tossed him a flirtatious look before greeting me. "Are you going to yell at me like you yelled at Claudio?"

"That depends on what you order. You look lovely, Joy-marie. Doesn't she, Dev?" I pointed toward her bright floral dress, which hugged her generous curves.

"Yes, I suppose." He gave her an absent smile before lowering his eyes to the register. That wasn't like him. Why was he acting so weird?

And how was it my super-smart brother, who'd graduated at the top of his class since kindergarten and had passed the bar on his first effort, hadn't noticed Joymarie's interest in him after all these years? Everyone else had. Odds were good she'd become a regular, at least until she realized Dev didn't work here full-time. He'd taken a few days off from his law firm to help out.

This weekend was our soft launch. We were closed Mondays and Tuesdays. Wednesday would be our official grand opening, then Dev would return to his firm the following Monday. It was anyone's guess as to how often we'd see Joymarie after that.

"Claudio's afraid of competition. He knows his dust-dry cookies are overpriced." The other woman's gaze kept drifting to Dev. "And he's rude to his customers. I bet you surprised him, though, Lyndsay. No one stands up to him. Not even Enzo, the wimp."

I'd experienced Claudio's rudeness years ago. When I'd gone to his bakery, he'd complained about how long I'd taken to make a selection. I'd left without buying anything and had never gone back. Rewarding discourtesy didn't sit well with me. But I responded to Joymarie's comments with a noncommittal smile. I didn't want a reputation of bad-mouthing the competition. My family would be so ashamed.

"What can we offer you?"

Joymarie studied the menu on the wall. "You have so many good choices. What d'you think I'd like, Dev?"

His eyes widened, shifting left and right as though searching for an escape. "I don't know."

She lowered her voice. A flirty smile curved her full pink lips. "Would you like to?"

His brow creased. "How else would I be able to ring up your order?"

I closed my eyes. *Oh, brother.* He wasn't this clueless. What was going on? I'd corner him later to find out.

Joymarie's shoulders slumped. The cheer in her voice dimmed and her choice of coconut bread and corailee tea seemed random.

The blonde who'd exchanged suggestive looks with Enzo was the final customer in line. "What d'you recommend?"

My mind went blank much as Dev's must have when Joymarie had asked the same question. In my defense, I'd never seen her before. How would I know what she'd enjoy? *Think fast.*

Did she have a sweet tooth? An image of our baked banana pudding came to mind. It mixed the flavors and textures of soft fresh bananas, crunchy pecans, and toasted almonds.

Or would she prefer something milder? Spice cake. Lime zest tempered the raw cane sugar and molasses. Cinnamon, nutmeg, and allspice rounded out the flavors.

"Do you like bananas?"

Her round, rosy features brightened. "I sure do."

Yes! I felt as though I'd passed a test. "Then I'd recommend the baked banana pudding."

"Sold! I'm Robin Jones, by the way." She presented her business card with a flourish. "I'm an event planner."

Networking with an event planner had infinite possibilities. I imagined my family providing cakes for business events and curried chicken dishes for weddings, each opportunity strengthening our bottom line—and shrinking our bank loan. "I'm Lyndsay Murray and this is my brother, Devon."

As Dev processed her order, I pulled on a pair of plastic gloves and cut a generous portion of the dessert. The knife slipped through the cake-like consistency, freeing the warm, heady aromas of nutmeg, coconut cream, coconut rum, and brown sugar. Wrapping the treat in parchment paper, I turned back to the counter.

Robin reached out and squeezed the pastry. "Oooh. Still warm."

I slipped her purchase into a bag. "Enjoy."

"I'm sure I will." She gave me a considering look. "I really think we can help each other."

I took a slow breath. I hadn't expected to make networking connections so quickly, but I couldn't let this opening pass. "I'm always interested in mutually beneficial business opportunities."

"Good to know." She collected her purchase, then nodded toward Dev before leaving.

That was promising. Hopefully, one taste of our banana bread pudding would seal the deal. We'd have another revenue stream keeping our bakery afloat, despite Claudio's threats.

CHAPTER 3

"All Souls' Day celebration, you know it?" Granny struck up a conversation with my last customer of the morning.

The young man was waiting for the fish cakes and callaloo take-out order he'd placed for his family. In addition to pastries, we offered a limited menu of hot, traditional breakfasts and lunches. I took the lead on cooking those dishes and poured my heart into every serving.

"No, Ms. Bain." Reggie offered her a shy smile. The teenager had just started high school. His house was a few blocks from us, but he often visited his classmates who lived on our street. Granny took pride in knowing everyone who came to our neighborhood. It was probably a holdover from her years working for the Grenville post office.

"Back home, during All Souls' Day, we'd set out a plate of food on a windowsill." She set down her doily-in-progress and tilted her head. The look in her eyes grew distant as though she was surrendering bit by bit to memories far in the past. "It's tradition, a sign of respect for our loved ones who've passed."

I'd heard this story before and loved it more each time. Granny was the keeper of so much of our family history and cultural traditions. I could listen to her endlessly. Putting together Reggie's order at the counter, my movements slowed as I let her carry me back into her All Souls' Day story again.

"This particular year, my sister, Winnie, and I were ten and nine." Great-aunt Winnifred was my grandmother's older sister. She'd immigrated to Toronto, Canada, to be with her children around the same time Granny had come to live with us. Great-aunt Winnie had passed of ovarian cancer a few years ago. Granny's tone was still wistful when she spoke of her.

She continued. "Our parents, aunts, and uncles had set out a plate. It was *big, oui*. Piled *high* with rice and peas, *thick* pieces of jerk chicken, a nice portion of boiled yam, plenty of callaloo, and a glass of coconut milk. The food smelled *so* good, and Winnie and I were *so* hungry."

My grandmother paused as though recalling the meal. She continued, drawing images with her words to draw us deeper into her memory. "Winnie and I were sitting beneath the window in a little piece of shade. It was afternoon. The sun was beating down on us. Hot. Hot. She told me to be quiet. Be patient. We had to wait until we heard the old heads move from the window before we could act. Then quick as a bird, Winnie grabbed the plate and the glass of coconut milk. We shared it. *Woi*, that food was *so* good. I've never had better. When we finished, we put the empty plate and glass back on the sill and waited beneath the window. Quiet. Quiet."

In my grandmother's smile, I saw the mischievous child she'd been. I also saw the satisfaction of a full meal for a too-often hungry little girl. "When our elders came back, they were *shocked*. They made so much ruckus, shouting and jumping. They were calling, 'Lord, Lord! The spirits ate the food! They ate the food!'"

Shaking my head, I smiled, just as every other time I'd heard my grandmother's story. Was it the memory itself or the way she told it? Maybe a combination of the two.

I'd met my great-aunt Winnie several times before her death and regretted never asking for her side of this story. Would her version be different? I couldn't imagine my intro-verted great-aunt being the mastermind of such a trick, but I had no problem picturing my grandmother in that role.

Reggie burst out laughing. Tears streamed down his brown cheeks. It was several seconds, perhaps a minute, before he controlled his hilarity and caught his breath. "Did you ever tell your parents the truth?"

Granny pressed back against her chair. Her hand rose to her chest to rest above her heart. "Boy, you crazy? They would've given us some licks for sure." She shook her head as though imagining the beating. "No, Winnie and I swore we'd never share the truth, at least not with them."

After wrapping Reggie's breakfast order with care, I placed it in a bag and presented it to him. He'd forever have a place in my heart for listening with such respect and pa-tience to my grandmother's story. Wiping tears of laughter from his cheeks, he stood to leave. He was still laughing as he held the door open for another customer.

"She's a practical joker." The voice carried to me from the checkout counter.

I straightened to see one of our guests who'd eaten alone at a table in our dining section. She was leaning against the counter near the cash register, smiling at my grandmother.

Her striking blue eyes sparkled with humor in her pale, square-jawed face.

"Yes, she is." I offered a welcoming but professional smile and crossed back to the register. "How can I help you?"

"I'm Jenna Frost." She extended a business card. "I wanted to compliment you on the delicious breakfast."

"Thank you. We hope you'll come back." I scanned her business card. *Jenna Frost, Blogger and Influencer, Subscribe to The Frost Forum.*

"I will. I'm impressed both by the food and the way you handled Claudio Fabrizi." Jenna's eyes searched my face as though trying to discern my innermost thoughts.

I forced myself not to fidget under her intensity. "Thank you."

Most guests didn't seem turned off by my altercation with the rival baker. Perhaps the angry scene wouldn't hurt the shop. I sent up another prayer and kept breathing.

"That man is immoral." Jenna's matter-of-fact statement seemed harsh. During the awkward pause that followed, I had the sense she was waiting for a response.

Time to change the subject. "I'm glad you enjoyed your breakfast."

"The portions were just right. Your prices are reasonable, and your customer service is wonderful. I'm going to write a glowing review about your bakery on my blog tomorrow."

I caught my breath. "Jenna, that's wonderful. Thank you."

I'd sent announcements about the opening to all the local print publications, radio hosts, TV reviewers, podcasters, bloggers, and other influencers. It was a strategy that had worked well when rolling out new products for clients of the marketing firm I'd worked for during the four years my family and I were preparing to launch our bakery. I hadn't heard of *The Frost Forum*, though. She must be new.

"You've earned it. And thanks for showing Claudio there are people he *can't* push around." Jenna marched out of the bakery.

Her parting words lingered with me. What had Claudio done to get on her bad side? Probably Claudio being Claudio.

"The butterflies are working." Granny must have overheard my conversation with Jenna. "First you met the event planner. Now this woman said she's giving you a good review." She nodded toward the jar of paper butterflies on the counter. "Told you."

I gave her a skeptical look. "Granny, they aren't real."

She kissed her teeth. I turned from her to scan the few dining tables we'd arranged on the opposite side of the shop. They were occupied by groups of friends enjoying breakfast and Buju Banton's music. They didn't appear to need anything. I sighed with satisfaction.

Reaching to play with my charm bracelet, I found my right wrist bare. The memory of placing it beside the cash register returned. I searched the area and the counter, but it wasn't there. "Granny, have you seen my bracelet?"

"No, love. You lose it?"

"It'll turn up, if not now, then later when I give this place a good cleaning after we close." But I felt agitated and out of sorts. My left hand reached for my right wrist again. Where could it be?

"You're not sweeping tonight, though, right? Leave that for the morning. We just opened the bakery. We don't want to stir up any duppies."

"No, we don't, especially since all we have for protection are fake butterflies." My answer was distracted.

"Oh, ho." Granny's reply was chastising, but I only gave it part of my attention.

My mind was still on my sterling silver jewelry. If someone had swiped it, I'd be *so* upset. And my parents would be heartbroken. They'd given it to me for Christmas four years ago and had added a new charm every season. Each one represented something about me, something I was proud of and that they celebrated. The nutmeg represented my Grenadian heritage. Boxing gloves referenced my kickboxing. Jogging shoes recognized my running, and the chef's hat celebrated our bakery's launch. It seemed silly, but losing that bracelet felt like losing parts of myself.

I pictured Jenna Frost, leaning against the counter. It was hard to imagine her taking my bracelet, then being so bold as to chat with me afterward. Wasn't it? Or what about the mysterious customer who'd thanked me but wouldn't tell me why?

I sent a baleful look toward the jar of butterflies. How could they send us so many customers but then let my bracelet slip through the cracks? What else were they missing?

CHAPTER 4

"Good morning, beautiful people!" My cousin Serena Bain was a force of nature. She blew into the bakery. Her mango orange dress was a splash of drama against the backdrop of our wood-and-glass entrance. Strokes of coconut green and lemon yellow filled a handkerchief hemline that fanned around her long calves.

Reena had inherited our grandmother's love of fashion and her outgoing personality. She was a showstopper, but even if she could enter a room quietly, she'd still draw attention. From her vivacious smile to her buoyant gait that moved to a beat she could make others hear, her presence radiated joy. Wherever she dragged me—happy hour at the Met rooftop, Off-Broadway musicals in the city, live tapings of late-night talk shows, or grand openings of soca clubs—Reena brought the party.

Setting aside the broom I was using during a much-needed lull in customers, I turned to greet her. "That entrance would've been so much more impressive when this place had been packed."

I adjusted my cap, ensuring my braids were covered. The

last thing we needed was for a diner to bite into a meat patty and find my DNA among the ingredients.

Reena's thick braids incorporated burgundy highlights, unlike mine. They swung above her shoulders as she straightened from our grandmother's embrace. "I saw the crowd, girl, which is why you're seeing me now." She pulled me into a hug and rocked us side to side. My cousin topped me by several inches. "I was like, 'I want to *capture* her attention. Not *compete* for it.' I'm so proud of you! Mommy and Daddy are stopping by later." Reena referred to her parents, my mother's older brother and his wife.

Mommy, Daddy, and Dev must have heard Reena's voice. They rushed into the waiting area to greet her. Laughter and cheer swelled out across the room. I felt like we were in a sports arena—or a family gathering.

"The line was *so long*." She hugged Mommy and Daddy in turn. "I had to go shopping until the crowd thinned."

Like Dev and me, Reena didn't have a discernible accent from either Brooklyn or the West Indies. We were born in Grenada but had immigrated to New York when we were very young. Somehow the Grenadian accent at home and the New York accent in school had canceled each other out.

"You *had* to, huh?" Granny snorted. "Since when do *you* need an excuse to shop?"

"Wait till you see what I got for you, Granny." Reena winked at our matriarch. "I even found items from your favorite designer."

A pregnant pause. Wait for it . . . "Clearance Sale!" we called in unison. But we pronounced it "Clarence" to make it sound like a person's name instead of a retail discount. Granny had an advanced degree in budget shopping, a talent she'd passed on to the rest of our family.

"So you left our long line to wait in someone else's." Dev smiled as he stepped back from Reena's embrace.

"I knew your opening would be a hit." Reena patted her flat stomach. "You're all incredible chefs. Well, Lynds, your baking still needs some finesse."

"Whatever, Reena." Used to my cousin's good-natured teasing, I rolled my eyes. The whole family knew my pastries made good door stoppers. For now.

Granny slid me a teasing look. Her dark brown eyes sparkled with amusement. "Reena, you missed the show."

Reena arched a well-shaped eyebrow. "You mean Lynds cursing up Claudio Fabrizi?"

I gasped. "I didn't curse him up. How'd you hear about that?"

Her smile was wicked. "Everybody's talking about it. Three groups of people stopped me on my way back here, and news is spreading fast. They were all like, 'You should've heard your cousin telling off Fabrizi.'"

I squeezed my eyes shut and groaned. "What a disaster."

"It's not that bad." Reena hugged my waist. "People are glad you gave him a piece of your mind."

Dev snorted. "Maybe she should've given him a smaller piece."

Reena jerked her chin toward him. "Spoken like an overprotective older brother. You don't have to fight Lynds's battles anymore, remember? She's a smart woman. And if words don't work, she can use her kickboxing moves to knock him on his butt. Besides, I bet even Enzo's glad Lynds told his father off."

Daddy folded his arms. "But doesn't Enzo work for his father's real estate business? Why wouldn't he be supportive of him?"

Mommy nodded. "The way he likes to spend money, he'd better be."

"You mad owah?" Granny questioned our sanity. "That boy and his father have been on the outs since his daddy forced him to stop dating that woman. He was looking at her *hard*, you see?"

An image of Enzo smiling at the woman in the navy skirt suit popped into my mind. "D'you mean Robin Jones, the event planner?"

"You saw it?" Granny did a quick impersonation of Enzo and Robin exchanging looks. It was really quite good, if a little overplayed. My grandmother might deny it, but I was convinced she was a frustrated actress. "They'd been dating before Claudio threatened to fire Enzo if he didn't end it."

Reena's voice was almost reverent. "Granny, you know everything. I wish I had your network of informants. I'd use it to get ahead of the fashion trends." Reena was a buyer for a chain of clothing stores, her dream job.

Granny tossed her hand dismissively. "Most things I hear on my own, you know. But Della's right. He'd better mind his daddy or he won't be able to buy his toys: Expensive watch. Pricey clothes. Fancy car. *Woi!*"

As he'd pulled Claudio from the store, I'd noticed Enzo's designer watch, too, which triggered another reminder. I rubbed my right wrist. "Dev, have you seen my bracelet?"

"No." He glanced over his shoulder toward the register. "Did it fall off the counter?"

"Oh, oh." Mommy's expression collapsed with concern. "Don't mind. It'll turn up."

I nodded absently, glancing again at the register before returning to Reena. Swallowing my disappointment, I focused on more urgent concerns. "I hope this negative gossip doesn't turn customers away from the bakery. People won't come if they think we're going to pick fights and throw them out."

Reena shrugged a slender shoulder. "That's what Claudio does and people still go there." She squeezed my arm. "Don't worry. It'll take a lot more than your arguing with Claudio to make people shun the store."

I hoped so. For now, I'd have to take her word for it. I turned to my parents. "Have you decided whether we should apply to be a vendor at the Caribbean-American Heritage Month Festival? We've been talking about this for a while. The application deadline's coming up."

"Why do we have to make up our minds now?" Daddy's tone was laced with dread. "The festival isn't until the end of June. It's only March."

June was Caribbean-American Heritage Month. It was a time for the West Indian community—those who'd emigrated from the islands, were born to people from the islands, or had been accepted into the fold—to recognize and highlight our culture and our contributions to our adopted home. The monthlong celebration's final event, the Steel Pan Day in Prospect Park, was three months away. My parents had been using that time frame to drag their feet on making a final decision.

"The festival planning's already started." I felt like a broken record. I threw Granny a desperate look. She motioned for me to keep going. I forced myself to relax. "The online application is due to the organizers next week, remember? The deadline's only five days away."

"Is doing the festival this year really a good idea for us?"

Mommy swept her arm, indicating the few customers still lingering in the dining area. "We have our hands full with the launch. We should focus first on building up the bakery."

"Exposure from the festival will help with that." I'd presented these reasons so often, I could recite them in my sleep. "We've been attending the event for years. You've seen the crowd it draws, and they're not just from Brooklyn. The festival advertising will help build our name recognition all over the city."

"Lynds has a point." Dev crossed his arms in a stance similar to the one Daddy had taken. "Being a featured vendor in the event will immediately increase our visibility. It's an opportunity too good to pass up."

"I agree with the children." Her declaration made, Granny returned to her chair like a queen to her throne. "I don't see why you wouldn't be able to take care of the bakery while you prepare for the festival. At least send in the application. You can change your mind later, if you can't manage."

Mommy pursed her lips, exchanging an uncertain look with Daddy. "Let's think about it a little more."

The bakery door opened. Several new customers had arrived. I welcomed them with a smile before turning back to my parents. "All right, but please don't take too long." I gestured between Granny, Dev, and myself. "The vote is already three to two."

Daddy gave me a teasing look. "Your granny and Dev have smaller investments, so technically the vote is tied, fifty-fifty."

He gestured for Mommy and Dev to precede him into the kitchen. Dev sent me a sympathetic look. Granny gave me an encouraging nod.

I swallowed a sigh as I turned back to the register. Was

I being too pushy? Every step toward launching our bakery had been a battle with my parents. Why should the festival be any different?

Reena stopped me with a hand on my arm. The concern in her dark brown eyes made my stomach dip. "Lynds, I'm proud of you for standing up for yourself, but be careful with Claudio. He's already ruined a lot of people. He's ruthless, and if he thinks you've crossed him, he's going to get revenge."

I swallowed as a cold wind crawled through my skin. "Understood, Cousin."

West Indians tended to be superstitious, but did I have cause to believe Reena had read my future?

CHAPTER 5

Sunday morning and all roads led to church. That's what Granny always said. After the early Mass—I took Sundays off from kickboxing—I'd hustled back to the home I shared with her and my parents. I'd needed to change clothes before going to the bakery to help prepare for its 10:00 a.m. opening.

Our neighborhood, like many in Brooklyn, was older. Well-maintained single-family homes rose with dignity from the sidewalks. Tall and narrow, they stood close together like supernatural guardians watching over the community.

I'd been traveling these blocks for more than twenty years. I could find my way with my eyes closed just by the sounds and silences of the streets. Barking dogs, shrieking children, and scolding parents led me through the residential area to the heavy traffic, angry car horns, and bellowed conversations of the commercial zone.

But it was when I stepped onto the corner of Parish and Samuel Avenues that the streets took on yet another vibe. Something shifted in the air, quick and subtle. I felt it and heard it. I even smelled it.

This tiny piece of real estate was the heart and soul of Little Caribbean. So many of our neighbors had West Indian roots and shared their heritage here. I'd grown up wanting to do the same.

I weaved my way through the pedestrian traffic. The cadence of my steps shifted as I instinctively responded to the syncopated beat of the soca music jumping from the produce market on the corner. Jerk smoke wafting out of the carry-out diner across the boulevard woke up my appetite. A Trini flag shared window space with cosmetics and medicines in the nearby pharmacy.

As I traveled the half block to the store, I was hailed by business owners on both sides of the street. Their compliments and good wishes confirmed my family was right to make the decision to open our shop. I entered the store through the back door off the rear parking lot.

Reggae fusion music already was playing in the kitchen. Mommy, Daddy, and Dev were working hard to fill the pastry trays with treats and prepping ingredients for the hot meals. Granny was overseeing their activities.

"Good morning, family. Listen to these great reviews." My words rushed together as I crossed the kitchen to turn down the sound system. Without taking time to shed my coat, I dug through my crimson backpack for my copy of the *Brooklyn Daily Beacon* and printouts of the online reviews.

Drawing a steadying breath, I read the *Beacon*'s glowing review first. "'Spice Isle's currant rolls melt in your mouth. The bakery brings the tastes and the ambiance of the islands to New York.'"

My family's cheers and shouts of relief overpowered my voice. Throwing my head back, I laughed with joy. "Wait! There's more."

I shuffled the printed sheets until I found a particular online review. After sharing the complimentary descriptions of our menu and the meal, I came to the closing sentences. "'You can count on this blogger becoming a regular patron. Try Spice Isle Bakery and tell them Jenna Frost sent you.'" I looked up from the sheet to find Mommy, Daddy, Granny, and Dev grinning back at me. "She included a link to our website."

"Wait. She gave them all the link?" Mommy turned from the counter where she'd been brushing melted butter over the rectangle of dough destined to become a currant roll. Her grin faded and her eyes stretched wide. "That's goin' to attract a lot of people. Will we be able to keep up?"

"If you need extra help, I'm here. After all, I taught you everything you know." Granny stood in the doorway between the kitchen and customer area. From that spot, she could monitor the bakery's entrance while participating in the behind-the-scenes action.

"Thank you, Genevieve." Daddy dropped cubes of butter and shortening into the commercial dough mixer. A cloud of flour puffed out of the stainless-steel bowl. "We couldn't have done any of this without you and Dev."

"After all the sacrifices you and Mom have made for our family, I was happy to help." Dev sliced the currant rolls he'd collected from the oven.

"I'm going to use these reviews in flyers and distribute them around the neighborhood tomorrow and Tuesday." I stored my coat and knapsack in the closet, then washed my hands before pitching in with the baking preparations. "With luck, they'll help bring customers to our official grand opening Wednesday. I'm sure we can keep up with the orders, especially if you let me help more with the baking."

Mommy wrinkled her nose as though I'd suggested adding honey mustard to the beef patties. "Keep practicing your dough. It's still not coming out right."

Accepting defeat—for now—I measured the dried currants, ground cinnamon, and brown sugar for the pastry filling, mixing them together in a clear plastic bowl. Their scents mingled with the smell of the melted butter. "I wonder if Claudio has seen the reviews." I dreaded the possibility of encountering our rival again.

Granny harrumphed. "You know he's never seen such strong reviews for his bakeshop. He's probably hiding in shame. He's a *bababooy*."

My grandmother wasn't the only one who thought Claudio was a fool. If we polled his business tenants, I had the sense they'd agree.

I'd be lying if I didn't admit a part of me hoped he was hiding. But I couldn't shake the sense Claudio wasn't done causing problems for us. I recalled Reena's words. "I don't know, Granny. It's more likely these reviews'll make him angry. I don't want him to bring his ugly temper here again."

"Don't worry about him." Dev spoke over his shoulder as he measured and sliced the currant roll, freeing its sweet, buttery scent. "Claudio's a bully. Bullies back down when others stand up."

With luck, my big brother would be proven right. I was tired of dealing with tyrants.

CHAPTER 6

"Since we now have confirmation that our pastries are a hit, do you feel comfortable enough to apply for the festival?" I slipped my parents a look as I continued mixing ingredients for the pastry fillings. Granny's sage counsel repeated in my mind: When we were at the bakery, I was my parents' equal partner. They could go back to bossing me around when we were home.

Daddy's wide-eyed expression seemed phony. "We weren't uncomfortable."

Granny kissed her teeth. "Of course you were. What other reason could there be for your cold feet?"

"They have a point, Dad." Standing beside me at the center island, Dev sent our parents a cheeky grin. "Lynds has been pushing for this since before we opened the bakery, but you and Mom always find an excuse to delay it: filing for the business license, getting the location and suppliers, opening the shop. We've done all that. Now what's holding you back?"

He'd laid out his summation like a TV courtroom drama. As usual, I was impressed.

Daddy glanced at Mommy, slipping easily into their silent communication. They'd always been a team, a unit. They faced every decision together, including the one to immigrate to the United States more than two decades ago. I'd been a baby and didn't recall their departure, but it couldn't have been an easy decision to leave Dev and me with Granny while they prepared a new life for the family in the United States.

"We want to focus on building our customer base before we expand," he said.

"But I keep telling you participating in the festival will help us do that." How could I get them to understand?

Mommy sent a look of appeal toward me. "Lynds, don't you think we're moving too quickly?"

Was she right? Was I pushing them too fast? I glanced at Granny. She rolled her eyes and shook her head.

"No." I returned my attention to my parents. "You're looking at this as, what do we have to bring to the festival? We have our product. I see what the festival can bring to *us*: more customers. And we need that."

Mommy hesitated. "Moving quickly isn't our thing." She waved a hand between Daddy and her. "It's your thing."

"And we know who you get that from." Daddy arched a thick black eyebrow toward Granny, drawing our attention to her.

"Whadayou?" Granny swept her eyes over us as though she didn't understand why we were looking at her. Today's fashion statement was a rich amethyst maxi dress. Images of tiny seashells covered the flowing material.

Daddy turned back to me. "'When horse reach, donkey does reach and pass.'"

My parents had been quoting that West Indian wisdom

since my childhood: The race was not for the swift; it was for the slow and steady.

"'Nuthin' beat a trial but a failure.'" Granny came back with an equally familiar expression: You can't succeed if you don't try. That sentiment had kept me going over and through every obstacle in our path as we struggled to launch our enterprise. "It's almost ten, you know. People lining up already. I'll open the store."

I yanked my cell phone from the front pocket of my tan khakis to check the time. Wow. It was a minute to ten. How had that happened? I picked up the tray of treats. "The festival is an opportunity that's too important to ignore."

Mommy darted a wide-eyed look at Daddy. Her features were tight. "Lynds, we're a small operation. Just your father and me. Dev's going back to his law firm next Monday. Suppose we can't keep up with the orders? What are we supposed to do then?"

"We'll be fine." Her panic pulled at me, trying to drag me under. It wouldn't take much. I stepped back to prevent myself from giving in to it. "Granny said she'd help. And I can handle the entrées. I'm going to complete the online application. We're not guaranteed to be accepted anyway. If we are, then we can decide whether we can do it."

Dev gave me an approving look. I answered with a grateful smile. He and Granny were two of my strongest supporters. I tried to present myself with confidence for my parents' sake, for my sake. But my insides were knotted with nerves. Carrying the tray of pastries to the display case, I reminded myself things always worked out in the end. Well, usually.

Was it my imagination or was the customer line even longer this morning than it had been yesterday? Many of the patrons were repeat customers. Some were new to the bakery but not new to me. Had the reviews lured them—or news of my confrontation with Claudio? I caught some of the knowing smiles and whispers spoken behind hands. It could be the latter. Either way, the tension in my neck and back relaxed at the sight of the crowd drawn to the shop. I squared my shoulders. *We can do this.*

For the next hour plus, I cleared my mind of everything but greeting and feeding our guests. A few of the patrons in line moved their hips and shoulders in time to the popular reggae fusion song spinning from our speakers. Others were chair dancing as they waited—not too long!—for their orders. So far, Daddy hadn't played one Bob Marley song. A good sign.

Granny entertained a little girl with an embellished telling of one of the many times in her childhood she'd allegedly come face-to-face with Papa Bois, the West Indian folklore protector of the forest. Some considered him our version of Bigfoot. The bakery was providing new audiences for my grandmother's tales. The small girl's huge eyes stretched. Her lips formed a perfect circle as she hung on Granny's every word.

I handed an older couple a tray with their banana breads and bush teas. "Thank you so much for your order. Enjoy."

I turned to greet the last guests in line. An electric current swept through me, freezing all of my muscles, including the ones that kept my smile in place. My vision narrowed to just one of the two men in front of me.

Bryce Jackson. Captain of the champion Flatbush Early College High School basketball team. Senior class president. Heartthrob. We lived in the same neighborhood, but somehow I hadn't seen him since he'd graduated from Flatbush

Early almost eleven years ago. He'd been a senior my sophomore year.

The native New Yorker's smile was slow and confident.
"Looking good, Lyndsay."

He recognized me? He remembered my name?

Just like that, I flashed back to my awkward teen years.
Creeping through the crowded high school hallways, I'd tried
to scrunch down behind my textbooks like a turtle, hiding
in my shell, hoping no one would notice me. Man, that's a period in my life I wouldn't return to on a bet. Now my adolescent crush was standing in front of me, telling me I looked
good. My heart was racing like Kirani James, the professional Grenadian sprinter who'd earned a gold medal in the
2012 Olympics.

He looked pretty good himself, but acknowledging that
would lead to madness, the kind that periodically duped me
into searching the internet for updates on him. I'd learned he'd
joined the New York Police Department and had risen to the
rank of homicide detective. That might explain why he'd cut
the braids he'd been so proud of. He may have thought the
more conservative style helped him blend in. It didn't. Instead
it enhanced his tawny angular features and deep-set hazel
brown eyes.

"Hello, Bryce." Battling the urge to rip off my chef's cap
and fluff my braids, I inclined my head toward his companion, an older white man with comfortable features and salt-
and-pepper bedhead. His partner? "What can I get for you,
gentlemen?"

"Information." The older man was a few inches shorter than
Bryce and outweighed him by several stones. He flipped a police badge and identification at me. "Detective Stan Milner,

NYPD. You seem to know my partner. You had an altercation with Claudio Fabrizi yesterday."

And Claudio had called the homicide *department?* This can't be good. "It wasn't an 'altercation.'" I used air quotes. "Why are you asking?"

Bryce scanned the dining area. "Is there someplace we can speak privately?"

I gestured to indicate our open floor plan and the guests who already were paying far too close attention to us. "Not unless you're willing to put on an apron and hairnet to question me in the kitchen."

"Then perhaps you'll join us at the station." Stan made the request sound like an invitation to his yacht.

"What's this about, Detectives?" I split my attention between Bryce and Stan. My heart knocked against my chest.

"Everything OK?" The sound of Dev's voice behind me had never been more welcome.

"These are homicide detectives Bryce Jackson and Stan Milner. They're asking about Claudio Fabrizi." My voice wobbled.

I sensed Dev stiffen beside me. Good to know I wasn't overreacting. What was going on?

He looked them over. "Has something happened?"

Stan returned Dev's assessment. "Fabrizi was killed last night—after an altercation with Ms. Murray."

Multiple gasps, including mine, rolled across the bakery. Patches of whispered conversations sprouted around the room. I barely heard the voices above the blood rushing from my head. Granny and I exchanged wide-eyed looks of disbelief and horror. Our lips were parted in shock.

Bryce considered my brother. "Who're you?" His words

came to me as though he was standing at the bottom of the sea.

"I'm her lawyer, Devon Murray." Dev's response was courteous but firm. The expression in his eyes was inflexible.

Another shock rattled my thoughts. With Dev's claim, the police interview had just gotten really real. I searched his grim profile. With him acting as my lawyer, was it permissible for us to hug? I had a feeling before this was over I was going to need one.

CHAPTER 7

Gray. Everything in the police precinct's interrogation room was gray: the faded and chipped plaster walls, the stained and pitted concrete floor, the dented and scarred wooden rectangular table, and the four identical hardwood chairs. Leaving the vivid colors of my bakery and finding myself in this monochromatic chamber was like Dorothy's trip to the Land of Oz in reverse.

My seat beside Dev was lopsided. Every breath I drew sent it rocking like a storm-tossed raft. I'd seen enough crime dramas to suspect the detectives were aware of this bonus feature when they'd offered me this chair. If it was an underhanded tactic meant to literally keep me off-balance, it was working.

The one miniscule window toward the top of the wall to my left had gray metal bars inside and out. Feeble sunlight strained through a thick layer of cobwebs, city smog, and—you guessed it—gray dirt, making Sunday's mid-morning seem like late afternoon.

In my entire life, I'd never been called on the carpet. Not to the principal's office in primary school, the dean's office in college, or human resources in my professional career.

How in the world had I ended up in a police interrogation room?

"Tell us about the argument you had with Claudio Fabrizi yesterday." Stan sat across the table from me. He'd made the directive sound like an invitation to help myself to hors d'oeuvres. His dark gray eyes were kind as he waited for my answer.

It was hard to guess his age under the weak fluorescent lighting. Despite his wealth of gray hairs, his soft, round features were relatively wrinkle-free. Botox? My attention dropped to his hands stacked in front of him. His skin looked smooth and soft, and his cuticles were perfect.

Uncertain, I looked at Dev. He'd driven his car to the precinct, practically tailgating the detectives, who'd insisted I ride with them. My big brother always knew what to do. I'd pay a king's ransom for a tenth of his confidence right now. His brown eyes were dark with concern, but he nodded almost imperceptibly, giving me the go-ahead to respond.

I sat straighter and split my attention between Stan and Bryce beside him. "Claudio came to the bakery early Saturday morning. It was the first day of our soft launch. The place was packed. He was already in a temper when he got to the counter."

"Why was he angry?" Bryce interrupted. He'd angled his chair toward me and seemed intent on boring into my brain with his eyes. Strange how someone's appeal faded when they suspected you of murder.

I drew a deep breath and almost gagged on the stench of burned coffee and stale pastries that had taken up residence in the broom closet masquerading as a meeting room. The movement of my seat beneath me added to my queasiness. *Note to self: Hold all deep breaths until we get out of here.*

Again, I looked to Dev before responding. "He said he was mad that I'd opened my bakery. He accused me of trying to steal his customers."

"And were you?" Was Bryce trying to goad me?

This time, I didn't check with Dev. "I'll tell you what I told Claudio: If he was so concerned about keeping his customers, he should return to his bakery and serve them instead of causing a scene in my shop." I turned to Stan, whose eyes twinkled with humor. "The entire exchange only lasted a few minutes. My parents and Dev came out of the kitchen and my father demanded Claudio leave. So he and his son, Enzo, left."

Bryce gave me a considering look. "I remember in high school, you were timid and quiet. You've developed a temper since then."

He remembered that about me? It blew my mind that he'd noticed me at all back then. We didn't say ten words to each other the entire two years we overlapped at Flatbush Early.

Dev responded before I could gather my thoughts. "Whether she has or not is beside the point. Having a temper is a far distance from committing murder."

"You're right, of course." Stan shifted on his seat, but his chair didn't rock. He returned his attention to me. "When was the last time you saw Mr. Fabrizi?"

"When Enzo took him out of the bakery." If only he'd prevented his father from coming to the bakery in the first place, I wouldn't have had that horrible confrontation with Claudio yesterday, and I wouldn't be sitting in this police interrogation closet now.

"Where were you between ten and eleven?" Bryce posed his question without inflection.

The hour before midnight; the time when duppies and other dangerous spirits are up to the most mischief. Was that the estimated time of Claudio's murder? "I was home, asleep."

"Can anyone verify that?" Bryce's follow-up question came before I'd finished responding to his first one. He must've expected my answer. Didn't he believe me?

"My cat." Ziggy Cat, named after the legendary Bob Marley's oldest son, usually slept beside me. His habit of kneading my waist each morning to wake me was much more pleasant than my alarm clock. I set the alarm each night anyway. "I closed the bakery at seven p.m., cleaned up, and got it ready for this morning."

Dev took over the report. "She called around eight thirty for me to pick her up. I got to the bakery about twenty till."

"That's right." I'd finished a few more chores before Dev's bronze compact sedan had pulled up in front of the shop. "He drove me home."

Stan interrupted. "How long of a drive is that, would you say?"

"Ten minutes." I looked toward Dev, who nodded his agreement.

"Thank you." Stan wrote something in his notepad.

It was a short drive and a quick walk. I'd made the trip at night alone many, many times. But since Dev was off this week and I was getting used to closing the shop, our parents had asked him to drive me home. I'm glad they had. Without him, I wouldn't've had anyone to vouch for even part of my alibi.

"Dev and I talked with my parents and grandmother for a while; then he'd left and I'd gone to bed. We have a security system at the bakery. Our camera footage will verify all of that."

Since Mommy, Daddy, Granny, and Dev arrive at the

bakery several hours before me to start the baking and the cooking, I insisted they leave early each day to ensure they got enough rest. But Saturday night, their adrenaline had been pumping from the bakery's success. So had mine. It had been even better than we'd hoped—except for the encounter with Claudio, of course. And although I'd been exhausted, it had been hard for me to fall asleep. There was no need to share that part with Bryce and Stan, though.

"But you don't have an alibi for the time of the murder." Bryce sounded like a TV detective. I half expected to hear the "duh-dum" from the original *Law & Order* series punctuate his statement.

Dev stirred beside me, leaning into the table. His chair didn't sway, either. "My sister couldn't have gone to Claudio's house to kill him. She doesn't know where he lives. No one in my family does."

"Thank you for that information." Stan's tone was almost apologetic. He shifted his eyes from Dev to me. "We were also wondering about the murder weapon."

I frowned. "What about it?"

Stan flipped some pages in his notepad before appearing to locate the information. "The weapon used to kill Mr. Fabrizi was a serrated bread knife. It was recovered at the scene. Is that something your bakery has, ma'am? A serrated bread knife?"

I exchanged a look with Dev. "Yes, Detective Milner. We have several serrated bread knives, and they're all accounted for in our kitchen."

"You're sure?" Bryce's appeal continued to wane during the course of this interrogation. I wanted to scream at him, *You remembered me from high school!*, which still blew my mind. *Had I seemed unbalanced to you at the time?*

"Very sure." I tamped down on the temper he'd mentioned earlier. "I washed all the dishes and put them away before leaving the bakery last night. I would've noticed if one had been missing."

Dev spread his hands. "Serrated bread knives aren't unique to my family or our bakery. Most bakeries have them. They can be bought in scores of stores and online."

"That may be, but our crime scene team's checking it for prints now." Bryce stood. "We'd like your prints, Lyndsay, to compare them to any we might recover."

Everything stilled except my lopsided chair. Fear like a cold fist tightened around my heart, but I forced myself to meet Bryce's impassive expression.

"Why do you think I would've killed Claudio? I barely knew him." I was proud my voice was steady.

Bryce didn't blink. "Because witnesses heard you say to him, 'If you dare to come back, your son'll be carrying you out.'"

Oh, yeah. I'd forgotten about that.

CHAPTER 8

Mommy and Daddy met us in the bakery's rear parking lot. Dev pulled into one of the two spaces reserved for my family's cars about two hours before the anticipated lunchtime crush. Although it felt like days had passed since we'd been taken to the precinct, we hadn't been gone very long. Had my parents been waiting in the lot the whole time or had someone told them we'd returned?

"Lynds!" Mommy pulled me into a strong embrace before I'd gotten all the way out of the car. Daddy crowded close behind her. "We've been so worried." She stepped back, holding my hands to steady me as I straightened from the car. Her attention switched to Dev. "Are you both all right?"

"Yes, Mommy." I squeezed her hands to reassure her and found a smile for Daddy. "But thank God Dev was with me."

It wasn't the first time I'd said those words. My big brother had always been there for me, which was one of the reasons I'd taken his going out of state for college so hard. I'd lost my safety net. I was only now starting to feel more confident in my decisions, starting to find my voice.

"Thank you, Son." Daddy spoke over the roof of Dev's sedan.

"No one should go through that alone." My brother's voice was grim.

I sensed the shift in my parents' mood. They went from being relieved their child hadn't been imprisoned to concerned I was still in danger. The knots in my shoulders and back tightened even more.

"Let's get inside." Mommy put one arm around my shoulder and used the other to beckon Dev to join us.

Daddy glanced back at us several times as he led the way across the small lot. It was as though he feared we'd disappear in the few yards to the bakery's back door.

Bob Marley's greatest hits were programmed on the compact disc player when I crossed the threshold into the kitchen. I recognized the opening chords of "I Shot the Sheriff." Not the best choice in light of the situation.

Moving farther into the kitchen, I realized the room held almost double the usual number of people. Extended family—an aunt, uncle, and cousin—had crowded into the modest space.

Under normal circumstances, I'd be excited to see them. I loved spending time with relatives. But not today. My nerves were shattered. My heart was racing, and my thoughts were all over the place. I needed space and time to think. My relatives had a bunch of wonderful, lovable qualities. Giving people space or time wasn't among them.

No one had noticed me yet. Perhaps it was because Granny was calling out instructions, putting everyone to work replenishing the bakery's inventory.

"Manny, ease up on the sugar, nuh? I'm watchin' you." She punctuated her words with an affectionate pat on my cousin's back. Manson Bain was Reena's older brother and an audio engineer with an up-and-coming independent record label. He had a weakness for sweets.

"Lynds!" Aunty Inez set down a measuring cup and rushed toward me. At her exclamation, everyone turned to me with various expressions of concern: furrowed brows, wide eyes, pursed lips.

Aunty Inez wrapped her arms around me, rocking us both from side to side. She smelled of pure vanilla extract and floral perfume. "We've been so worried. We knew Dev would take good care of you, though." She stepped back, holding me at arm's length to look me over. Her voice dropped to a stage whisper. "But they took you in for questioning about a murder. Oh, Lord."

"If the bo-bo had wanted to arrest her, there was nothing Dev could've done, you know. She would've been locked up for sure." Romany Murray was Daddy's older brother. He'd worked for the U.S. Post Office as a mail carrier for almost thirty years. We believed he'd been born under a dark cloud. But he was family.

His comments prompted curt protests from my other relatives. They also replaced the warmth of Aunty Inez's embrace with the cold slap of fear. Still, I turned to my aunt, forced a smile to my lips, and lied. "I'm all right, Aunty Inez."

Inez Minnis Bain was my aunt through marriage and I loved her dearly. She'd married my mother's older brother, Alrick Bain, more than thirty years ago. Reena was their second of three children and their only daughter. We were all proud of Aunty Inez's position as an Equal Employment Opportunity Officer in the Brooklyn Borough President's Office. It was a stressful job, but she was doing important work. Although she claimed she'd heard stories that would undo my braids.

With my business owner's eyes, I surveyed the kitchen. Granny had made sure everyone was wearing a hair cap and apron. I gave her a grateful look. She returned it with troubled eyes. Distress deepened the creases bracketing her bow-shaped lips.

I left the kitchen to check on our customers. Startled, I stopped at the sight of my Uncle Alrick working the cash register. I hadn't expected to see him there, nor had I known the technophobe could operate the digital device. But there he was, helping Reena process an order for several loaves of freshly baked hard dough bread. The buttery scent spread across the bakery, reminding me I hadn't eaten anything since before 7:00 a.m.

"Lynds, why'd the bo-bo take you in?" At well over six feet tall, Uncle Al had to bend to embrace me. His brown features were tight with concern. He stepped back to the counter. "Why'd they think you'd have anything to do with Claudio's murder?"

Uncle Al had worked in the New York City Department of City Planning office for decades. No one in the family understood what he did.

I exchanged a hug with Reena before circling to the front of the counter. From that angle, I could check on the customers and assess how many were watching this drama unfold. A handful of people were seated in the dining section, openly listening to our conversation as they lingered over their beverages or took their time with their pastries.

I lowered my voice and tried to appear more confident than I felt. "They're claiming my argument with Claudio makes me a suspect. And no one can verify where I was between ten and eleven p.m. Saturday when Claudio was being killed."

Uncle Al's heavy black eyebrows knitted. "Ten and eleven? Weren't you sleeping?"

"Yes, but I can't prove it." I folded my hands in front of me to keep from wringing them.

Reena snorted. "Everyone knows you don't have a social life."

"This is the reason she hasn't had a social life the past few years." Uncle Al spread his arms, encompassing the bakery. "An active social life won't help you build the American dream."

"Daddy's right." Reena's features glowed as she smiled at me. "We're all so proud of you."

"Thank you." I squeezed her hand as it rested on the counter.

I surveyed the bakery. I'd worked hard and saved for years to make this dream a reality. I didn't regret a second of it. Yeah, the horrible boss at the marketing firm where I'd worked for three years could've been nicer, but he taught me how to promote a business. Turning down dates to spend Friday nights alone, researching my business plan, had been a necessary sacrifice. Or so I'd told myself. I'd known what I'd wanted and had gone after it. Now what? What happens to my dream now that I'm—and by extension, the bakery— caught up in a murder investigation?

Aunty Inez came through the kitchen door behind me and hustled into the dining area. "They need to stop asking questions about Lynds's life and focus on Claudio's if they're serious about finding his killer."

Granny settled down at her table across from the cus- tomer counter and picked up her crocheting. She hummed her agreement to her daughter-in-law's comment. "He had plenty enemies."

"Even he and his son were on the outs." Uncle Roman's voice came from behind me.

My uncle was notoriously unlucky in love. Twice divorced, he claimed his alimony and child support payments were the reasons he worked all the time, requesting extra shifts from the post office. Even so, you'd be hard-pressed to find anyone more tightfisted with a dollar than Romany Murray.

"How d'you know that?" Aunty Inez wove her way through the dining area, cleaning empty tables and graciously nudging lingering customers along. She was incapable of remaining still, though her lack of restraint was only awkward in strangers' homes. Her son Manny trailed her, carrying the dishes and plastic drinkware she took from the tables. Uncle Roman followed the pair, wiping the table surfaces clean with a damp cloth. "I does hear things on the route, OK. People they don't see the postman, but we do hear and see everything."

I took the plates and glasses from Manny. Reena held the kitchen door open for me. Dev helped me stack the plates in the dishwasher; then we followed my parents out of the kitchen.

Granny's eyes remained on the yellow-and-green doily she was making. "So, Roman, what did you hear about Enzo and his daddy?"

Uncle Roman slouched onto a seat at the table he'd just wiped clean. "Their business office's on my route, right? One day, a coupla weeks ago now, me walk in to give the receptionist some letters and a package for she to sign, but she not there. So I think, let I wait a coupla minutes. And as I waitin', I hear voices raised in the back. Angry voices. One shouting, 'Sell the bakery. It's taking all our profits. Sell it before it destroys the business.'"

I froze. Interesting. "This happened two weeks ago?" I turned to my family. Some were seated; most were standing. Aunty Inez was cleaning the glass front door. "If Enzo and Claudio were arguing about their real estate business and about the bakery, wouldn't that give Enzo a motive for the murder?"

Granny gave a slow nod as though processing the conversation. "Claudio liked his bakery, but he made money with his real estate business."

"Sounds like the business was Enzo's passion." Uncle Al ran his hand over his tight dark brown curls. "They have several commercial real estate properties all over Brooklyn."

"Yes, a couple of office buildings and a few storefronts." Reena set the checkout counter to rights and wiped it down with sanitizing cloths. She was so like her mother with her need to be in constant motion, especially when it came to cleaning.

"The police should speak with the business owners renting offices in his buildings." Granny shook her head without looking up from her crochet needle. "Any one of them would have reason to kill him if he really was doing the dirty tricks I'd heard of."

Reena had pointed out to me a couple of the office buildings and storefronts. Most were in need of repairs. But could any of his tenants have killed him? Wouldn't finding other office space be easier than planning murder?

"Didn't he also teach at a cooking school?" Mommy asked as she assembled the fresh pastries into the showcases. "The police should talk with the people there."

Daddy swept the broom across the waiting area. "People there probably had bad feelings for him, too."

With cousins, uncles, and my aunt helping Dev, Mommy, and Daddy tidy the bakery and place fresh pastries on display, there wasn't anything for me to do to prepare for what I hoped would be a lunchtime rush. I replaced Uncle Al behind the cash register.

Dev rested his hand on my shoulder. "How're you holding up?"

"I don't know." It wasn't much of a response, but it was the best I could give. "When I'd planned my future, I'd never imagined being a murder suspect."

A cloud shifted over Dev's sienna features before his eyes sharpened with determination. "Lynds, the truth will out." That was something Mommy and Daddy had taught us. He gave my shoulder an encouraging squeeze. "The police have only started their investigation. They're just doing their due diligence to rule you out before they move on to better suspects."

"Is that what they're doing? It didn't feel that way." Checking the time on my cell phone bought me a moment or two or three to collect my composure. It was half past ten on Sunday morning. In a few minutes, customers would come in for lunch, or so I hoped. "You know me. I have to prepare for a worst-case scenario: the good, the bad, and everything in between."

He let his hand drop. "I'll get a defense lawyer for you. You won't need one, but as you said, we should be prepared just in case."

Never in my most horrific nightmares had I envisioned defending myself against murder charges. But here I was preparing to do just that during what should be one of the happiest times in my life, right up there with earning my U.S. citizenship, and graduating from high school, college, and graduate school. Opening this bakery was supposed to be another triumphant accomplishment in my twenty-seven years.

I cut him a skeptical look from the corner of my eye. "I hope they take IOUs. I need someone who's in my budget. My savings are tied up with the bakery." I swept my arm, drawing his attention to the room and the relatives who showed their love and support with brooms and dustcloths. "I may need a public defender."

Dev shook his head. "I'll pay for the lawyer."

"I'll help." Granny's offer reminded me that there were others who could hear our conversation.

"We will as well, of course." Daddy spoke for himself and Mommy.

"We'll all help." Uncle Al jerked his head toward my aunt and cousins.

"With everyone else helping, all you don't need me." Uncle Roman hunched his shoulders under the barrage of rebukes and chastisements that fell on his head in response to his statement. "I'm joking."

Was he really?

I swallowed the lump in my throat. I wasn't used to asking for help. I'd always been so desperate for my family to see me like Dev, self-sufficient and confident. I'd never wanted them to suspect I was nervous and unsure all the time.

"Thank you." My voice seemed steady enough. "I really appreciate your offers, but I'm sure it won't come to that."

A chorus of agreements rose from them. Their voices sounded more determined than convinced. I couldn't blame anyone for having doubts. I had several of my own. I wanted everything to return to normal so I could focus once again on growing the bakery.

If only I could turn back the clock to before Claudio had stormed into our bakery and threatened to shut us down. Could I have done more to convince him I wasn't his competition during one of his many visits before the bakery had opened? Should I have appealed to Enzo to talk some sense into his father earlier? What if I hadn't said Enzo would have to carry Claudio out of my shop if he ever returned? Would that have made a difference to the police investigation?

Probably not.

Dev continued. "One of my mentees, Alfonso Lester, is a defense attorney. I'll tell him what's happened and let him know we may need his help if the police charge you—which they won't."

I raised my eyebrows. "Exactly how many mentees do you have?"

After graduating from Harvard University with a bachelor's degree in history, Dev had graduated from the University of Michigan's Law School. He was an active alumnus of both institutions.

"I enjoy mentoring." He shrugged. "Anyway, now you have a plan if we get into a worst-case scenario. You'd be in good hands with Alfonso. So put this investigation out of your mind. The detectives were fishing and came up empty. Focus on the bakery."

Really?

He wanted me to pretend I wasn't a murder suspect. That would take greater acting skills than I had.

CHAPTER 9

Jab! Cross! Hook! Uppercut! Body blow! Front-right kick! Squat! Front-left kick! Squat! Repeat!

I called out the moves in my mind with each execution as I pummeled the heavy foam-filled punching bag at my neighborhood gym. The feel of the freestanding black vinyl against my fists was satisfying. With each kick, the six-foot, high-density bag anchored by a round sand-filled base snapped back before rocking forward again.

It was about a quarter till six on Monday morning. I'd already stretched; done my cardio with a three-mile run on the gym's elevated track; and lifted weights. Mondays were upper body. I was dripping with sweat even before I started the kickboxing routine.

The gym was old. The stench of perspiration had fused with the walls and flooring, but the equipment was in excellent condition. The rooms were spacious enough so patrons weren't exercising on top of each other. Best of all, it was walking distance from home and the bakery.

As I finished my kickboxing workout, other gym members strolled into the weight room where the punching bag was stationed, including the Watcher. In my peripheral vision, I marked her entrance. She was back.

Urgh.

The Watcher was a tall, attractive woman—perhaps five-nine, five-ten—with warm brown skin. She was around my age, perhaps a few years older. Her black unitard hugged her dancer's figure. It covered her to her ankles, but left her sculpted arms bare. Her hair was a short natural that followed the shape of her head. Its deep red color must have come from a bottle, but it flattered her.

For weeks, the Watcher would arrive at the gym toward the end of my kickboxing routine and stare at me. She'd stretch and stare. Pump weights, and stare. Do abdominal crunches. And stare. At first I thought she wanted to be next on the punching bag, but she continued to stare at me even after I'd stepped away.

If this was happening to Reena, I had no doubt my assertive cousin would approach the other woman, snatch her cell phone, take a selfie, then hand it back with the comment, *Pictures last longer.*

I didn't have that much gumption.

But I had to do something. She was staring at me again. And it was creepy.

Jab! Cross! Hook! Uppercut! Body blow!

Breathing hard, I stepped back and removed my thick yellow vinyl gloves. Shoving them into my green nylon gym bag, I tugged out my towel. I hoisted my bag onto my shoulder and used the towel to wipe the sweat from my face and neck. Then I turned, steeling myself to confront her.

I closed the distance between us. After my workout, I smelled pretty ripe but didn't care. "May I help you?"

She stood from the black vinyl weight bench and offered

me a smile. "You don't remember me, do you?" Her Brooklyn accent was strong.

"Should I?" My belligerence was expanding.

A faint chuckle preceded her words. "You're Lyndsay Murray. I'm Roxanne Stewart. Friends call me Rocky. We started in the same adult beginner kickboxing class."

My frown cleared as recognition replaced confusion. "Rocky! I remember now. Your hair's different." Back then, it had been dark brown, longer, and straightened. She hadn't been quite as fit. Overall, she'd undergone a pretty radical transformation. She looked great.

"I see you're still kickboxing." Rocky looked down the aisle, past the row of weights to the punching bag I'd been using, before returning her attention to me. "Are you still taking classes?"

"Yes. What about you?" I recalled her moving on from beginner to intermediate at the end of our class.

I'd enrolled in the adult beginner class about seven years ago while I was still in school. I'd stayed with the class for five years before advancing to adult intermediate. What can I say? It takes me a while to let go of people, places, and things. Besides, I was more focused on fitness and basic moves. I wasn't interested in being able to beat up on people. Although, if I was falsely convicted of killing Claudio and ended up in prison, it would be a useful skill set.

"I see you in here all the time and wanted to say hello." Her comment distracted me from my worries about the murder case. "But I wasn't sure if you were one of those people who don't like to be interrupted when you're working out."

That explained the staring. She must have been willing me to come to her. *Ha!* "I don't mind, although I'm usually in a rush to get to work."

"You know, you're really good. Kickboxing." Her words rushed out almost on top of each other. "You have good form, power, speed, and what have you. Have you considered entering an exhibition? There's one in the fall."

I would've laughed if she hadn't seemed so sincere. Me? Enter a kickboxing exhibition where people would judge me and compare me to other participants? No, thank you.

"I'm not interested in competing." I smiled to soften my response. "I just like the workout."

"Why not?" Her dark eyes sparkled with enthusiasm. "This will be my fourth event. I've gotten great feedback from the professional kickboxers who judge the entrants. They've helped me improve so much. I feel stronger and my workouts are better."

I stepped back, shaking my head. "I'm not much of a competitor."

She closed the widening distance between us. "But that's just it. I'm not competing against other entrants. I'm competing against myself. Challenge yourself. It's another way to get better. And you clearly enjoy it."

"Yes, but I'm very busy right now, getting the bakery up and running." Even to my ears, that excuse sounded flimsy.

"I understand." Her disappointment was tangible. "At least consider it, though. We need more women to enter so we can diversify the events. Too many young, white guys and not enough sisters in the mix."

I struggled against a smile. "I get it. OK, I'll think it over for next year. My schedule's pretty full with the bakery this year."

Rocky raised both hands, palms out. "Just think about it."

"OK." I wanted to end our conversation.

I strode out of the weight room, heading for the gym's exit.

I still had to get home and clean up before going to the shop. A blast of chilly early-morning air smacked me as I pushed open the facility's front door. It felt good against my hot, damp skin.

Challenge yourself.

I was doing that already by launching a business and improving my baking skills. Oh, and convincing the NYPD I didn't kill a rival baker. I had all the challenges a person could reasonably—or unreasonably—handle.

Maybe if the detectives removed me from their list of suspects I'd find myself with free time. *Ha!*

I exhaled a breath and closed my eyes briefly as I hurried home. Could I trust the detectives would come to their senses and remove me from their list on their own? What more could I do or say to prove my innocence?

CHAPTER 10

"Granny! What're you doing here? The bakery's closed Mondays, remember?"

My grandmother looked at me as though she was reconsidering my IQ. "What you think I'm doing here?" She closed the kitchen's back door and crossed to the storage cabinet to set aside her bulging faux-leather orange purse and plantain-green nylon gym bag. "I've come to help with your lessons. How're you going to improve your baking without guidance? You think of that?"

It wasn't yet eight o'clock Monday morning. I looked askance at her outfit. She didn't seem dressed for baking lessons. Her flowing satin ankle-length dress skimmed her slender figure and featured an orange, yellow, and brown abstract design. With her matching head wrap, she didn't need the chef's cap, but she covered her dress with one of our red aprons with the screened image of Grenada in the lower corner.

Granny was close to my height. She kept herself fit at the same neighborhood gym I belonged to, using the facility as an outlet for two of her passions: dancing and swimming. She took Zumba classes and used the indoor pool every evening. She also preferred to walk everywhere, a habit I suspected she'd developed from her years with the post office.

I went back to gathering the ingredients for my practice currant roll baking session: all-purpose flour, shortening, margarine, salt, cold water, and one tablespoon of our secret ingredient.

Granny crossed to the long center island where I was setting up to make the pastry dough. "Stick to the basics. You're not ready for the secret ingredient yet. Don't waste it."

She tore off a strip of the plastic wrap from the box on the table, covered the cup, then carried it to the industrial refrigerator. On her way back to join me at the table, she made a detour to the CD player on the counter near the door to the main bakery. With the press of a few buttons, she freed Harry Belafonte—or at least his voice—to perform his calypso classic "Island in the Sun."

Swaying her hips to the mesmerizing music, she continued on to the table and stopped beside me. "A little mood music to relax the nerves. Did you know this is from a movie filmed in Grenada?"

"I remember, Granny." I felt like she told me that every third time this song played. *Island in the Sun* was a 1957 movie, starring Harry Belafonte and Dorothy Dandridge. Part of it also was filmed in Barbados, but Granny never mentioned that.

Her frown returned. "You're always trying to do things yourself. I've told you before, Lynds, you need to ask for help sometimes. There's no shame in it."

"I didn't want to ask you to come in to work on your day off." I shook the flour into the mixing bowl and reached for the salt.

"Chutz!" Granny slapped my hand to stop me. "This is our bakery, nuh? It's not work. It's a labor of love."

"I know." I sighed. "For us, cooking's always been an expression of love. It comes from the heart to nourish us and those we care for. That's one of the reasons I wanted to open this bakery, to share that feeling, those memories, with our community and, hopefully, other people."

Granny's heart-shaped face softened with a smile. Her wide dark eyes twinkled. "When people bite into the currant roll, they'll remember family gatherings, the closeness and the laughter. Others who haven't had the pastry before will feel the love that went into baking it."

"That's right." She always understood me, even when I struggled to express myself. Being a professional baker was a dream I'd cherished since I was a young child. As a baker, however, I made a pretty good marketing professional. My breads, pies, and pastries couldn't hold a candle to those my granny, parents, and Dev made.

Why not? What was I doing wrong?

"I know you're frustrated." Granny spoke as though she was eavesdropping on my mental conversation. "But there's hope for you. You can cook, yes. Your entrées, soups, and appetizers are exceptional."

"Thank you." My tension eased a bit.

"It's just your pastries that taste like rocks."

Harsh. But she wasn't wrong.

This wasn't the first baking lesson Granny was giving me. Mommy, Daddy, and even Dev had tried to help. Nothing worked. But I couldn't—wouldn't—give up. Ever.

"I love to cook and to bake." I loved the scents, textures, and creativity of cooking. Those senses carried me back to my most cherished memories of being in the kitchen with my family surrounded by love and laughter after school and work, and on weekends. How could I bring that passion out through the pastries?

"I know, love. You just have to believe in yourself."

"I do."

"Maybe you believe in yourself here." Granny touched the side of my head. Her fingers were soft and warm. "But you don't believe in yourself here." She tapped her index finger against my chest. "It's true. It's reflected in your baking. You have to work on your confidence." She hunched her shoulders. "When you're expressing your feelings, you can't be bashful and second-guess yourself." She stood straighter. "When you tell someone you love them, speak up. Otherwise why bother? It's the same when you bake."

"All right." I nodded, feeling the muscles in my shoulders and arms tightening.

Granny patted my back. "Let's get started."

I added salt to the flour already in the mixing bowl, then the margarine. I pinched off pieces of the cold shortening into the bowl as well.

Granny placed her hands on my forearm. "Gently. You're baking, not kickboxing."

"Yes, Granny." I struggled to clear my mind and focus on the joy of baking. It had to come from the heart.

"I can feel your tension from here. What's troubling you, love?" Granny gave me a searching look.

What wasn't? So many concerns were trying to sink their teeth into my conscious: Improving my baking skills. Launching the shop in two days. Being suspected of murder. That last one was a biggie.

Before coming to our shop, I'd stopped by Claudio's Baked Goods. A notice in the storefront stated it would be closed for several days while the family mourned his death. It would reopen in five days. Was I reading too much into the fact that there weren't any notes of sympathy to the family or tributes to Claudio in front of the store? Perhaps Enzo had already collected them.

Or perhaps no one had liked Claudio.

"It's nothing," I lied. I mixed the ingredients together in two separate bowls. "There's just a lot left to do to get the shop ready for Wednesday."

She huffed. "Knowing you, you've already checked everything four times, so the bakery's in excellent shape. Something else's bothering you. Claudio's murder."

I parted my lips to deny it. But the worry in Granny's eyes stopped me. And I didn't want to tell another lie. With Granny's help, I broke the dough into four parts and wrapped them in separate plastic sheets.

"I don't understand how I could be suspected of killing him. I barely knew him. One quarrel makes someone a credible suspect for a homicide investigation? Really?" Gaining steam for my argument, I flung my free arm toward the front door, which was out of sight of the kitchen. "If that's true, then if you're killed while riding the bus, the police could have three suspects by the time the bus gets to your stop."

"That's true." Carrying her two packages of wrapped dough, Granny led me across the room to the silver industrial fridge. "That's why I believe everything will work out. So don't worry so much."

I set my dough on the shelf beside Granny's. We needed to let them chill in the fridge for a few hours before continuing the creative process. I set the alarm on my cell phone. In the meantime, I'd planned to review the shop's inventory and work on the week's marketing and promotion. I needed to check our supplies, not just cooking ingredients, but takeaway containers, bags, soaps, and napkins, among other items. Some packages were due to arrive today. And I needed to update our website.

"Granny, that's easier said than done." I closed the refrigerator door. "It was scary enough in that interrogation room. How much scarier would prison be?"

"You'll never have to find out." Granny removed her apron, turning to put it back in the storage closet. "Come on, nuh? Claudio had plenty of enemies. The detectives will have more suspects than they'll know what to do with."

My muscles were heavy as I trailed Granny. I would have believed her prediction if I hadn't heard a hint of concern in her voice.

Our bakery's official launch day. The last Wednesday of March. I checked the time on my cell phone. It was minutes to seven. Today was supposed to be a joyous occasion. A triumph. There was just one problem: Yesterday's *Brooklyn Daily Beacon* had identified me as a "person of interest" in Claudio's murder.

The reporter, José Perez, seemed to relish the possibility of a rival baker killing Claudio. His enthusiasm had cast a shadow over everything and every feeling. My family had been subscribing to the *Beacon* since my parents had bought their house almost thirty years ago. Our extended relatives were subscribers, too. Uncle Roman enjoyed reading the obituaries. I'd never imagined reading about myself in its crime section. How would the article affect today's turnout?

Granny, Mommy, Daddy, and Dev were nervous, too. It

showed in their jerky motions and unblinking stares. Daddy had performed three duets with Bob Marley before Granny turned off the CD player.

"The family that prays together, stays together." She gathered us at the front of the kitchen to lead us in a prayer for strength and guidance.

Afterward, I tried a smile and reached for some humor. "So this is what it feels like to be excited and terrified all at once."

To my family's credit, they made an effort to laugh at the weak joke.

This feeling was way worse than the nervous excitement I'd felt during the product unveilings for the marketing firm's clients. I'd cared about my former employer's customers and had been committed to their events. Their triumphs were my triumphs. But this time, the promotion was personal. The soft launch had been a great success, surpassing my modest expectations. But that wasn't a guarantee of success for our hard launch, even though I'd calculated my measurements for today's event with conservative numbers.

From her position beside the kitchen's swinging door, Granny caught my attention. She pointed toward our front picture window. "No matter what happens, remember *you* made that possible. All of this is thanks to you."

I stepped forward hesitantly to see what she meant. Through the glass, I could see people waiting in a line for our door to open. The line was long. I couldn't see the end of it. I wanted to jump, laugh, scream, and cry all at the same time. Thank goodness Dev would be helping me at the counter.

Take that, Beacon *reporter!*

"And all of you." Blinking back tears, I spread my arms

to encompass my family. "It's your baking that's bringing them into the shop. Thank you for supporting my dream."

The aromas of sugar, melted butter, cinnamon, baked fruits, and fresh breads rolled across the kitchen and escaped through the air vents in search of potential customers for our bakery.

"It was one of the best ideas you've ever had." Daddy embraced me. "We're so proud of you for all you've accomplished."

He stepped aside so I could exchange hugs with Mommy and Dev.

"Your gran's right." Mommy held me close. "You did all of this. We're so proud of you."

"Great job, Sis." Dev's hug lifted me from the floor.

The memory of my jealously squirreling away my allowance, birthday, and holiday money and as much of my earnings as I could manage in a separate savings account since the age of nine blinked into my mind. It no longer felt like a faraway dream. This was real. The day had arrived.

"I'll let our customers in." Granny gave me a delighted smile, showing how much she relished being able to say those words.

There were new guests among the familiar faces, which meant our marketing and probably—hopefully—our word of mouth was spreading. Twin surges of hope and excitement rushed through me as I readied to take our customers' requests while Dev rang up their order.

A few of the customers wanted to take their time perusing the menu when it came their turn at the counter. That didn't make some of our other patrons very happy.

"Hurry up and order, nuh?" one irritated female voice called out. "I have to get to work!"

"We all have to get to work!" An aggravated male voice supported her complaint.

"I just now coming from work." An aggrieved man spoke up for himself. "I need to get to bed!"

The two older, well-dressed women before me appeared to be sisters. They cast dirty looks over their shoulders toward the grumbling crowd. After they made their requests for hard dough bread and fish bakes, Dev processed their order and I prepared their takeaway bag.

Granny left her table and collected a handful of our colorful menus from the display shelf near our entrance. With pointed looks, she distributed them to the people in the line. I was grateful for her not-so-subtle hint for people to make their order decisions before getting to the counter.

A tall man in his late twenties was next in line. It was the same guy who'd worn the gray jersey with the New York Knicks logo to our soft launch Saturday. Today, he was in a suit.

I did a mental fist pump. Another repeat customer. "Good morning, sir. What can I get you?"

He frowned, searching my face. "The paper says the police are looking at you for Claudio's murder. That's wack."

My smile froze. My mind went blank. I sensed Dev stiffen beside me. Holding the Knicks fan's eyes, I spoke clearly. "I did not kill Claudio Fabrizi."

Near the counter, Ms. Nevis kissed her teeth. "We know that, Lyndsay. What we don't understand is why the police don't."

A snap sounded near the entrance. A young woman stood near the door, chewing gum. Based on the bump extending her right cheek, she must be working on more than one piece at a time. "That shows you how out of touch the cops are with this community."

"Humph!" An imposing older woman in a white blouse and black slacks considered me from the center of the line as though she was assessing me at a lineup. "It's the quiet ones we need to mind, you know."

"Grace Parke!" Granny flung the name across the room like a blade. "If you're so suspicious of my granddaughter, why're you waiting in line for her to feed you?"

Grace's shoulders slumped. "I wanted some fish bakes, Genevieve."

Granny snorted. "Order them with your mouth closed."

"She wasn't quiet Saturday." The gum chewer adjusted her heavy book bag on her narrow shoulder. She stared at me with eyes bright with admiration.

I exchanged a tense look with Dev. A second ago, everyone had been in a hurry. Now they'd found time to discuss the murder investigation that I was in the center of. He shook his head, signaling I should let the debate run its course without getting involved. Was he crazy? Ms. Parke was basically putting me on trial.

"Listen." Ms. Nevis reclaimed the audience. "I'm telling you. They should be looking at the son before anybody."

A chorus of agreements rolled across the store. The Knicks fan who'd started the debate silenced them.

"I don't know." He split a look between Dev and me. "Lemme get a coconut bread and guava nectar to go." He looked over his shoulder at the guests behind him. "I can't see Enzo knifing his dad in the gut. I think it was someone he was doing business with. Fabrizi was a con artist."

I didn't know anything about Claudio's business practices,

but I also had a hard time accepting the idea of a child killing a parent. I'd read enough Greek tragedies in school to know it wasn't unheard of. I just wasn't comfortable with the idea.

However, Ms. Nevis had grabbed ahold of it with both hands. "Claudio was killed in his home late at night. What kind of business meeting is that?"

The Knicks fan—I should ask his name; I couldn't keep calling him that—paid his bill, accepted his to-go order, then turned to Ms. Nevis. She barely reached his shoulder. "I'm just guessing like everyone else." He shrugged as he stepped backward toward the exit. "But if Enzo killed his father, why didn't he make it look like a break-in? Why would he want people to think Claudio knew his killer? That makes him look suspicious."

The fan had a point. I exhaled as the debate ended after his disappearance. Thank goodness. After two or three more orders, the atmosphere in the bakery relaxed and I was able to greet our customers with a natural smile.

"Good morning, Joymarie. You look lovely." I glanced at my brother as I greeted her.

Joymarie wore a formfitting navy suit with a pencil-slim skirt. Dark, chin-length curls framed her round face. Her matching I-Mean-Business stilettos added at least three inches to her height, lifting her even closer to Dev's six-foot-plus.

She gave me a warm smile. "Thank you, Lyndsay. Congratulations on your grand opening." She boosted the wattage of her smile as she faced my brother. "Good morning, Dev. Congratulations to you, too."

His expression was frustratingly impassive. "Joymarie."

Her expression dimmed just a bit in the second before she

rallied. She struck a pose, cocking her right hip. "You can't wish me a good morning?"

A flicker of amusement feathered across Dev's spare features before he regained control. Interesting. "Good morning."

"Flirt on your own time." A grumpy order rose from the line. "Some of us have to get to work, you know."

Dev scowled at the speaker. "We're not flirting. This is customer service."

An elderly woman, fourth in line from the counter, grunted. "I hope I get such customer service when I reach the front." Her voice was as dry as dust.

Laughter rose and bounced around the waiting area.

Our guests had given me a lot to think about. I mulled over the earlier debate as I processed Joymarie's order. By making it seem as though Claudio knew his killer well enough to welcome them into his home, was someone trying to frame Enzo? If that was the case, why were the police looking at me?

CHAPTER 11

Granny burst through the kitchen's swinging door hours later. "The phone's been ringing off the hook with calls from businesses placing lunch orders for their staffs." She was practically singing. Her body trembled with excitement. She'd tucked her hair into a black chef's cap and tied a red Spice Isle Bakery apron over the blush pink pantsuit she wore with matching heels.

"What!?!" Wide-eyed and slack-jawed, I spun toward her from my spot behind the service counter. "Are these local businesses?"

The morning wave—and it had been almost a tsunami—had slowed to a steady stream of one or two customers every twenty minutes or so. We were taking advantage of this slower period to ramp up for lunch. Those guests should begin arriving in another hour. Daddy would probably start his duets with Bob Marley about half an hour before that.

I was due to join my family in the kitchen to help prepare the lunch selections. Entrées I could handle. It was the pastries that gave me grief. But first I wanted to tidy the customer service area. We had to be mindful of the bakery's need to make a good first impression. With that goal in mind, I was wiping down the countertop and straightening the napkins, order pads, pens, and large acrylic jar of paper butterflies. Those butterflies had done their job and then some this morning. And it looked like their luck would continue into the afternoon.

"They are around the neighborhood." Granny glanced at the forms in her hands. "They all said they'd come pick up their food."

"Oh, my gosh! This is amazing!" Aware of the few customers seated at the dark wood tables in our modest dining area, I struggled to keep my voice down to a stage whisper. "It must be those great reviews we received after our soft launch. Word's spreading."

In my mind, I was screaming, break-dancing, and jumping up and down. On the outside, I'm sure I wore a goofy grin as I held on to Granny's hands.

"It's the marketing you've been doing. All of your hard work to let people know where we are and that we're open is paying off, you know." Granny wrapped me in her arms.

I returned her embrace, holding on tightly, then stepped back. "How many orders do we have?" I took the forms from her.

"Twelve so far, but the phone's still ringing." She pointed over her shoulder toward the kitchen. "I put Dev in charge of answering it."

Granny executed an intricate hip shimmy, proving she still had it.

I skimmed the yellow sheets. Curried beef with rice and peas. Jerk chicken with fried plantain. Jamaican beef patties. I made a mental note to add online order forms to our website. My head was spinning. The cloud of the newspaper article on Claudio's death had been replaced by the triumph of these lunch orders. Some of the calls had been from places we knew, like the pharmacy across the street and the hair salon on the corner. Other company names weren't familiar to me. That must mean we were extending our reach. Thrilling! These must be additional signs that everything was going to work out.

"Oh, this is so exhilarating." I passed the slips back to Granny. "I'll come help with the orders after I check on our customers."

Granny turned toward the swinging sand-toned kitchen door. "In the meanwhile, we'd better get started."

Still smiling, I started around the counter to check on our guests, but the sound of the soft chimes above the entrance diverted my attention.

Robin Jones, the event planner who'd exchanged flirtatious looks with Enzo, stepped into the shop. She strode to the counter with confident, decisive steps. I admired that. She also had a distinctive fashion style. Her black-and-white–checked wool box coat hung open over her scarlet knee-length sheath dress. She'd accented her outfit with a chunky sterling silver necklace and matching earrings. Reena would say she had a bold statement. Or something like that.

I returned to the register. "Good morning, Robin." Did my greeting sound as tentative as I felt? She was friends—if not more—with Enzo. Had she seen the article in the *Beacon*? Perhaps she didn't read the paper. One could hope. I braced my hands on the cool sand-toned counter on either side of the cash register and waited for her response.

"Lyndsay, how are you?" She swung her blond tresses over her shoulder and swept off her black designer sunglasses.

Her blue eyes were wide and searching. "I read in the news that the police are questioning you about Claudio's murder?"

Of course she had. I swallowed a sigh. "I'm fine. Thank you."

"Good." Her eyes remained glued to mine. "I spoke with Enzo on Monday, after I read about his father's murder. We've known each other for so long. I mean, Claudio was his last living relative."

I couldn't imagine how devastated Enzo must feel. He was all alone now. Good friends like Robin were a blessing, but they weren't the same as having family around you. I felt so bad for him. Still, I couldn't say anything that might be misconstrued if I ended up behind the defendant's table in a New York City Criminal Court. "That was thoughtful of you. How long have you known each other?"

Robin wrinkled her face as she considered her answer. "About a year." She nodded as though for emphasis. "I'd hired Claudio's bakery to make a client's wedding cake."

I shook my head, thinking I'd misunderstood. "Wedding cakes? I didn't know Claudio made those."

"They didn't until I convinced him to give it a try." She flashed a grin, displaying large, startlingly white teeth. "I loved their cakes. I was sure they could make a wedding cake. And I was right."

That was shocking. Wedding cakes were vastly different from regular cakes. I wasn't just thinking about stacking, assembling, and transporting them. Those issues would be challenging enough. Wedding cakes used high-quality ingredients and much more elaborate presentations than anything I'd seen from Claudio's shop. For him, baking was a hobby. I couldn't see him excelling at something as complicated as a wedding cake.

Maybe I was wrong. "Were Enzo and his father partners in the bakery?"

Robin waved both hands as she chuckled. "Oh, no, no. Claudio kept the bakery for himself. Enzo worked for his father's real estate business."

"Did they have a good relationship?"

Surprise blanked her expression. She lowered her voice even more. "You can't think Enzo would kill his own father?"

"That's not what I was asking." Wasn't it? "But I saw the way Claudio treated Enzo. It wasn't very nice. Did that ever bother him?"

"Enzo was devoted to his father." Robin didn't look convinced by my explanation. I couldn't blame her. I wasn't completely convinced, either. "It was one of the things that attracted me to him. How can you not like a man who loves his family? I'm not saying Claudio didn't have enemies. He had a lot of them, mostly business investors and tenants. And a student. Claudio actually took out a restraining order against her."

My jaw dropped. "Are you serious?"

"As a heart attack."

"And the police are questioning me? Do you remember her name?"

Robin frowned, seeming to search her memory. "Marissa? Marguerite?" She shook her head. "I don't remember. I think her last name is Beauvais. Something French. But that's not what I came here to discuss. I want you to give me a bid."

I blinked. "Pardon?"

Robin pulled her business card and a packet of information on her event-planning business from her black leather attaché case. "I want to partner with your bakery to provide catering services for some of my future events. Now, some of your food might be a little too spicy for some of my customers. But I believe the majority of my clientele would adore your entrées and desserts."

I took her materials. "We'd love that. And we can moderate the heat levels of some of our dishes."

"Even better. Do you have a brochure on your catering services?"

"Yes, let me get that for you." My hands were shaking with excitement as I pulled a brochure from one of the drawers beneath the cash register.

"Thank you." She glanced at the cover of the marketing piece. "I have an event in a couple of months. I included a description of it with the material I gave you and a request for pricing for a basic curry chicken plated dinner. Could you work up an estimate?"

I found her email address on her business card. "I'll send it to you by tomorrow." If not sooner. I was excited to make a good impression. From my experience with the marketing firm, providing an accurate, detailed presentation ahead of schedule always caught the attention of potential clients.

"Thanks, Lyndsay." Robin adjusted the strap of her case on her shoulder.

"Thank you for the opportunity." I watched her long, confident strides carry her out of the bakery.

My attention turned to the jar of paper butterflies. *Maybe you weren't a mistake after all.*

CHAPTER 12

The bakery's phone was still ringing when I leaped into the kitchen, trembling with excitement over Robin's request for a catering bid late Wednesday morning.

Was it too soon to think about setting up a second phone line?

The broad grin I felt stretching my cheeks wavered and faded when my mind registered the concern on my family's faces. The air was heavy with disappointment and alarm. My eyes swept across the room from Daddy, Mommy, and Dev to Granny. She was framed by the office threshold as she sat behind the desk, speaking in somber tones with someone on the phone.

My heart dropped into my stomach. I could barely breathe. Was a relative sick? In the hospital?

Dead?

I braced myself against one of the counters. "What's happened?"

Dev's features were tense. "People are canceling their lunch orders."

My legs felt weak with relief. Everyone was fine. Thank

goodness. I drew a deep breath. The scents of cinnamon, sugar, and fresh bread soothed me. "All right. Well, that's disappointing, but the food won't go to waste. I expect at least as many people to come for lunch today as we had over the weekend."

"Lynds." Daddy's soft tone claimed my attention. "Almost half of the orders were canceled."

I lost my breath. "That many?" I looked to Mommy and Dev. Their silent nods confirmed Daddy's report. "But . . . Did they say why?"

Mommy's shoulders lifted in a sigh beneath her black cotton chef's smock. "They said they'd seen the story in the *Beacon*, and that they didn't want to patronize someone who was suspected of murder."

I didn't think my jaw could fall any farther. My wits scattered to the four winds. I hadn't been charged. They didn't have any credible evidence against me. I was barely a suspect, yet already the cloud of suspicion hanging over me was damaging our bakery. What would happen if I was arrested?

Something seemed off. "Did they all say the same thing? That they didn't want to patronize a suspected murderer?"

Dev started to drag his hand over his head but dropped his arm when his palm encountered his chef's cap. "Something like that. They all gave variations of the same excuse."

I frowned. "But that story was in *yesterday's* paper. How could it be that so many of them didn't know about it before they placed their orders today?"

"I was wondering the same thing." Granny appeared in the office doorway. A scowl of irritation creased her forehead.

"What're you saying?" Daddy looked from Granny to me and back. "You think they're lying?"

Granny gave a curt nod. "Yes."

I raised both hands, palms out. "I don't know if they're lying exactly, but this whole thing is suspicious. A bunch of companies order lunch, then half of them cancel and give the same excuse?"

Granny waved the order pad. "Not half, eh? Most kept their orders."

I exhaled. "Well, that's good news at least. Still, it feels like someone was pranking us."

"You think so?" Daddy seemed shocked, which wasn't surprising. He tended to see the good in people, unlike his older brother, my uncle Roman, who never saw a glass half-full.

"Who would do something like that?" Mommy was more cautious.

"I don't know." My eyes drifted away from the kitchen's black-and-silver appliances against its stark white background to the vivid design across its far wall where Mommy had painted the images of our Caribbean music greats Buju Banton, Harry Belafonte, and Bob Marley above the red, yellow, and green illustration of the Grenadian flag. "But the possibility that those orders were a hoax is something we should be prepared for. There could be more."

"I agree." Granny folded her arms across her chest.

"Someone would've had to coordinate that, though." Dev voiced his skepticism. "They would've had to contact all of those companies, told them when to call, what to order, and when to cancel. Who would've had that many contacts to plan such a scheme?"

Mommy looked pensive. "And the time to put it all together?"

The real killer perhaps. For example, how many of those

businesses rented space from Enzo? "Those are good questions. Just because we don't have answers doesn't mean we weren't being played."

"It's too fishy." Granny dropped her arms and came farther into the kitchen.

I turned to her. "In the future, let's get credit card numbers for preorders and let customers know there'll be a charge for last-minute cancelations."

Dev's frown cleared. "Good idea, Sis. That should help us separate the people who really want to place an order from those who're playing games."

His support confirmed I was on the right track. My shoulder muscles relaxed. "That's the plan."

Granny praised me with her smile. "You have a good head for business."

My parents' dark eyes glinted with approval as they added their support for this new, on-the-fly policy.

"I'm glad we're all in agreement." I looked at each family member in turn. "Now for some good news. Robin Jones, the event planner who attended our soft launch, has asked us for a bid on a catering event for one of her clients."

The kitchen filled with exclamations of approval and excitement.

"That's wonderful." Granny hugged me.

"Great news!" Dev applauded.

"Things are really coming together fast." Daddy exchanged a dazed looked with Mommy.

"We're so proud of you." Mommy's smile was misty.

"Thanks." I flashed a grin. "Now, what can I help with?"

The bell above the bakery entrance pealed, signaling a new arrival.

"Another customer. We're getting good traffic today." With

a grin, I rushed back to the cash register. I didn't recognize the person. "Welcome to Spice Isle Bakery. What can I get for you?"

"Information." The tall, good-looking Latino gave me a smile that could've melted butter. "I'm José Perez. *Brooklyn Daily Beacon*. Why're police investigating you for Claudio Fabrizi's murder?"

CHAPTER 13

It was him. The reporter whose article in Tuesday's newspaper gleefully identified me as a "person of interest" in an active homicide investigation.

My back stiffened. Heat filled my cheeks. I stared into his inquisitive bright brown eyes and reached for something—anything—to say that would distract him from his current line of questioning. I parted my lips, but no words came out.

I tried again. "I have nothing to say about Claudio Fabrizi or his death." My tone was firm. I hoped my message was clear.

His smile broadened. "Did you and Fabrizi have a dispute?"

I narrowed my eyes. "I told you I'm not talking—"

"Witnesses said the two of you had argued about your opening this bakery." He scanned the shop, taking in our green, red, yellow, and sea blue color scheme. His eyes gleamed as though he approved. "They said you were really going at it."

"I said—"

"Did you know you were going to make him angry when you opened this place?"

"José!" I raised my voice to make him listen to me. His monologue reminded me of my former boss. He used to talk over me, too. I never had the satisfaction of shouting him down, though. "I'm only going to say this once more. I am *not* discussing Claudio Fabrizi or his death. Now is there something from our menu I can get for you? If not, please leave. This is my place of business."

His smile remained in place. *Baffling.* "Lynds—may I call you Lynds?"

I unclenched my teeth. "No."

"Really?" His eyebrows shot up as though I'd caught him off guard. He must be used to charming information from people. He paused, seeming to expect me to change my mind. I didn't. "All right. I'm the *BDB* crime beat reporter with the rep for getting all the relevant info on crimes in Brooklyn *first.* I got the scoop on you being a person of interest before anyone else."

"Congratulations. Would you like to buy a currant roll to celebrate?"

"Sure." He flashed a grin and some cash.

My sarcasm was lost on him. *Oh, brother.* I rang up his order and turned over the pastry. "Enjoy and goodbye."

"Are you sure you don't want to say anything?" He took the order bag and his change. "This is your chance to get your story out before the police take over the narrative. And believe me, with those two, you'll need the head start."

My mouth went dry. "What does that mean?"

"Jackson and Milner caught this case."

"I know." Their interrogation had made that crystal clear. So much for his "scoop."

"Jackson's a new detective. He's been on the job less than a year. Some people think he's moved up fast. Too fast. He's young and Black. He's heard those rumors. And they've made him anxious to prove himself. Let people know he was promoted on merit and nothing more." José gave me a pointed look.

If he was trying to scare me, he was succeeding. Still, he'd have to spell out his warning. I wasn't going to cave on rumors and theories. "How does that affect me?"

José's eyes widened. "Are you serious? Jackson's going to use this case to prove he has what it takes to be a homicide detective. He'll want to show he earned this promotion. If he's already tagged you as a person of interest, they're probably building a case against you right now."

Oh. No.

My body temperature plummeted. My muscles were shaking. I gripped the checkout counter and locked my knees to hold myself upright. The hard laminate surface was cool beneath my clammy palms. "How do you know this? Are the two of you friends or something?"

José shrugged broad shoulders beneath a pale salmon shirt and black tie. "It's my beat. I make it my business to know. That's how I'm always able to get the info first."

I nodded, still struggling to maintain my composure. "Thank you for sharing your insights with me." The question was, were his insights accurate or was he saying these things to scare me into talking?

José gave me an assessing look. "Are you sure there's nothing you want to tell me? Let me help you get your story out before the police take control of the talking points. Whaddya say? You need to do this for your own protection."

I was so scared and his offer was so tempting, but was he

encouraging me to speak with him for my benefit or his? I had the impression he was interested only in himself.

"All right. I'll give you a quote."

"Great." José flashed a toothpaste commercial–worthy grin and pulled a notepad from his tan satchel. "I'm ready."

"Spice Isle Bakery is open for business. We serve breakfast, lunch, and lots of snacks. We cater events. Visit our website for our location, hours, and menu. You're not writing any of this down."

His eyebrows knitted. "I'm on the crime beat, not the food section. This doesn't help me."

"I'm not here to help you. Food—specifically my shop's— is all I'm willing to discuss with you."

"Well played, Lyndsay." José closed his notepad and returned it to his bag. "Let me know when you've changed your mind. Sooner or later, people always do. Just don't wait too long. The police are already telling their side of the story." He left his business card on the counter. With a wink and a wave, he turned and left.

Insufferable. But was he also right?

A weight pressed against my shoulders. I didn't want to be one of the people who "changed their minds sooner or later." But I didn't want to be someone who waited until it was too late, either. Were there other options?

Judge Spice Isle Bakery's opening day only on the breakfast sales and the lunch crowd and it was an indisputable success. I could almost imagine the mysterious canceled lunch orders and my encounter with the crime beat reporter—who was his source?—had never happened.

A glance around the shop confirmed the lunch rush was ebbing. I was amazed by and proud of how well Granny,

Mommy, Daddy, and Dev had kept up with the orders. Every customer had seemed satisfied with the quick turnaround on their requests and pleased with the quality of the food. I finished cleaning the counter, then grabbed the broom to give the floor a good sweep.

"Mind you don't sweep over my feet." Granny spoke without looking away from her latest doily creation. This one was lavender and white. "I may want to get married again."

I smiled at her reference to the belief that sweeping over a person's feet will cause them to never wed. "You have your eye on someone, Granny?" I maneuvered around her table, careful to avoid her blush pink pumps with their pointed toes and spool heels.

"The day's young, love."

I flashed a grin at her cheeky reply.

The chime from the bell above the door and a movement in the corner of my eye let me know we had a post-lunch-rush guest. My smile grew when I recognized Jenna. Her blog post praising our bakery and menu had contributed to the success of our launch. I was certain of it. The air vent that directed the scents of my family's cooking onto the street had played a major role, too.

Jenna returned my smile and added a brief but friendly wave as she crossed to the order counter.

I set my broom in a corner beside the kitchen door and joined her. "Hi, Jenna. It's good to see you. Thank you for stopping by on our launch day."

"Lyndsay." Her blue eyes were wide with distress in her pale, square-jawed face. She searched each of my features three or four times. "How are you?"

It was good to know the *Beacon* had such an extensive readership. Note: That was sarcasm.

"I'm fine." If I'd answered any other way, I had the feeling she'd dissolve into tears. "Thanks for asking."

My attention dropped to her long fingers, gripping the edge of the customer service countertop. They were tipped with lavender nail polish. She had an artist's hands: elegant, slender. Strong.

Strong enough to thrust a serrated bread knife into Claudio?

Where had that thought come from? I shook free of the image.

"I'm glad." Keeping eye contact, she leaned into the counter and lowered her voice. "I know *you* didn't kill Claudio."

"No, I didn't." I kept my voice down, too. Was I imagining things or was she trying to give me a signal?

She glanced over her shoulder as though she didn't want anyone sneaking up on her. "The person who did deserves a medal."

"Excuse me?" Did she just say a murderer should be rewarded? Claudio had a lot of issues, but wishing him dead seemed many steps too far.

Jenna's eyes stretched wide as though she realized she'd used her outer voice. She shook her head, sending her thick blond hair over her broad shoulders. "You're another one of his victims. Everything that's happening to you is his fault. First he attacks you in your own bakery and now the police are investigating you for his murder."

The pulse in my throat played a drumroll. I narrowed my eyes. "Jenna, what do you know about Claudio's murder?"

"Me?" She looked startled. Was she faking? "How would I know anything about it?"

"You sound as if you do." It was getting harder to keep

my voice down. "Jenna, if you know *anything*, you have to go to the police."

She looked horrified, stubborn, and impatient. "No, I don't."

"Yes. You do." I gritted my teeth. "The police think *I* killed him."

Again, she looked on the verge of tears. "I know, and I'm really sorry about that."

"You're sorry?" I couldn't stretch my eyes any wider. "Then go to the police."

"I'm not doing that." Jenna shook her head as though re-inforcing her decision. "Claudio's killer shouldn't be punished. That would be like giving him justice when he denied it to other people."

My cheeks were burning with anger. "By withholding information, you're denying *me* justice. Is that what you want?"

"I'm sorry, but I can't go to the police." She tightened her lips.

"Then give *me* the information. *I'll* go."

She kept shaking her head. "But I promise to do everything I can to prove you didn't kill him."

The bell above the entranceway chimed. In a learned re-action, my attention shifted to the front of the store. A man and woman, both appearing to be in their mid-twenties, were approaching the counter. They'd be here in seconds. I was running out of time to get Jenna to help me.

Shifting my attention back to her, I made the effort to keep my voice low. "Withholding information could send an innocent person to prison. Do you want that on your con-science?"

"I'm sorry, Lyndsay, but I'm not going to let the person

who did this to Claudio get in trouble. I owe it to my mother."
With that parting comment, Jenna turned and hurried out of
the bakery.

What did her mother have to do with this?

I started to circle the counter to go after her. I'd force her
to call the police and tell them everything she knew. But a
sharp cough pulled me up short.

Turning my head in the direction of the interruption, I
found my grandmother. During my exchange with Jenna,
she'd sat in her corner without saying a word. Now she gave
me a pointed look, then nodded in the direction of our customers.

Urgh!

Stepping back to the cash register, I faked a smile. "Welcome to Spice Isle Bakery. How can I help you?"

Chasing after Jenna would have to wait. I had her business card. I'd call her and get to the bottom of her strange
behavior. She wasn't going to give me any information now
anyway. Maybe time would help her to see how unfair she
was being. Why was she opposed to going to the police? Was
she afraid of the killer—or afraid of getting caught? And
what did her mother have to do with any of this?

I'd have to dig into the blogger's background. There was
more to her than I'd originally thought.

CHAPTER 14

An hour later, I was still fuming. Jenna wasn't returning my calls. It was late Wednesday afternoon. I'd called three times, each time leaving a message. I'd even sent a text and an email. No response. Could she make it any more obvious she was avoiding me? My frustration was building along with my suspicion that Jenna had something to do with Claudio's murder and she was cutting me loose to take the fall.

I wanted to scream. But that would have to wait. The bell above the entrance pealed, signaling the arrival of more customers. I popped up from behind the display case where I'd been restocking pastries. Products were depleting at a satisfying pace. The fresh, hot treats had the added benefit of refreshing the shop's enticing smells.

My smile of welcome froze. What did Bryce and Stan want now? A stack of ice collected in my gut. Granny and I exchanged frowns of concern. Fortunately, there weren't any customers to overhear whatever had brought those two back to our door.

Watching Bryce's loose-limbed gait carry him to the

counter, I recalled José's warning. Bryce was anxious to prove himself. At my expense? My throat went dry.

I switched my attention to Stan. The older detective gave me a toothy smile. His eyes crinkled at the corners, generating a web of wrinkles that stretched almost to his rumpled hairline.

Straightening my shoulders, I forced my lips into a smile. As Reena would say, even if you don't feel confident, fake it till you do. She made it seem so easy. "Good afternoon, Detectives. What can I get for you?" My voice was several octaves higher than normal. I sounded like a scared mouse.

Stan's warm gray eyes were glued to the menu on the wall behind me. He shoved his beefy hands into his front trouser pockets and rocked forward onto his toes. "I'd like to try a couple of your currant rolls. Please."

I nodded, keeping my eyes on the cash register. "And what can I get for you, Detective Jackson?"

"Bryce," he corrected. "We've known each other too long for you to call me 'Detective.'"

I blinked. What was he talking about? We didn't know each other at all. There'd been a time when I'd wanted to, though. He'd been so handsome in high school. Maturity had made him even more attractive. He'd also been smart and funny, and had seemed kind. But he'd always been surrounded by the cool kids. And I hadn't belonged. Besides, when your secret crush thinks you could be a stone-cold killer, schoolgirl fantasies quickly fade under grown woman resentment.

Shrugging off those embarrassing memories, I gave him a cool look. "Am I still on your suspect list?"

His smile wavered. "We're looking at a few people."

I crossed my arms. "Including me, *Detective Jackson*."

Stan looked uncomfortable. "Actually, that second roll's for him." He glanced at Bryce. "They sound good, right?"

Bryce's smile warmed his eyes. "I'm sure they're delicious."

With a sniff, I turned my attention to Stan. Bryce's flattery may have meant something BTI, or before the interrogation. After the interrogation—ATI—it didn't even rate.

Stan pulled his wallet from his front pocket. "Let me have three. I think my wife would like them, too."

Bryce pressed his hand against Stan's, forcing his partner's wallet back into his pocket. "I'll get them."

From the corner of my eye, I caught a movement at the kitchen door.

"Good afternoon, Detectives." Dev stopped beside me at the cash register. His bland tone was as cautious as the look Granny and I had exchanged earlier. It also held an edge of intimidation. My brother must be a formidable lawyer. I felt such pride. If only I could be more like him.

"Good afternoon." Stan and Bryce spoke in chorus.

Bryce's features were impassive, but I sensed him taking in everything about me, Dev, Granny, and our shop. Stan was doing the same. The seasoned detective gave the impression of being an open book, but I suspected he had many hidden chapters. The quick looks he tossed at us and around the room were casual, even friendly. He wanted us to believe he and his partner had stopped by for a quick snack; that's all. But he was shrewd. From the tension circling Dev, I could tell he wasn't buying the rumpled detective's act, either. As for Granny, she could smell pretense from a borough away.

"Three currant rolls. I'll get those for you." I tore a sheet of wax paper and pulled a pastry bag.

Mommy and Daddy joined us. If they were trying to mask

their concern, they were failing. Their apprehension was obvious in the lines bracketing their mouths and creasing their brows. I wanted to shake Bryce and Stan for worrying my family.

"Detectives," my mother greeted them. "I'm Lyndsay's mother, Cedella Murray. My husband, her father, Jacob. You've met our son, Devon." She gestured toward Granny. "And this is my mother, Genevieve Bain. Are there any updates on your investigation?"

"I'm afraid we can't discuss ongoing investigations, ma'am." Stan softened his rejection with a smile. "I'm Detective Stan Milner and this is my partner, Detective Bryce Jackson. He and Lyndsay went to the same high school. Small world, right?"

Every eye in the bakery was drawn to me like the tide to the shore. I pretended not to notice. Wrapping the currant rolls in separate papers, I placed them in a Spice Isle Bakery bag. Dev rang them up.

"Is that so?" Granny huffed. "Then he should know better than to think Lynds would've done this thing."

"That reminds me." Stan made a production of searching his pockets. He withdrew a mid-sized clear plastic bag with a single piece of jewelry inside.

"That's my charm bracelet." I blurted the announcement without thinking. Leaning into the counter, I took a closer look and confirmed it was indeed my missing jewelry. "Where did you find it?"

As soon as the words left my mouth, I knew the answer. Joy and relief chilled into fear and dismay.

Stan looked sad. "I thought it might belong to you. I noticed that little plant-shaped charm. It's like the image on the flag there." He pointed to the nutmeg on the bracelet as he looked up at the Grenadian flag behind the counter. He handed the bag to me.

The plastic carrier had a bloodred border. The word "Evidence" was stamped diagonally across the front in big red block letters, obscuring the view of my bracelet. I shook the baggie to move the jewelry free of the text. Nutmeg, boxing gloves, jogging shoes, and chef's hat. Yes, that was my bracelet, or an impressive duplicate.

My stomach turned to think someone was using it to frame me. "My parents gave this to me for Christmas years ago. I thought I'd lost it."

"When?" Bryce watched me closely.

I didn't like the expression in his eyes. It made me feel like a villain. I wanted to scream, *I'm not a murderer!*

Straining to steady my voice, I drew a shaky breath. "Saturday during our soft launch. I'd removed it when I was taking breakfast orders."

"We noticed it gone sometime around the lunch rush." Daddy looked at Mommy, Granny, and Dev. "Lynds asked us if we'd seen it."

"Yes, and I'd said . . ." Mommy's words faded away. I could almost hear her gulp of horror. "I'd said, 'Don't worry. It will turn up.'"

I turned back to Bryce and Stan. "I was standing here when I took it off." I pressed my fingers against the counter. "It kept getting caught on the cash register keys."

"Did you find it at the crime scene?" Dev's tone was grim.

I drew a sharp breath. Did anyone else hear it? Granny put down her doily-in-progress and rose from her table. She joined Dev and me behind the counter, wrapping her right arm around my waist. I leaned into her. It was the only thing I could convince my rubbery muscles to do.

Stan looked at me with what seemed like compassion. It was as though he knew I was scared spitless. "I'm afraid we did."

"*Bunjay!*" Granny's shocked exclamation crashed over me like an ocean wave. I was drowning in fear.

Why was this happening? Who was behind it?

How could I make it stop?

"If you found it at Claudio's home Sunday, why did you wait to show it to me now, three days later?" I was trembling. Granny rubbed my back.

Stan ducked his head. "I'm embarrassed to admit we missed it during our first search of Mr. Fabrizi's home. We just finished going through it a second time. That's when we spotted it and noticed the charms could connect back to you."

This was madness. "I don't even know where Claudio lives. Lived."

"Then how do you explain your bracelet ending up at the crime scene?" Bryce's question triggered another echo of José's claim. Bryce was anxious to prove himself. By any means necessary.

"It's obvious." Dev's voice was cold. His fist was clenched at his side. "The killer stole my sister's bracelet with the intention of planting it at the crime scene to frame her for Claudio's murder."

I hadn't seen him so upset since I'd been in the fourth grade. He'd been in the ninth and had confronted the bullies in my class who'd been taunting me as they followed me all the way home from school.

Stan held out his hand to me. "May I have the evidence bag, please?" He sounded as though he was inviting me to waltz with him.

Everything in me rebelled against relinquishing my brace-let. "When will I get it back?"

He stored the bag back into his pocket. "All evidence is returned at the end of the trial."

"This isn't right." Mommy raised a hand to her chest. "It must have happened the way Dev said."

"Of course it did." Granny squeezed my waist. "One of the customers must be the killer. That would explain how the killer came by the bracelet."

Bryce furrowed his brow. Waves of disbelief rolled off him. You'd think Granny had been talking about aliens landing in our rear parking lot rather than someone's efforts to frame me. "Someone else is using your spontaneous ar-gument with the victim to frame you for their premeditated murder? That seems like a stretch."

I clenched my teeth. "No more of a stretch than my kill-ing Claudio over a petty argument."

"An argument over your livelihood." Bryce spread his hands to encompass the shop. "Either his premeditated mur-der was spontaneous or your spontaneous argument was planned."

Stan stepped backward toward the door. "We're going to have the bracelet tested for prints. If we find some other than yours, it would back up your theory about one of your cus-tomers planting it at the scene."

And if you don't? I couldn't bring myself to ask.

The silence was deafening in the seconds after the de-tectives left the shop. I felt numb, cold, and isolated. This was worse than the fear I'd felt when the school bullies had chased me home. Or when I thought I wouldn't get accepted to grad school, or the possibility of defaulting on our busi-ness loan. It was so much worse.

"I've spoken with my mentee, Alfonso Lester." Dev's voice sounded so far away. "He's a criminal defense attorney. He'll represent you, *if* it becomes necessary."

My attention was drawn back to the door. "I think it just did."

CHAPTER 15

"What're you doing?"

I jumped at the sound of Dev's voice behind me at the bakery counter late Wednesday afternoon. I pressed my left hand to my heart to keep it from diving out of my chest. With my right fist, I punched him in the arm. "What's *wrong* with you? You scared twenty years from my life."

Still vexed, I tried to punch him again, but he hopped out of reach. "Stop now." He rubbed his arm as though I'd hurt him. *Oh, brother.* "Nothing's wrong with me. I want to know what you're doing." From a safe distance, he peered over my shoulder at the laptop. I'd carried it from the office to the front counter so I could do research while keeping an eye out for customers.

"I'm researching how to investigate a homicide, nosy." I turned back to the web page I'd been reading before he'd annoyed me. "I've got to do something. Someone's trying to frame me, but I don't know who and I don't understand why."

"The *who* is the killer." Granny spoke without looking up

from her crocheting. "The *why* is they don't want to go to prison." Sometimes I forgot she could hear my every word.

"Not helpful, Granny." I expelled a breath in frustration. "The only prints they're going to find on my bracelet will be mine. And I am *freaking out*."

Dev interrupted. "You don't know that."

I ignored him. "Every time I turn around something more horrible is happening to connect me to Claudio's murder."

Dev put his hand on my shoulder. "Lynds, I know you're scared. That's why I contacted Alfonso. Let him handle this. He's an excellent defense attorney."

His words made me cringe. How did I get to a place where I needed a defense attorney? "I'm grateful for your help, Dev. Really. But I can't sit here and do nothing while the police build a case against me. It's already beginning to affect the bakery."

"You mean those canceled lunch orders?" He shook his head. "Those were cranks, Lynds. Someone was trying to rattle you."

And they succeeded.

"You didn't believe me when I'd suggested that earlier. Now you're on board with it?" I rolled my eyes. "Cranks or not, the negative publicity the shop's getting—*I'm* getting—led to that dirty trick. It has to stop. Someone at the *gym* asked me about Claudio's murder. It's too much." I turned back to the laptop. "I've got to clear my name and protect the bakery."

"Lynds's right." Granny looked at us over her shoulder. "We can't let people take advantage of us."

I wasn't surprised she'd agreed with me. Granny had always been a fighter. After our grandfather had died, she'd fought his employer and the Grenadian government to get her benefits as his widow. She hadn't been motivated only by her dire situation, raising two children on a postal worker's salary. She'd also been driven by a need for justice. She'd wanted what was rightfully theirs. I needed that same inner strength and courage if I was going to get myself out of this mess.

Dev folded his arms. He still wore his black smock and matching chef's cap. "We're not sitting around. We found a lawyer to represent you *if* the case goes to trial—which it won't."

I wanted to tell him those words weren't as comforting as he seemed to think they were, but I didn't want to hurt his feelings.

"So, we're just sitting so." Granny folded her arms over her chest. "And waiting for the bo-bo to charge her? I can't accept that. We need answers. Don't they always look at family first? Enzo's going to inherit Claudio's bakery and real estate company, no? Why aren't they following the money?"

I'd wondered the same. Enzo had stood at the bakery counter with his father after I'd removed my bracelet. "Claudio spent most of his time with his bakery, but his family's wealth came from the commercial properties he owned and rented."

"One of his tenants could've killed him." Granny set down her doily-in-progress and joined us at the laptop. "He ran a crooked business, cutting corners on maintenance and safety. He promised upgrades but never did any. Charged some high, high late fees even if the tenants' rent was just a few days late. And you should see the contract. *Woi!* They called him the Wolf for his dirty practices."

I arched an eyebrow at her. "Are you sure *you're* not the one who gave him that nickname? It sounds like something you'd do."

Granny's silence was proof I was right.

Dev shook his head in disbelief. "How do you know so much about the Fabrizis' business?"

Granny sniffed as though his question wounded her. "I told you. I hear things. That's how you learn."

Dev rubbed his chin. "Those are predatory business practices, but I can't see a tenant killing him for any of that."

"Humph." Granny slipped him the side eye. "You haven't seen the contract."

Dev tilted his head as he considered her. "You have?"

Granny gave him a brusque nod. "I know some people who rent from him. I may have mentioned you'd take a look at it."

I shook my head in amusement. Granny was always offering Dev's services for pro bono legal advice. And he always accommodated her.

"The tenants may have a motive." I shifted to give my grandmother more room in front of the computer. "But we're looking for someone who'd been here Saturday morning. Someone who could've seen me take off my bracelet and put it on the counter. That's when it disappeared from the bakery." And turned up at the crime scene. My muscles tensed at the wretched turn of events.

Dev seemed deep in thought as he stared at the blue-tiled flooring. "You're right. That narrows the suspect pool."

"That's still a lot of people, *oui*." Granny looked from Dev to me. "That first morning, we were packed. And one of the customers could've been a tenant. We don't know."

"True. But we *do* know Enzo was there." I brought the events of that morning back to mind. "He was at the counter when I took off my bracelet. And his inheritance gives him a motive. I want to know his alibi for the night of his father's murder."

Dev dropped his arms. "You're not the police. You can't walk up to someone and ask for their alibi. Besides, Enzo wouldn't have to kill Claudio to get his hands on their business. Didn't Claudio put him in charge of the properties so he'd have more time to focus on his bakery?"

Granny was shaking her head even before Dev finished speaking. "The bo-bo should be spending more time on Enzo. The business had something to do with it. I'm—"

"What're all you doing?" Daddy asked.

He and Mommy joined us at the counter. We'd entered the lull between the lunch rush and the anticipated frenzied after-work foot traffic. There were still a few hours before we'd need to get back to work baking fresh pastries to add to our inventory and create the aromas that drew customers in.

"We're investigating Claudio's murder." Granny's blunt response caught me off guard.

I'd planned to handle my parents delicately to ease their concerns. Instead, Granny had heaved me into the deep end. I braced myself for their reaction.

"You're what?" Mommy's jaw dropped.

"What did you say?" Daddy frowned his confusion. There was a sweep of wheat flour on his black chef's smock as though he'd tried but failed to wipe an ingredient from the garment.

Mommy set her hands on her hips above her tan khakis. "How're you going to investigate a murder? It's too danger-ous."

Daddy raised his hands chest high, palms out. "There's no

need for you to do that. Dev's got an attorney coming to meet us."

Mommy put her hand on my shoulder, humming her agreement. "We're not going to let them put you in jail. But you can't run after this homicide investigation. Someone's steady trying to frame you. How do you know they won't kill you to cover up their crime?"

I hadn't thought of that. A chill raced through me as the temperature in the bakery seemed to plummet forty degrees. "You have a point."

Mommy nodded decisively. "I know."

"I'm not actually trying to find a killer, though." I pushed past the fear my well-meaning, overprotective family tried to generate. "I want to put together a list of more likely suspects to take the police's focus off of me."

Daddy gestured toward the laptop. "What do you know about homicide investigations? It's not like TV, you know. People go to school for years to learn about that. Police get special training."

"I didn't know how to start a business, either. But I learned and I'm still learning." I gestured toward the laptop. "I feel like I have to try or the police'll railroad me into a murder charge."

Mommy looked to Dev. "The sooner we meet with Alfonso, the better. Perhaps with his help, we can bring Lynds back to her senses."

I rubbed my forehead, trying to ease the tension-induced headache. "The only thing that'll bring me to my senses is clearing my name."

"She won't be doing this on her own. I'll help." Granny lifted her voice as though she wanted everyone to know she approved of my decision.

"That's not reassuring." Dev stared at Granny in slack-jawed disbelief. "Now we'll have to worry about both of you."

Curious. Had Granny been waiting for me to take an active role in clearing my name? Did she think my decision had been inevitable? I wouldn't put it past her. She was a risk-taker and she'd been encouraging me to join her since she'd come to live with us seven years ago. I'd rather find another way to prove my innocence, though, one that didn't involve risking my life.

"What d'you have to worry for?" Granny shrugged her shoulders under her pink jacket. "Me, I'm not worrying. Lynds's a kickboxer. I've seen her practicing. She's more than capable of defending us both, if need be."

My cheeks heated at her praise even as the thought of Granny being threatened chilled me to the bone.

Dev hooked his hands on his slim hips. "You can't investigate a homicide."

"Why not?" I gave my brother an incredulous look. "Don't I have the right to prove my innocence?"

And yet, I didn't have a clue as to how I would do that. What were the things I could and couldn't do as a civilian? Could I ask Enzo to account for his time for the night in question? How would I convince people to confide in me? And how could I avoid crossing paths with Bryce and Stan?

Daddy tossed an arm toward the door. "You heard the customers. No one believes you had anything to do with killing anyone."

"This isn't just about me." I faced my family gathered behind the counter. "It's about protecting all of you." I gestured toward them. "And all of this." I swept an arm around the bakery. Lowering my voice, I continued. "If I'm charged with killing Claudio, I don't want our family's name dragged through the mud. If we're in the news, I want it to be because we have a successful bakery. I want people to enjoy our food. I want them to want to come here. The only way to return the focus to our shop is to clear my name."

Dev rested his large right hand on my left shoulder. "Let the professionals handle it. Your way could make things worse."

I blinked. "What could be worse than being framed for murder?"

"Having the real killer come after you." Dev's eyes reflected the fear in his words. "This is serious, Lynds."

I clenched my fists to hold back the chill coursing through my body. "I know how serious this is."

Granny gestured toward me. "So we have to sit on our hands while someone runs free, framing my granddaughter for murder?"

"I'm not suggesting we don't do anything." Dev shook his head. "There are things we can do. We just have to be smart about it."

Daddy interrupted. "When can we meet with Alfonso?"

Dev glanced at me before looking to Daddy and Mommy. "I'll ask him to meet with us tomorrow after the shop closes."

"Good then." Mommy glanced from me to Granny and back. "Dev's right. We should work with the defense attorney. Since Dev's his mentor, I'm sure he's smart." She gave Dev a proud smile.

"And he has experience," Daddy added. "He could give us advice on what we should do and how we could handle the detectives."

"But we have to wait till tomorrow. That's another day wasted." I drew a calming breath, smelling fear along with cinnamon, nutmeg, and sugar. Closing the laptop, I stepped back from the counter. "Fine. Set up a meeting. Thank you. But my mind is made up. I'm doing my own investigation, starting now."

Granny's cheers of encouragement followed me back to the office along with my parents' and Dev's entreaties to change my mind. This was only the second time I hadn't deferred to the trio's judgement. The first had been opening this bakery, but I'd been able to change their minds. Something told me they weren't going to reconsider this time. As scary as this situation was, I had to do what was right for me. And I needed to figure out how. Quickly.

CHAPTER 16

"Good afternoon, Genevieve. Your little shop's so tidy. Have you had any customers a'tall today?" Tildie Robinson's voice reminded me of a chirping bird.

I looked up from my account ledger late Wednesday afternoon. I'd been working on it for the past hour, since making the decision to investigate Claudio's murder despite my parents' and Dev's objections.

The older woman, a contemporary of my grandmother, was resplendent in magenta from her stylish, angled hat to the mid-calf dress that hugged her generous curves. The rich jewel color complemented her dark brown skin. I glanced across the table I shared with Granny to see how she was reacting to the arrival of her nemesis.

Her dark eyes had narrowed with barely concealed dislike. The two women had known each other since school days back in Grenada, and had worked for the Grenville post office together. Granny had confided they'd once been friends. I didn't know Tildie's side of the story, but according to Granny, Tildie had always been jealous of her and had never missed an opportunity to show off.

Now they were both members of the Caribbean American Aid Society. Granny had been a member of CAAS almost since the moment she'd arrived in the United States. It was an association of Caribbeans in the United States dedicated to helping new immigrants settle into their adopted home. They also organized charitable projects like sending financial and other types of assistance to Caribbean nations devastated by hurricanes, earthquakes, pandemics, and other tragedies.

"Afternoon, Tildie." Granny's voice was cool. "You must be anxious for company if you can leave your shop unattended and walk the two blocks to our place just to say hello."

Tildie's store, Lester's, carried West Indian–themed novelty items like jerseys that read: "Someone in Aruba Loves Me." And nightshirts with the Bahamian flag and a caption that stated: "I left my heart in Nassau." She had a large collection of classic and current reggae, soca, and calypso CDs, as well as paintings and sculptures.

With her smile still in place, Tildie looked to me. "Good afternoon, Lyndsay."

I stood. This woman might be my grandmother's adversary, but good manners had been drilled into me from the womb. "Hello, Ms. Robinson. Is there anything I can get for you?"

She glanced at the menu on the wall behind the counter. "Perhaps a cup of mauby tea. Hot. Thank you, sweetheart."

"You're welcome." I carried the ledger to the counter with me.

Tildie claimed my vacated seat, a bold move. "I know what hard work it takes to achieve the type of success I've attained with my store." She set her cream handbag beside the hot pink and cloud white threads on the small table.

Granny was using those materials for her new doily project. "I thought all you'd appreciate my making the effort to come down and offer my insights."

Fact-check: Tildie had inherited Lester's. Her deceased second husband, Lester Robinson, had passed nearly five years earlier. God rest his soul. Mr. Lester, as everyone had called him, had established his business with his first wife almost eleven years earlier. It was their hard work that had made the store a success long before Tildie had married the widower.

"Offer away." Granny packed her threads, needles, and half-finished doily into her red canvas craft bag. Probably as a precaution from having Tildie stain the materials with her hot tea. "But I doubt you have any information my granddaughter hasn't already addressed. She's very thorough."

Granny's praise made me blush. I filled three cream porcelain cups from the industrial-sized sterling silver tea maker labeled "Mauby." The tea was brewed from the orangey brown bark of the mauby tree or its fruit. You could drink mauby cold or hot. At first, the taste was sweet, like a root beer soda, but it had a bitter aftertaste. It wasn't nearly as unpleasant as corailee, though. My body shuddered thinking about that bush tea. Dev and I had tried to ban it from the shop but were overruled by Daddy, Mommy, and Granny. Now with Joymarie ordering it every day, we were never getting it off the menu.

A medical study had shown mauby helps lower blood pressure and ease arthritis pain. It also was thought to be an aphrodisiac. I tried not to think about that last fun fact as I offered the cups to Granny and Ms. Robinson.

"Thank you, sweetheart." Tildie took one of the cups and

saucers and two packets of sugar from the tray I balanced. She'd removed her hat, placing it on top of her handbag. Short, bouncy silver curls framed her round face. "How much do I owe you?"

"It's on the house." I sensed rather than saw the sharp look Granny gave me. Later, I'd have to explain I wasn't betraying the family. This was business. If Ms. Robinson wanted to share some of the secrets of her late husband's success with us, I wasn't going to let her pay.

"That's very kind of you." Tildie turned her smile to my grandmother, who pretended not to notice as she took her own cup and saucer and three packets of sugar.

"You're welcome." I returned to my seat behind the cash register. Despite my grandmother's reservations about the widow, I hoped to pick up some business tips from her. At the very least, the two women could be entertaining. Tildie was the only person I knew who could fluster my grandmother. And Tildie often seemed undone after their encounters.

Turning away from Granny, Tildie scanned the interior of the shop. "Did Cedella paint all of this?" She gestured toward the murals on the wall behind the counter.

"Yes, she did." Granny's cool tone couldn't mask her pride in my mother's work.

Tildie nodded. "She was always very talented, even as a child. And very practical. I'm sure she would've been a successful artist, but she chose to teach math instead."

Granny's expression softened. "You never hear of them laying off math teachers, but art programs are cut all the time."

Tildie hummed as she sipped the hot brew. "A lot of people have been talking about your bakery. The neighborhood's impressed. But if you're going to grow, you're going to need more staff, you know. Especially if you're going to take part in the festival."

"We're managing fine."

Tildie scowled. "You can't manage a festival with just four people. Trust me. I know. I've had a lot of success at the festival for many years. We're one of the vendors people demand for the event."

Granny rolled her eyes. "We don't need an army of people to make a currant roll. And you don't need one to sell your novelties. I've seen a lot of idle hands in your booth."

Tildie gasped, then grunted. "Suit yourself, Genevieve. You always did. I doubt you'll be applying this year anyway, not with this murder scandal hanging over you."

Straightening on my seat, I started to respond, but Granny's clipped tone beat me to it. "My family didn't have anything to do with Claudio's murder."

Tildie looked shocked. "Of course not, and I never said you did. But the bakery was named in the news. Give people time to forget it first. Some people won't let it go, you know. And they'll keep the bakery connected to the murder. But you do what you want. You always do."

I felt guilty admitting even to myself that Tildie's advice made sense.

Granny sniffed in dismissal. "Thank you, Tildie, but we've already applied for the festival. All of this confusion with Claudio's murder will be long over before then."

She nodded, but I sensed her doubt. "Hopefully, the police will have caught the real murderers by then. If you ask me, it was one of his tenants who killed him."

Granny and I exchanged a look. Imagine Granny and her

nemesis having the same theory about the case. Was it possible they'd find other common ground, too? The mind boggles.

I took a sip of tea, then winced. It needed more sugar. I stirred two more packets into my cup. "There are plenty of bad landlords in Brooklyn, though. That's not much of a motive for murder." Although it was more than the one the police had pinned on me.

Tildie's brown eyes widened in her round face. "They practically threatened to kill him at a tenant meeting just last week. At least that's what I'd heard."

I blinked. That was worth looking into.

The darkness crushing against the windows of my neighborhood gym at five Thursday morning matched my sour mood. I went another round with the freestanding punching bag. My yellow boxing gloves slammed into its black vinyl.

Jab! Jab! Cross! Hook! Bryce!

How could he think I was a killer, then eat at my bakery? He'd barely known me in high school. We'd overlapped my freshman and sophomore years. Had I seemed unbalanced?

Uppercut! Body blow! Claudio!

Was he trying to shut down my bakery from beyond the grave?

The heavy, six-foot-tall bag snapped back with each blow, mocking me.

Front kick! Squat! Right kick! Squat!

Well, I wouldn't let him destroy my business, even in the afterlife. I'd do everything I could to raise the bakery's profile in the community, starting with submitting my catering bid to Robin, which I'd done before leaving for the gym that morning.

So there. Take that, Claudio!

Jab! Cross! Hook! Uppercut! Body blow!

"Who're you trying to take out?" Rocky's greeting, laced with amusement, came from behind me.

Oops. I turned, panting a bit. "Good morning. How're you?"

The taller woman arched a thin eyebrow as she looked from me to the bag and back. "Better than you, I think."

She was in another black unitard that clung to her figure but bared her arms. This one had a diagonal red stripe across both calves.

"I'm fine."

Rocky looked dubious. "Can I give you a suggestion? It's about your stance."

Startled, I raised my eyebrows. "Sure. I'd appreciate that."

"Great." She tapped her right palm on her right thigh. "You have good speed and force, but you can improve that if you change your stance just a bit to enhance your stability."

"OK." I moved to stand beside her and mimic her pose.

"You should have an equal amount of weight on both of your feet." Rocky gestured toward me. "Keep your feet and your knees pointed in the same direction. That will keep your stance stable and help increase the force of your blows. And remember to stay on the balls of your feet. That will give you more speed with your movements."

I looked up as she straightened and stepped back. "Thank you. I appreciate the tips."

"No problem." She shrugged. "You know, they really emphasize form and stance to increase speed and force in the advanced class. Why haven't you enrolled in that one yet?"

Good question. "I just haven't gotten around to it."

Another dubious look. "OK. So, you know I've gotta ask.

Have you given any more thought to training for the exhibition?"

"I'm thinking about it."

"Why're you hesitating? What's holding you back?"

"Time." I gestured toward the bag. "I can find time to exercise." And boost my self-confidence. "Training takes a bigger commitment."

"But you've got skills."

"Thank you, but my family's just opened a shop. Getting it up and growing takes a lot of effort." Oh, and there's the issue of my clearing my name in a homicide investigation.

"Right. Spice Isle Bakery on Parish off Samuel. That's not far from here. A friend tried your bakery opening day and recommended it to me. She said your food's great."

More organic, word-of-mouth marketing. *Yay!* "That's great to hear. Thank you."

"She also told me you threw Claudio Fabrizi out of your shop." Rocky grinned. "She loved that."

"Why?" *Oh, brother.* How many people had heard about my encounter with Claudio?

"She and Claudio had a disagreement back in the day. It's a long story." She shrugged. "Maybe you know her. She's in event planning. Marisol Beauvais."

I blinked.

Marisol Beauvais? Was that Claudio's student with the French-sounding name Robin told me about? The one he'd gotten a restraining order against? She'd been in my bakery Saturday morning?

I took a breath to steady my voice. "Her name sounds familiar, but I don't think I've met her. What company does she work for?" And where was she the night Claudio was killed?

"Events by Chique. It's not far from here." She waved a hand in the general direction of the neighborhood outside. "I tried to get her into kickboxing, but she doesn't have the discipline for it."

"Maybe she'll come around." I'd heard of Events by Chique. Its specialty was high-end events for the rich, famous, and infamous. My mind was racing. "Perhaps the three of us could get together and I could help you convince her to give kickboxing another try." And question her about Claudio's murder.

Rocky chuckled, shaking her head. "I don't know. Maybe it's for the best that Marisol doesn't get involved in the sport. She has a temper. I don't want to even think about what she could do if she knew how to disable a person."

Is that right?

CHAPTER 17

"Sweep up the dust toward the door, *oui*. We don't want to trap any duppies in here." Granny called out another reminder late Thursday morning about sweeping out evil spirits.

"Uh-huh." I changed the direction of the broom as I moved across the floor.

I could sweep fifty-leven times a day but not after nightfall. Disturbing the dust could stir up the ghosts that were always nearby. I did what Granny asked out of respect for her beliefs and also because I didn't want to tempt bad luck. Or rather, any more bad luck.

We'd had another hectic morning at the bakery. It was thrilling and gratifying, and so very satisfying. I hoped I never took the community's support of our venture for granted. At the same time, it was puzzling and stressful.

Could we keep up with the pace once Dev went back to work next week? At first, I'd calculated that we could. Now I was beginning to doubt myself. On the other hand, would customer demand continue if, say, I was charged with murder?

"What's on your mind, Lynds?" The worry in Granny's voice stopped the tumble of images in my head. I didn't want to share any of them with her, though. I wanted her to think I had everything under control. I wanted everyone to think that. Hopefully, I'd get it together soon.

Setting aside the broom, I took the seat opposite Granny at her table. "There's a woman who goes to our gym, Roxanne Stewart. She goes by 'Rocky.'"

"Oh? What does Rocky want with you?" Granny continued her crocheting. Today, she was making a green, gold, and scarlet pullover sweater. She must have moved on to her Christmas gift list. Between friends and family, Granny had a lot of people to crochet for, and someone's feelings would be hurt if she missed them.

The entrance bell chimed its announcement of another customer. I offered a smile of greeting to our guest as I returned to my post behind the counter. "Welcome back, Ms. Nevis." I didn't recognize the dapper older gentleman beside her. "How's the day treating you?"

"It's all right." She brushed a flirtatious look toward her companion before turning to Granny. "Hello, Genevieve. You remember Benny Parsons?"

"Of course I remember." Granny set aside her project. "We met at the last CAAS meeting. How are you, Benny?"

"Good to see you, Genevieve." The older man's voice rumbled like the bottom of the Caribbean Sea.

Granny turned back to her friend. "What're you doin' back here so fast, Tanya? We just saw you this morning."

In fact, Ms. Nevis had once again been one of the first customers through our doors when Granny had opened the store this morning. In the more than four hours since we'd last seen her, she'd styled her gray chin-length hair into an attractive flip and had changed into a modest soft green dress that complemented her warm brown skin.

She folded her hands over her tan purse and sneaked another look at her gentleman friend. "Benny wanted some good fish bakes for brunch. I told him I knew just the place he could get them."

"Thank you, Ms. Nevis." I smiled at the compliment. "Is there anything else I can get for you, Mr. Parsons?"

After taking care of the couple's brunch order, I watched them choose a table in the dining area before returning to Granny. "Rocky thinks I should enter the fitness center's annual kickboxing exhibition. It's in the fall and open to kickboxers with intermediate to advanced skills."

"Why does she want you in the competition?" Granny's voice was edged with suspicion.

Skepticism was my family's default reaction to pretty much everything. We didn't agree to an idea, opportunity, or offer the first time someone made it. Or even the third time. You had to sell us on the proposal. And oh, boy, were we tough customers.

When preparing my Spice Isle Bakery presentation, I'd created a slideshow with graphs illustrating a conservative five-year financial projection animated to a soundtrack of Harry Belafonte's greatest hits.

"She wants more women to compete."

"Oh, ho." Granny's eyes remained on the developing pullover.

"She thinks I have talent."

Granny snorted. "Of course you have talent. You've been kickboxing since you were thirteen. But what do *you* want?"

I shrugged restlessly. "I don't know, Granny. Like you said, I've been kickboxing for fourteen years. But for me, it's exercise like swimming or Zumba." Two of her favorite activities.

Granny looked up from her project. "We don't try to hurt people in Zumba."

"That's another thing. I've never used any of the techniques on a person. Mommy and Daddy wanted me to know how to defend myself, but I never wanted the bullying to go beyond words. I never wanted to get into a fight."

"Your parents didn't want that, either." Granny lowered her crocheting. "They wanted to know—and they wanted *you* to know—that if you needed to defend yourself, you could. But no one wanted it to come to that."

"I know."

"Do you have to fight other people for the exhibition?"

I waved my hands, palms out. "No, thank goodness. The fitness center doesn't carry insurance for actual matches. Competitors are judged on form, speed, and power."

"All right, then." Reassured, she returned to the pullover. "So are you going to do it?"

Deep sigh. "I don't know."

I looked around the bakery. Ms. Nevis and Mr. Parsons were the only customers in the dining area. They seemed to be enjoying their fish bakes and fried plantains. And each other's company. Our shop was off to a good start. But each time I recalled the murder investigation, my blood ran cold.

"There's already so much to do." I looked to Granny. "Now that the bakery's open, we have real business transactions. I'll need those numbers to update our order supply, bookkeeping, marketing, and promotion." And on and on.

"Listen." Granny held my eyes. "This is your business. You own the largest share of the bakery. But we're all here to help. We're a family. You don't need to do everything by yourself, you know. Even Dev, who has his own busy career, is helping."

"Yes, but—"

"No 'buts,' Lynds." Granny held up her hand. "We're a *family*. That's what family does. So if you want to enter this event and kick things, then do it, nuh? We'll handle the shop."

What about Claudio's murder? I needed to investigate that on my own. "Thanks, Granny."

"In the meantime, finish up the sweeping before nightfall. We don't want any duppies, including Claudio's, finding their way into the bakery."

"Yes, Granny." But I had the feeling Claudio's ghost had already taken up residence in our shop.

Alfonso Lester's appearance didn't inspire confidence.

My parents, Granny, Dev, Reena, Alfonso, and I had gathered around a couple of tables after closing the bakery Thursday night. I tried not to let my dismay show. It wasn't easy.

What was it about him that made me question his credentials? Was it his smooth, brown baby face; slight build; plain brown suit; guileless ebony eyes; or black-and-white polka-dot bow tie? I was leaning toward the tie. Dev had told me he was thirty. He looked fifteen years younger. Was he shaving yet?

My brother had confidence in him, though. I reminded myself of that before I spoke. "I'm sorry to ask you to meet with us so late on a work night. I know it's inconvenient, but we're anxious to discuss the situation with you."

"This isn't an inconvenience." He was seated between my mother and me. His deep voice was a surprise, coming from that baby face. It had a hint of a Trinidadian accent. Dev had mentioned Alfonso and his parents had emigrated when he was twelve. "Dev's a good friend and I'm happy to work around your schedule."

His tone was low and unassuming. I couldn't picture him in a criminal court proceeding, defending someone from a murder charge that could land her in prison for the rest of her life.

Did he wear that bow tie in court?

Seated across the table from Alfonso, Dev filled him in on everything that had happened since Claudio and I had exchanged cross words. I used that time to read my family's reactions. Mommy and Daddy wore the expression of worried parents all over the world. Their eyes were wide and fixed. Tension bracketed their mouths. They leaned against each other as though sheltering together in a storm.

Granny was animated as she interjected her opinions and made comments, adding her impressions to Dev's. Reena was the only one focused more on Alfonso than Dev. The look in her narrowed eyes seemed as skeptical as I felt.

Dev finished his report. "Then yesterday afternoon, the detectives returned to the shop. They claim to have found Lynds's bracelet at the crime scene."

Alfonso's thick dark eyebrows rose. "The one she'd lost the morning before Claudio was murdered?"

Dev nodded.

Granny gestured to me. "Obviously someone's trying to frame her."

Alfonso's eyebrows drew together as he turned his attention to my grandmother. "Why would someone do that?"

Reena's jaw dropped. "So that *they* don't go to prison."

I winced at the underlying *duh* in her response. Reena had a lot of positive traits. Tact wasn't among them.

Alfonso took a moment to consider her, seated diagonally across from him. It was during that silent assessment that I saw the tough defense attorney Dev had described. Panic swayed toward hope.

"But why Lyndsay?" Alfonso's voice was expressionless. I couldn't tell whether he'd learned anything about my cousin from his brief study of her. "If this was premeditated murder, the killer would've had time to frame someone with a better motive than hers."

"That's what I'm saying." I leaned into the table. He was rising in my estimation. "There're people who're better suspects than I am. I've been researching them. So why are the police focused on me?"

"Because of the evidence against you." He counted off the points on his fingers. "The bracelet found at the scene and the bread knife used as the murder weapon in addition to your argument in which you threatened him."

I'd changed my opinion too quickly.

Reena was impatient. "We've already explained all that."

Alfonso spread his arms. "I'm afraid the circumstantial evidence against Lyndsay is strong. That's why the police would consider her their top suspect."

"He's right." Dev sighed. "Right now, the only thing we have in our favor is timing. I found Claudio's home address. Even if Lynds had known where he lived, she wouldn't've had enough time to get there and kill him Saturday night."

My throat was so dry, I couldn't swallow. I gripped my hands together on my lap and struggled not to shake them apart. Was this really happening or was I having a nightmare?

This was supposed to be one of the happiest times of my life. I'd realized my dream of opening our bakery. Instead of celebrating, I was preparing my defense against a possible murder charge. It was crazy.

"But Enzo has a stronger motive: money. And Claudio took out a restraining order against Marisol Beauvais. And during a meeting, several of his tenants threatened to kill him." I didn't bring up Jenna. She had a lot of hostility toward Claudio, but I didn't know why. And since she'd disappeared, I was beginning to worry I never would. Maybe she was capable of murder, but had she killed Claudio?

"We shouldn't try to solve Claudio's murder." Alfonso shifted his earnest eyes to mine. "Leave that to the police."

"I'm not trying to solve it. I'm trying to take the focus off me." I swept my arm to encompass the bakery. "Every day I'm considered a person of interest in this case is another day that hurts my bakery. We've just opened and the media's included me in every article about the investigation."

Daddy exchanged a look with Mommy. "We don't want people telling lies about our daughter."

"That's right." Mommy's lips thinned with anger. "She's not a murderer. We don't want people to think she is."

Granny's warm brown eyes were shadowed with concern. "It's one thing if they were criticizing our prices or service. Or even the food, which they could never criticize because it's exceptional. Those are things we can address. But the suspicion? We're going to need help dealing with that."

"I understand, but our best strategy would be to focus on how to defend Lyndsay." Alfonso inclined his head toward me.

"Defend me?" I gaped at him. "That sounds like you're not going to do anything unless I go on trial."

Alfonso threw a startled look at Dev across the table before turning back to me. "If you're not charged with Claudio's murder, there's no need to collect evidence."

Reena interrupted. "You're not listening. We can't risk a trial. What's your strategy to clear Lynds's name *before* that happens?"

Alfonso's brow furrowed. His eyes were wide and uncertain as they bounced between Reena and me. "It would be a waste of resources to do anything *before* she's charged."

Breathe. Breathe.

I fisted my hands as though I could hold on to the last shreds of calm. "I don't see it that way."

"The investigation's not hurting the business, Lynds." Dev reached across the table and gave my forearm a tight squeeze. "Our neighbors know us. They support us. They know you're not a killer."

Wide-eyed, I searched his features. Didn't he understand? "Dev, our neighbors are great. I know that, but if our bakery is going to stay open, we have to expand our reach beyond this immediate neighborhood. This investigation will make that impossible."

Alfonso shifted to better face me. "If the case goes to trial—and I hope it doesn't—we'll list all the reasons we know you're innocent. That will build reasonable doubt."

"Reasonable doubt?" I heard the thin, sharp pitch of hysteria along the edges of my words. "I don't know who killed Claudio, but it wasn't me." I sounded like that popular Shaggy song. I clenched my teeth to stop the flood of words.

I was light-headed and dizzy as though the blood had drained from my head. I couldn't collect my thoughts. He was going to wait until I was charged before doing anything to protect me? Then I was on my own with this investigation.

CHAPTER 18

"What d'you think?" Dev reentered the dining area after escorting Alfonso from the bakery Thursday night.

Torn between my faith in my brother's judgement and a sense of unease with Alfonso's strategy, I sat back, waiting for the rest of our family to share their thoughts.

Mommy leaned back onto her seat. "He's sharp. He asked good questions and seems to have a lot of experience with these situations. I have confidence in him."

I inclined my head in silent, though hesitant, agreement. Alfonso was knowledgeable and capable. But did I have confidence in him? Not yet.

"Yes, he's got a lot of experience." Daddy studied the table as though looking for insights in its pale wood. "But I was hoping there was something we could do now."

Waves of tension radiated from him. I felt them from across the table. Knowing I was the cause of his concern weighed me down like waterlogged driftwood.

"Me, I want to do something now, too." Granny shifted on her chair. "I don't like sitting and waiting. I want to act."

Dressed in dark khakis and a red jersey, Dev rested his

hips against the table facing us. "Alfonso knows what he's talking about. He's been a criminal defense attorney for five years. He has a solid reputation and a lot of courtroom experience. If he says we should wait, we should listen to him."

Granny kissed her teeth. "How many cases has he won?"

"A lot." There was pride in Dev's voice. "He's negotiated lighter sentences for clients who were guilty. For those who were innocent, he was able to prove it."

But how many of those clients was he able to prove innocent *without* entering a courtroom?

"He's not the one." Reena crossed her right leg over her left. Her movements were as decisive as her tone.

All eyes swung to her, waiting for an explanation for her pronouncement.

"Why do you say that?" Dev didn't seem surprised. Perhaps he'd also heard that unspoken *duh* in Reena's earlier response to Alfonso.

"Did you see his suit? And his tie? He's too cautious."

Dev regarded her in confusion and disbelief. "You're basing your opinion on his clothes?"

I agreed with Reena, but I based my opinion on his decisions, not his outfit. I lowered my eyes in embarrassment. *Reena. Reena. Oh, brother.*

She leaned forward as though emphasizing a point only she could make. "I'm in fashion. I can tell a lot about a person by their wardrobe. His clothing tells me he's risk averse. We need someone bold, dynamic, even charismatic."

"She's right, you know." Granny's agreement didn't surprise me. My cousin had been influenced by my grandmother's sense of style. "Where's his fire? We need to be on the attack, not on defense."

Daddy pinned me with his eyes. Their dark concern made my heart clench in fear and regret. "Lynds, you haven't said a word. You're the one who'll be most affected by this decision. What do you think?"

Everyone turned to me. An expectant silence lay heavily on the air around me, threatening to cut off my oxygen. In their eyes, I read their expectation that I'd accede to Dev's judgement. This time, they were wrong.

I faced my brother. "I'm sure you're right. Alfonso would do a good job defending me at trial. But I don't want to go to trial. I can't afford to."

"I'd help pay whatever legal fees we have." Dev's tone was persuasive.

"We all would." Mommy spoke for our extended family.

Shaking my head, I stood to pace. "I'm not talking about money. A trial would destroy my reputation both personally and professionally. Every cent I have is tied up with this bakery. If it fails, I'll be ruined."

My voice was clipped as I strode the length of the dining area. I'd give the floor a good scrubbing with the lemon-scented cleanser in the morning. Granny wouldn't stand for me disrupting the dust and stirring up duppies this late at night.

"What is it you want to do?" Mommy asked.

I definitely didn't want to wait. The injustice of my situation made my stomach hurt. "My own investigation."

"Lynds, we talked about this. Listen to Alfonso." Dev spread his hands. "He's the one with experience, not you."

My big brother was my hero. I didn't like arguing with him, so I rarely did. But in this instance, I couldn't go along with his plan. I'd never before considered him to be so very wrong. "It's fine for *him* to say wait until the trial. *I'd* be the one on trial. The case would help his business and be a death knell for ours."

"All right, all you. Let's calm down." Mommy's voice came from behind me.

Dev sighed, dragging a hand over his tight curls. "I know you're scared, Lynds. I am, too. But you're being rash."

I stared at him. Really, right now? "How's it rash to want to prove I didn't kill anyone?"

"Let's stop arguing, nuh?" Mommy persisted.

Reena blew a breath. "Let them argue, Aunty Della. They need to work through their disagreements."

"How're you going to prove a negative?" Dev's impatience reached out from behind me.

I stopped pacing and turned to him. "By proving other people have stronger motives. That's what the police should be looking for. They should follow the money; look at all of Claudio's enemies, past as well as present. If they're not going to, I will."

Dev froze. "No, Lynds. What makes you think a *murderer* will stop at framing you? If you try to find them, they might kill you, too."

Mommy gasped. "Dev's right. No, Lynds. It's too dangerous."

Daddy scowled. "This isn't some TV show. You aren't trained for this kind of thing."

"She might be on to something, *oui*." Granny gave me a considering looked. "It's not safe to not do anything, either. Besides, she won't be investigating on her own. I'll help."

Reena raised her arm. "So will I."

My conviction for my plan stood on shifting sand. I didn't want my eighty-one-year-old granny and leap-before-we-look cousin putting themselves in harm's way.

Dev turned his frown on them. "No. Way."

Reena scowled back. "You're not the boss of us."

Granny lifted her chin. "I changed your diapers."

Daddy looked from Granny to Reena, then me. "How are you going to do this investigation?"

Think fast. "We'll follow the money, starting with Enzo's inheritance."

CHAPTER 19

Confrontations. I've tried to avoid them all my life. So it was even more absurd that I was suspected of killing Claudio because of an argument. One of the few times I stood up for myself, I ended up a person of interest in a homicide investigation.

"Just take a deep breath and open the door." Reena's calm advice repeated over the cell phone. It was as though she could see me, standing frozen on the sidewalk in front of the shoe store next to Claudio's bakery late Friday morning. The bakery had reopened after being closed for five days in observance of Claudio's death. Had it only been five days ago that Claudio had been found murdered? It felt like a month. At least.

"I heard you the first time." But I still couldn't move. I stood and stared at the bakery instead.

The building was a basic cement structure. Black iron bars clung to its glass entrance. A large, empty display window glared at the neighborhood. Signage stretching across the top of its façade read "Claudio's Baked Goods" in bold black cursive against a plain white background. Based on the little

I knew of him, the store reflected Claudio well: unimaginative, unwelcoming, and abrupt. *OK, that was uncharitable.*

The bakery's name made it seem as though it was all about Claudio, not his family or his culture. My bakery was my dream, but I dreamed it because of my family and wanted it to reflect my culture. What had motivated Claudio? Vanity? Or was I judging him too harshly?

"All right. I'm going in." I squared my shoulders.

"Good luck. Holler back."

"I will." I ended the call.

With grim determination, I took a deep breath as Reena had suggested and strode forward. I lifted my hand toward the door—then froze. The nape of my neck burned as though warning me I was being watched. Turning from the bakery, I swept my gaze up and down the street. A dozen pedestrians and even more cars were within view of Claudio's shop. Any one or more of them could be watching me either consciously or unconsciously. Or I could be imagining things.

I shook off the discomforting feeling and pushed the bakery's door open. Similar to Spice Isle Bakery, a bell chimed, announcing my entrance. Enzo ignored it.

Was he here alone? The last time I'd been here, which was some time ago, Claudio had had two or three employees to help with the store. Where were they?

The shop was silent. No music. No laughter. Not even a whisper of conversation. Of course, it was just after ten in the morning and there was only one other customer. Business at Spice Isle Bakery slowed around this time, too. That made it easier for me to leave Granny to handle the register on her own. And people may not know Claudio's had reopened.

As I waited for Enzo to notice me, I took in the surroundings. The bakery was spotless but didn't feel welcoming.

Claudio had decorated it with a simple black-and-white pattern: floor tile, wall accents, and ceiling fixtures. The effect should've been elegant and timeless. Instead it was cold and impersonal, like its previous owner.

There wasn't a dining area, inviting people to linger and relax. But there was plenty of space for a carry-out line. At the counter, Enzo waited on a dapper gentleman with a wealth of snow-white hair. His black-and-white plaid hat made him seem like part of the bakery. He counted out dollar bills with great reluctance. A dubious expression deepened the wrinkles rolling across his pale forehead. Was he having second thoughts about his purchase?

Enzo finally glanced up from the transaction. His body stilled when he recognized me. His eyes widened beneath thick black eyebrows. I nodded a greeting before continuing my survey of his store.

Whiffs of flour, yeast, butter, and smoke floated on the air, but I was too nervous for the aromas to tempt me. The menu on the wall behind the counter displayed a long list of baked goods, but the display case was almost bare. Was he signaling to customers that Claudio's Baked Goods would soon be closing? How sad. I didn't like Claudio. His bakery was more about making money than serving the community. But this wasn't the way I would've chosen for the shop to close.

I dropped my gaze to the counter. Enzo was using a large serrated knife to slice the customer's loaf of white bread. Seeing his familiarity with the item filled me with satisfaction.

He bagged the loaf, then presented it to the customer. The man hesitated before accepting it and leaving. The entire time I'd been in the bakery, they hadn't exchanged a word.

"What're you doin' here?" Enzo's greeting was more curious than hostile.

He wore a black apron with the white Claudio's Baked Goods logo over a white shirt and blue-and-red-striped tie. Was he going back to his office later?

I locked my shaking knees and forced myself forward, stopping at the counter. "I wanted to express my condolences for your father's death. I didn't know him. I don't know you, either. But losing a loved one is hard and I'm sorry for your loss."

"Thanks." His tone was grudging. His wary dark eyes searched my features. What was he looking for, sincerity? Guilt?

"I also want you to know I had nothing to do with his murder."

"Yeah? Well, we only have your word for that, don't we?" He folded his arms, sandwiching his hands in his armpits. He was going to change those plastic gloves before serving another customer, I hoped.

"I don't mean to speak ill of the dead, but your father rubbed a lot of people the wrong way. Do you know if any of them had threatened him?"

"Besides you? No." He eyes slid away from mine. Understandably. We both knew he was lying.

I pressed my palms against my tan cargo pants to keep from fisting them. "Were you at the meeting with your commercial property tenants when they threatened to kill him?"

His eyes shot back up to mine. "Not all of them. Just a couple."

Oh, well, that was so much better. "Did you tell the police?"

Enzo scowled at me from the other side of the white-and-black laminate counter. "Whaddya tryin' to do? Set up someone else to take the fall for killing my father?"

My brow furrowed in confusion. He knew I didn't murder Claudio. Didn't he want to know who did? "He was your father. Why aren't *you* trying to find his killer?"

Enzo stepped back from the counter. His movements were clumsy and abrupt. His face was tight as though he wanted to mask his thoughts from me. "The cops're handling that."

Not if they were focusing on me. "Had your father been troubled by anything?"

"Besides your opening your bakery?"

I pounded down my rising temper. Why was he so determined to turn my questions back to me? Was I wasting my time? I thought of my family, my shop, my dream. My debt. No, I wasn't wasting my time, but he was wasting his. I wasn't going to be chased away. There was too much at stake.

I locked eyes with him. "Why did it take you so long to report your father's murder?"

"Whaddya mean?" His gaze shifted slightly.

Something about the timing of Claudio's case had struck me as strange the first time I'd heard it. "Your father was killed between ten and eleven, but you didn't call nine-one-one until after one Sunday afternoon."

Enzo shrugged. "So? I don't live with my father. I didn't know anything was wrong." He sounded defensive.

"Your shop opens at ten a.m. Sundays, the same as mine. Claudio would've been at the bakery by seven. If my father hadn't shown up at our bakery by seven, I would've called him at seven-oh-one."

"I don't like what you're suggesting." His scowl darkened. "I don't work with my father the way you work with yours."

"What about Claudio's staff? Didn't they call you?" I looked around the bakery as though the staff was hiding behind the counter or something. "Is that why you fired them?"

His jaw dropped. "Did they tell you that?"

"Your display wouldn't be so bare if you had help in the kitchen." I pointed at the cases. "And since you don't have much experience baking, when you tried to fill them on your own, you burnt whatever you were making. I can smell the smoke. So what happened that morning?"

He watched me in silence for several beats. I could almost hear him arguing with himself. Should he toss me out of the bakery—or should he set the record straight? I returned his look without blinking. Finally, he spoke. "Yeah, they called. But I was with someone."

"With whom?" Did that mean he had an alibi for his father's time of death? Was that the reason the police didn't consider him a suspect? My eyes stung with disappointment.

"That's none of your business." His voice was almost a growl.

It was worth a try. Still, just because he was with someone when his father's employees called didn't mean he had an alibi for the murder.

"Did your father want you to take a greater interest in the bakery?"

"Of course he did." Enzo released a heavy, choppy sigh and, with it, some of his aggression. He appeared resigned to my presence. In the end, he seemed to need someone to talk with. It might as well be me.

He was silent for a moment as though reviewing memories and perhaps regrets. "We argued about it all the time. Baking was *his* hobby, not mine. I don't have any interest in this place." His voice shook and he blinked quickly. "It's not even making money. I told the staff I'm selling it. That's why they're all out looking for new jobs. I didn't fire them."

"When you closed the business, you essentially fired them. Is either one interested in running the bakery for you? Or do you know someone who would be?"

"I've put out a few feelers." He looked closely at me. "Are you interested?"

I shook my head. "I've got my own bakery, remember?"

Enzo glared at our surroundings. His features were compressed with resentment. "I don't know what made Pop think this bakery would be a good idea."

"Did you disagree with his using money from the real estate business to open it?"

Enzo looked surprised. "He didn't use money from the family business to start this place."

I frowned. "Did he take out a loan?"

"I don't know what he did." He looked away. Was he lying again? What was he hiding?

"You must've asked him where the money came from. What did he say?"

"I didn't ask him. I didn't care. And it didn't matter. That money wasn't enough to keep the bakery in the black. He used money from the business for that." Enzo still wouldn't look at me, but I heard the bitterness in his words.

Did Claudio taking money from their business to sink into his bakery make Enzo angry enough to kill him? "Did you see your father the night he was murdered?"

Enzo gave me an irritated look. "Are you trying to set me up for my father's murder?"

I raised my hands, palms out. "I was just curi—"

The chime of the bell above the entrance interrupted us. A warm, welcoming smile transformed Enzo's face.

A tall, slim woman crossed the threshold. Her mango pantsuit and nutmeg spring coat were welcome splashes of color against the sparse black-and-white décor. Her delicate, pale brown features and wide ebony eyes stirred a memory. Where had I seen her before? My frown cleared with recognition. She was the mysterious customer who'd thanked me for making Claudio leave our bakery.

She'd also been near the counter when I'd taken off my charm bracelet. Who was she? Struggling against my introverted nature, I stepped forward. "Hi, I'm Lyndsay Murray. I recognize you from your visit to Spice Isle Bakery. Thank you so much for your patronage."

Her elegant features brightened with a surprised smile. "Of course. Your food is delicious. I've recommended it to my friends."

I felt a warm rush of pride. "Thank you. I appreciate that."

"Sure. Sure. I'm Marisol Beauvais, by the way, with Events by Chique."

I blinked. *No. Way.* What was she doing in Claudio's bakery?

And what had that cryptic "thank-you" been about? I slid a glance at Enzo. She probably wouldn't explain her comment in front of him. I'd have to find a way to speak with her in private—ASAP.

"It's a pleasure to meet you formally. I should get back to my shop." I gave Enzo a curious look. "Again, my condolences on your loss, Enzo."

I looked back as I hurried out of Claudio's bakery. Enzo

was meeting with the person who'd threatened his now-deceased father. I had to tell Bryce and Stan. If Enzo hadn't been on their suspect list before, they needed to add his name now—and put it above mine.

CHAPTER 20

Spice Isle Bakery was bumping. The shop was noisy with animated conversations and shouts of laughter. The sound system was playing Billy Ocean's "Caribbean Queen," an oldie but goodie. In the customer order line, hips were swinging, shoulders were shaking, and wannabee background singers were chiming in on the chorus. Their efforts displayed more enthusiasm than talent.

The lunch rush had started almost an hour before noon, minutes after I'd rushed back to the bakery from my reconnaissance at Claudio's Baked Goods. I'd barely had time to tell my family what I'd learned about Enzo's plans to sell the bakery—Claudio's other pride and joy—his familiarity with the bread knife, and his meeting with the student who'd threatened his father. Dev and I hustled to keep up with orders while Mommy, Daddy, and Granny performed magic in the kitchen. The scents of chicken, beef, and vegetable rotis swam through the order window.

As I turned to greet our next guest, my smile froze in place.

"Hi there, Lyndsay. How've you been?" Stan smiled as

though we were former college classmates, meeting for an alumni trip to the Caribbean. Bryce stood in silent support beside him.

I sent a look at Dev, my eyes stretched wide. He gave me a look that warned me to stay calm. *How?* The memory of the last time they'd "dropped by" our bakery was still fresh. It was right after they'd found my charm bracelet at the crime scene.

"You tell me, Detectives. You're the ones investigating a murder." I struggled to keep my voice low as nearby guests strained to catch our every word.

The sharp, tearing sound of someone kissing their teeth interrupted our exchange. I turned to find Tanya Nevis leaning forward from behind Bryce.

She slapped the counter. "I'm knowing Lyndsay since she was a child. You know how much taunting and teasing and *meanness* she's taken from the school and on the block? And I ain't never once seen her raise a hand against nobody. She's peaceful just so. And now you want to come up and say she's killed someone? No, sir. That can't be."

My face flamed as I listened to my neighbor's passionate defense of me. It wouldn't have been so bad if she hadn't used the fact that I'd been a loser in school as evidence of my innocence. Isn't that what they often said about serial killers?

And who's to say New York's finest wouldn't find a way to twist those anecdotes into evidence of my culpability? They might claim Claudio's threats had been the straw that broke the camel's back into becoming a serrated knife-wielding murderer who left charm bracelet calling cards.

Bryce's eyes fixed on me. His broad forehead wrinkled as though in concentration. "I remember you were always being picked on in high school. Now look at you. You own your own business."

He sounded admiring. I dragged my eyes from his and cleared my throat. "My family and me. And the bank."

The way he was looking at me made me wish I was wearing something other than tan khakis and a blue Spice Isle Bakery jersey. Maybe one of Reena's outfits with accessories and perfume.

Don't let those hazel eyes fool you; he's not on your side.

Stan gave Tanya a friendly smile. "Ma'am, I'm afraid we can't discuss open cases."

Tanya repeated her teeth-kissing sound. Other guests in line murmured their agreement with the elderly neighbor and urged me to have faith. My heart filled with gratitude for their kindness and support even as my stomach churned at having my business "out on the street," as my parents would say. Perhaps Dev was right and the bakery could withstand this attack against my reputation. They gave me hope, and that's what I needed right now.

Dev spoke up. "If you remember my sister from school, you'd recall she was a good student. She was never in any trouble and always followed the rules. Continuing to include her in your investigation would be a waste of your department's time and resources."

Our guests' voices rose in support of his statement.

I gave Dev a grateful look before addressing the older detective. "Can you at least tell me whether you're looking at other suspects or if you're just focusing on me?"

He gave me the same innocent and friendly smile he'd given Tanya. "I'm afraid we can't do that, ma'am."

I refused to be drawn into either that smile or his kind dark gray eyes. "What have you learned about Claudio or his dealings with other people?"

Bryce shook his head. He seemed almost regretful. "Like we said, Lyndsay, we can't discuss an ongoing investigation. But we'll get to the bottom of this."

Not good enough. "Did you know Claudio had filed for and received a restraining order against a former student? I saw that student meeting with Claudio's son, Enzo, this morning at his bakery."

A ripple of excitement worked through the crowd as this update circulated the customer service area. Several guests checked their watches and cell phones as though anxious to place their orders, then hurry to Claudio's Baked Goods to see what was happening.

The look the detectives exchanged made me think they weren't aware of the restraining order's existence.

Bryce shoved his hands into the front pockets of his black slacks. "We can't discuss the case with you, Lyndsay. We're sorry."

Gritting my teeth, I planted my hands on my hips. "Why're you here if not to discuss the case?"

Stan chuckled. I wished he'd share the joke. "We're here for the same reason everyone else is. We want to order lunch."

My eyes stretched wide in disbelief before narrowing with suspicion. I drew a deep breath, catching the aroma of peppers, salts, and savory sauces. "You think I'm a cold-blooded killer, but you're willing to eat at my bakery?"

"My wife loved your currant rolls," Stan said.

"Of course she did." Granny had joined us from the kitchen. She obviously wanted to know what was going on.

Had she come on her own or had Mommy and Daddy sent her to do surveillance? "We wouldn't sell them if they weren't exceptional."

Was I the only person who saw the contradiction between my being a person of interest in a homicide and the investigating detectives ordering currant rolls from me?

I shook with outrage. "Detectives, I didn't drop down with the last rain. You chose our bakery for your lunch break so you could spy on me. You have me under surveillance."

"Just take their money and feed them, nuh?" Granny tossed over her shoulder as she returned to the kitchen.

Dev shrugged. "Granny's right. They're paying customers. And you're not doing anything wrong."

"Fine." But I wasn't happy about their spying. "What would you like?"

Stan stared at the menu behind me. "What would you recommend?"

"That depends." I arched an eyebrow. "How much heat can you handle?" Because I was prepared to make it as uncomfortable for them as they were making it for me.

"Marisol Beauvais met with Enzo this morning?" Reena gaped at me. "What's the four-one-one on that confab?"

I'd parked my car at a meter Friday afternoon. My cousin and I were walking up the two blocks to Events by Chique, Marisol's employer. The name and address had been on her LinkedIn profile. The company specialized in planning events for personal and corporate clients. They also provided craft services for production crews and hired chefs for families wealthy enough to afford those services.

The hairs on the back of my neck stirred. That creepy feeling of being watched was back. As casually as I could, I looked around. I glanced up and down our block, and the one across the street; scanned every car parked at both curbs. I lived in one of the most populated cities in the country, but I'd never had this feeling of being stalked before. Was this case making me paranoid?

I shook off the sensation and responded to Reena's question. "I don't know what it's about. That's what I want to ask Marisol." I'd filled Reena in on my conversation with Enzo on the drive over.

"And those detectives didn't seem to know about the restraining order, but they didn't ask you about the meeting." Reena rolled her eyes. "What was that about?"

"I came across an article on the *Beacon*'s website that referenced the order. In the article, Marisol accused Claudio of stealing one of her original recipes. Claudio took out the restraining order because he claimed she'd threatened him with bodily harm."

"Um. Can't blame her."

"But if Claudio had stolen her recipe and then taken out the restraining order against her, why would she go to his bakery? Ever?"

Reena nodded, co-signing my question. "Although Claudio's dead, so I doubt that order's still in effect."

I arched an eyebrow. "If Uncle Al had a restraining order against someone, would you want to talk with that person? Ever?" I asked, referencing her father.

"Definitely not." Reena's voice was grim.

"I didn't think so. We need to know the connection between Enzo and Marisol. Do you think they could be working together? Maybe Enzo wanted his inheritance now and Marisol wanted revenge for Claudio profiting off of stealing her recipe."

Reena pursed her lips in disgust. "How cold is that? Plotting to kill your father with someone who's already threatened him. That's next level."

"Marisol has a temper." I thought back to my conversation with Rocky. "A friend of hers confirmed that."

Reena slid me a look. "Then you'd better be careful questioning her. How're you going to do that?"

Uncertainty made my knees shake. I guided my cousin out of the heavy pedestrian traffic and stopped to face her. "I'll use our catering services as a cover, then guide the conversation to Claudio."

"Hmmm . . ." Reena's dark eyes looked unsure but determined. She put her hands on my shoulders to turn me around. "Let's get this over with."

"It's not like I have much to lose. The cops came to the bakery again today."

"The handsome one?"

"Focus, Reena. He's the enemy. Try to remember that." I should work harder to remember that, too.

"Funny how you knew right away who I was talking about." She gave a careless shrug. "What did they want?"

"They claimed lunch, but I think they were spying on me."

"Well, that's not creepy much." Her tone was dry.

The company's offices were more spacious on the inside than they appeared on the outside. The illusion may have been accomplished by design. There was a lot of silver metal, bright white walls, and clear glass.

"May I help you?" The handsome young man behind the reception desk had a hint of a Puerto Rican accent.

His clean-shaven angular features were set in polite inquiring lines. A hands-free headset was camouflaged within the glossy curls of his thick jet-black hair. An emerald short-sleeve shirt hugged his biceps. He wasn't the best pick to represent a catering company, though. He looked like he ate only once a day.

I cleared my throat. Nerves. "I'm—we're—here to see Marisol Beauvais, please."

"Is she expecting you?" His smile never faltered, but the twinkle in his onyx eyes suggested he knew we weren't on the priority guest list.

"No, but she'll want to see us." Reena used her I'm-in-Charge voice. It worked 100 percent of the time and that lucky streak wasn't going to be broken today.

After a barely noticeable hesitation, Mr. Circumspect spoke. "Who can I say's here?"

My muscles relaxed. "Serena Bain and Lyndsay Murray of Spice Isle Bakery."

He tapped in an extension. "Marisol, Serena Bain and Lyndsay Murray of Spice Isle Bakery are here to see you." After a moment, he nodded. "I'll direct them to your office."

I struggled to mask my amazement as he gave us the promised directions. We climbed a winding acrylic-and-metal staircase to the second floor. Her corner office had acrylic walls and a wooden door. White slats afforded some privacy, although at the moment the blinds were open. Seriously, the interior was a lot larger than the exterior had led me to believe.

Marisol stood and opened her office door as we approached. "It's good to see you again, Lyndsay. And you must be Serena. Hello. How can I help you both?"

I gave her my salesperson-in-training smile and a marketing brochure. "You'd mentioned that you'd enjoyed our food. We wanted to speak with you about our catering services and suggest the possibility of partnering with you for some of your events."

Marisol's eyes widened as she took the brochure. "Really? Enzo said you'd asked him a lot of questions about Claudio's death. I thought that's why you were here to speak with me, too."

I exchanged a look with Reena. Her wide dark eyes appeared as dazed as I felt. "Well." I turned back to Marisol. "There is that."

CHAPTER 21

I accepted Marisol's invitation to make myself comfortable in her office Friday afternoon. I took one of her two gray guest chairs. Reena sat beside me. The room was comfortably cool, but Marisol gathered a thin curry-colored sweater around herself.

Her office exposed a scary obsession she had with time. A monthly calendar lay on the center of her white modular desk with notes and tasks covering the month of April. A three-month, erasable calendar hung on the acrylic wall behind her computer. She'd dotted it with color-coded project notes. A daily calendar stood on her desk in the space between her computer monitor and phone.

She'd balanced her punctuality preoccupation with personal touches. On the shelf behind her were framed photos of smiling people who bore a striking resemblance to her. Trinkets from international trips were positioned around her office: Ottawa, Canada; London, England; Paris, France; Kingston, Jamaica.

Drawing my attention from the mementoes, I tracked

Marisol as she stepped past us. "At our bakery Saturday, you thanked me before you'd even placed your order. Why did you do that?"

"Because you impressed me when you threw Claudio out of your shop." Marisol closed her office door, then returned to her black faux leather executive seat behind her desk. "That puts you and me in a very exclusive group of people who've ever 'confronted' him." She used her index and middle fingers to draw air quotes around "confronted." "And for our trouble, I got a restraining order and you're a suspect in his murder."

She was making this investigation almost too easy. Why was that? Was there nothing for her to worry about because she was innocent? Or was she trying to make me believe she had nothing to hide because she was guilty? Confusing.

Reena settled back on her chair, crossing her legs. "We'll keep it one hundred. That paper def blew everything up. Claudio came into the bakery, ready to spar, threatening to shut down my cousin's bakery." She waved a hand toward me. "She told him to step."

"Like Claudio would listen to anyone ever." Marisol interrupted in a dry tone.

"Truth." Reena nodded before continuing. "The next day, he's dead and five-o's at our door. But you know what he was like."

"Yes, I do." Marisol gave me an assessing look. "He was a lazy man who imagined himself to be a great baker. He was all about taking shortcuts. Baking and cooking are labors of love. But you know this. They're hard labors, but Claudio wanted all the recognition without any of the work."

Hearing the resentment in her voice, I was even more curious about her dispute with Claudio. "Why were you at his shop?"

Marisol rolled her eyes. "Normally, I wouldn't have gone to that place if it were the last safe building in New York, but Enzo has been asking to meet with me and he wouldn't take no for an answer."

"Why?" Reena and I asked at the same time.

Marisol pressed back against her chair as though taken aback by our interest. "He's trying to sell the bakery. Can you believe that? The day after his father was found dead, Enzo's busy calling all over New York for someone to buy the place. I've told him no more than once. This time, I told him in person. Claudio *stole* my recipe. Now his son wants me to *buy* his business? What would I want with Claudio's except to burn it to the ground?"

I exchanged a wide-eyed look with Reena. *Why aren't the police looking at Marisol?* "Why would Enzo think you'd be interested in buying Claudio's?"

Marisol's shrug communicated irritation, disdain, and resignation. "Years ago, I'd wanted to own a restaurant. But things have changed. Now I have different goals."

"I see." Had her goals changed because she'd changed or had someone put obstacles in her path? It had been almost two decades, but my dream had never changed. That was in part because of my grandmother's encouragement. "When had Claudio stolen your recipe?" My research wasn't clear about the timing.

"It's been almost a year, eleven months ago." She sighed. "I was getting a culinary degree at a community college and he was teaching a pastry class my last semester. The school said he was one of the best pastry chefs in the city." Marisol rolled her eyes again. "I don't know why. It was obvious to all of us we knew more than he did."

"It's all about the papers." Reena rubbed her fingers together. "The better they make him sound, the more money they'll bring in."

"Good point." A spark of admiration brightened Marisol's eyes. Reena had that effect on people. "We had to develop new pastry recipes every week for his class. He stole at least one of mine." The look in her eyes hardened with contempt. "I found out when I tried to include the recipe at a restaurant where I worked after graduation. I was so excited—until he came into the shop and accused *me* of stealing the recipe from *him*."

Reena's jaw dropped. "But couldn't you prove it was your recipe? Did you show your boss your classwork?"

Marisol was shaking her head even before Reena finished speaking. "It didn't matter. The restaurant owner was renting the space from Claudio. It's not a question of who he believed. It was about who had more power over him. So he fired me."

"What?" Reena's outrage scorched the air between us and Marisol on the other side of the desk. "I'm shook."

My mind was blown, too. Anger robbed me of speech. How furious had Marisol been over that unfairness? Claudio had felt he'd needed a restraining order. Had she been angry enough to kill him? But this had happened almost a year ago. Would she have waited that long for revenge?

My voice returned. "Had he stolen anyone else's recipe?"

"Not that I could tell." Marisol's one-shoulder shrug was too stiff to be as careless as she wanted us to believe. "I asked a few classmates. They didn't think he'd stolen their work, but it was easier for me to prove because he'd also taken the name."

"What a sleaze." Reena tightened her lips in disgust.

"I'm so sorry that happened to you." That was an understatement. She'd experienced a monumental injustice.

"So am I." Reena scowled. "Now that Claudio's dead, will you take back your recipe?"

"Are you kidding? Claudio ruined it for me. But, you know, after that horrible experience, things turned out pretty well." Marisol swept her arm to encompass her office and the company beyond. Her features relaxed into a smile. "This is a good company. It's growing, and I'm in line for another promotion. So there's no point in looking back. I'm looking forward."

I studied her closely. "Why did he steal *your* recipe?"

"The same reason I wanted it for the restaurant at the time." Marisol spread her hands. "It's a signature pastry, fancy enough to make a bakery or restaurant stand out."

I exchanged a confused frown with Reena. "Claudio's doesn't have a signature pastry."

Marisol's chuckle was deep and full of spite. "Even though he had the recipe, he couldn't make it. No one who worked for him could. So it didn't do his bakery any good. His business failed anyway. And now Enzo's hot to sell it."

"Have the police spoken with you about Claudio?" I asked.

"Why would they?" Marisol rested her elbows on the arms of her chair. "I didn't kill him."

Reena's eyebrows flew up her forehead. "Claudio had a restraining order against you."

Marisol rolled her eyes again. "He was a coward. One argument and he went running to the cops."

"Must've been some argument," Reena grumbled.

"The police think Claudio was killed between ten and eleven." I folded my hands together to stop them shaking.

I wasn't looking forward to asking this question. "Where were you that night?"

Marisol's lips thinned. "I don't like what you're implying."

Neither did I. She didn't have a compelling reason to kill Claudio. And if she was going to kill him, she wouldn't have waited almost a year, I thought, glancing at the calendars surrounding her. She didn't seem like a procrastinator. But I had to ask. Reena gave me an encouraging nod.

I turned back to Marisol. "Humor me. What were you doing the night Claudio was killed?"

"Sleeping." Marisol's response was abrupt. "As a matter of fact, it was the best sleep I'd had in almost a year."

"I'm taking Marisol Beauvais off my suspect list." I parked my car in the lot behind our bakery late Friday afternoon.

"She doesn't have an alibi, but she does have a motive." Reena repeated her argument as she climbed from my car.

"I have the same alibi. I was home asleep." I followed her across the lot. "And her motive isn't any stronger than mine. Why would she kill Claudio over a pastry recipe she didn't want anymore?"

Reena threw her arms up. "To pay him back for stealing it in the first place. *And* his lies got her fired."

"That happened almost a year ago. Does she seem like the kind of person who'd wait that long to take her revenge?"

Reena stopped, turning to me before she pulled open the bakery's back door. "She seems like the kind of person who can hold a grudge. Almost a year later, she's still angry."

I hurried to catch up. "That doesn't make her a killer. Besides, she said she has new goals and she's up for *an-*

other promotion with her company. I don't think she's our killer."

Reena held the door open as I walked through. "We're not looking for the killer. We're looking for other suspects. Tell Alfonso to give Marisol's name to the police. Maybe then their investigation could be her problem."

"I don't know, Cuz." I called the words over my shoulder. Her idea made me a little squirmy. "That doesn't seem right. I don't want to prove my innocence by throwing another innocent person under the bus." I checked my watch. "I've gotta get ready. Robin's coming to discuss my catering bid in about ten minutes."

"Hey!" Granny's irritated interjection pulled me up short. I spun toward the sound. Reena was scurrying from the staging table, holding three fish bakes she'd pilfered from Granny's platter.

She waved over her shoulder as she hurried toward the back door. "Goodbye, beautiful people!"

Ten minutes later, I was seated at a back table with Robin, reviewing my catering bid for the June event she'd been hired to organize. Had she noticed my nervousness as I'd answered her questions? Expanding our services into catering wasn't something I'd planned to do for at least six months, but when opportunity called it would be foolish to put it on hold.

Robin returned her copy of the estimate to her lavender manila folder. "Your proposal is thorough and your menu ideas are creative. I especially like your blending traditional American and island dishes."

"Thank you." *Just breathe. Breathe, breathe, breathe. If we get the event, great. If we don't, better luck next time.*

With my peripheral vision, I kept an eye on the few customers who'd stopped by for a late-afternoon snack. Quiet conversation and occasional laughter accompanied the soca music streaming through our sound system.

An older couple at a nearby table could use a refill of their water. Catching my grandmother's eye, I inclined my head toward their table. She nodded as she set down her crocheting to retrieve the jug of ice water from the refrigerator behind the counter. I thanked her with a smile.

"Your contract states you'd want half of your invoice paid in advance and half within thirty days after the event." Robin made the question a statement.

"That's right. It's standard contract language." I pressed my lips together to keep from babbling further.

"It is and my client can work with that." She put her folder away. "I'll present your proposal to them Monday morning."

I nodded. "Thank you again for the opportunity, Robin."

"Don't mention it." She waved her hand in a casual gesture. "Working with a new kitchen before other caterers discover you is exciting." She glanced around the bakery. The lack of foot traffic and handful of diners might not seem impressive now, but she should've seen the lunch crowd. "How're you holding up?"

I followed her gaze. "We're managing. The community has been very supportive."

She gave me a faint smile. "It helps that people knew you and that you had a good reputation before launching your business. That's something Claudio never had. People here didn't know him at first. And when they got to know him, they didn't like him."

No, they didn't. Claudio had built a reputation for being

rude. His pastries were overpriced. His serving sizes were stingy, and his customer service stunk. Those last three marks against a restaurant spelled disaster in Little Caribbean and explained why his shop was failing.

"What did *you* think of his bakery?"

Robin crossed her legs in her pale gold sweaterdress. Her shrug was almost apologetic. "He was a good baker, but working with him on that wedding had been tough. That's why we never worked together again. He was hard on his office tenants, too."

"I'd heard he had some questionable invoicing practices and that he didn't reinvest in the buildings' maintenance." That was one of the reasons I was determined to purchase a shop rather than rent one. The stress of being in that much debt kept me up most nights, but at least I didn't have to worry about being ripped off.

She nodded. "Enzo told me he gets a lot of complaints about that. Parking lots need to be repaved. Landscaping's overgrown. He said, before his father bought the bakery, he'd been very proud of their properties. They were pristine. But his father lost interest in their real estate holdings after he opened Claudio's Baked Goods. That's when everything started to crumble. Enzo was very upset."

I narrowed my eyes in concentration. Enzo's motive could be more than getting his inheritance early. It could be saving it from his father. "Do you think that's why Enzo's in such a rush to sell the bakery?"

"I'm sure this is very hard for him. He and his father were close, but he has to protect his inheritance."

"Isn't the bakery also his inheritance?"

"Enzo isn't a baker. He can't even make a sandwich."

Robin giggled. "He told me he wants to sell the bakery and reinvest the sale into his properties."

That was something he couldn't do while Claudio had been alive. Enzo's motive for murder had just gotten stronger.

CHAPTER 22

"José, you're back." *Lord, save me from journalists. Amen.*

"Yes, I am." The reporter strode to the bakery counter late Friday afternoon. His long strides were confident, almost cocky. He looked sharp in narrow black slacks, cream shirt, steel gray blazer, and cream-and-gray tie. He put his large, ringless hands on the counter between us. His black-and-crimson wristwatch peeked out from his cuff. "Have you changed your mind about letting me interview you about Fabrizi's murder?"

"My granddaughter? Change her mind?" Granny barked a laugh. "You mad owah?" She laughed again, her attention still on the sweater she was crocheting.

Ignoring Granny's suggestion that I could be unreasonably stubborn, I turned back to José. "No, I haven't and don't expect to. Is there anything else I can do for you? Perhaps you'd like to *buy* something? After all, this is a bakeshop." I swept a hand, encompassing the dining area. "I'd suggest the currant rolls. You had those before and seemed to enjoy them."

Granny scoffed. "*Seemed to?* Of course he enjoyed them. They're exceptional."

This late in the afternoon, there were very few people at the dining tables. But the soca music still played, and the sweet scents of coconut bread and currant rolls and the savory aromas of curried beef and jerk chicken blew across the bakery. In the kitchen, my parents and Dev were preparing for the after-work rush, which had been significant earlier in the week.

"If I order something, will you let me interview you?" His smile was disarming.

"Tell you what." I gestured to the menu board behind me. "If you order a pastry and pay for it, I'll put it in a bag and give it to you."

José sighed and stepped back. "You're making a mistake, Lyndsay."

I crossed my arms over my chest. "How so?"

"I'm giving you an opportunity to get your side of the story out to the public: your customers and potential customers. The police have already given *their* side and named you as a person of interest. Don't you want to clear your reputation, assert your innocence?"

Anger stirred in my gut. "I *am* innocent. What I don't want is to give any more oxygen to the idea that I'm not. If you're serious about wanting to help me and my bakery, stop speculating about my connection to Claudio's murder. I don't have one."

Granny set down her crocheting project. "There's plenty of crime in Brooklyn, enough to give you a different news story every day of the week. Why're you so focused on Claudio?"

José shifted his stance to face Granny. "Fabrizi's real estate holdings made him a major player in this borough."

"We know." I gestured between Granny and myself before lowering my arm.

His smile was sharp around the edges. "His tenants flat out hated him, though. I doubt any of them shed a tear when they heard he'd been killed. There's already been a lot of heated exchanges between him and the tenant of the building he'd just bought."

That caught my attention. "He bought a building right before he died? But wasn't Enzo running the family's real estate business?"

"No-o-o." José drew the word out. "He handled the paperwork. Claudio made the deals. And it looks like he was making enemies right up to the end. It was just a matter of time before he pushed someone too far."

Granny glanced at him before turning back to her needlework. "What're you saying? That you predicted someone was going to kill him? What good's having all this great information if you don't give it to the police?"

Confusion clouded José's dark eyes. He opened and closed his mouth as though uncertain whether he should answer her question. My grandmother had that effect on people.

"Police don't take reporters' intel seriously, especially when it comes to criminal investigations. That's why I usually work around them."

I jumped at his words. "So you're looking into the murder on your own? Who've you interviewed?"

José extended his hand and waved his fingers in a come-on gesture. "I've already given you information. Now it's your turn."

I exchanged another look with Granny before turning back to José. Leaning into the counter, I lowered my voice. "I'm not an investigative reporter. I've never done anything like this, but I do have a theory. It's possible Claudio's bakery's financial problems could be the motive behind his murder. It seems Claudio was taking money from the real estate business to keep the bakery open."

José's eyes gleamed with interest. "So you think Enzo killed his father?"

Horrified, I sprang back from him, raising my arms in surrender. "That's not what I'm saying, and if you print that I'll sue you and your paper for libel." That could be one way to pay off my business loan. "All I'm saying—off the record—is the police should pay more attention to Claudio's businesses."

"Then why aren't they?"

I narrowed my eyes, giving him a suspicious look. "You're trying to trick me into giving you an interview. It's not going to work."

"It was worth a try." José shrugged. "It seems to me we could help each other."

I shook my head. "I'm not interested in helping you keep my connection to this story alive."

He looked from me to my grandmother and back. "I'll see you again, Lyndsay."

I stopped him on his way out of the bakery. "Where's this building Claudio bought?"

He named the street the building was on. "Events by Chique's renting it now." Then he was gone.

I blinked. *Seriously?* Granny and I looked at each other. I was certain I wore the same wide-eyed look of amazement. Marisol worked for Events by Chique. Had we just found the connection between the angry tenants and my stolen bracelet?

"Are you sure you don't mind working at the bakery on your day off?" I led Dev from the kitchen to the counter at noon

Saturday as we prepared for the lunch rush. "Don't get me wrong. I'm grateful for your help, but I feel bad putting you to work on the weekend."

"Are you kidding?" He chuckled. "I love being here."

The customer line was gratifyingly long. With Dev's help, we made quick work of the requests. Everyone seemed to be in a good mood when they came in. That mood became even better as they listened to the old-school reggae bouncing into the dining area from the sound system, engaged in lively conversations with friends and neighbors, and took in the scents of seasoned meats and sweet pastries.

"Afternoon, Lyndsay, Dev." Joymarie stepped forward in the line. She looked like a warm summer day in a form-fitting aquamarine dress. Her smile was bright and confident, but her eyes were cautious.

"Good afternoon, Joymarie." I matched her welcoming smile. "You look lovely as always. Doesn't she, Dev?"

Dev peeked up from the register and nodded before returning his eyes to whatever he was focused on at the register. "Yes, she looks nice."

Oh, brother. What had such a hold over his attention that he could only spare the measliest glance for Joymarie?

I closed my mouth and cleared my throat. I wanted to shake my big brother. Joymarie was smart, kind, independent, and ambitious. She was perfect for him. Why was he being so dense?

Boosting my smile to make up for Dev's cluelessness, I turned back to her. "What can we get for you today?"

A shadow moved across her heart-shaped face. "Dev, are you dating anyone?"

I blinked. That was direct. My lips curved in a small smile. Good for her.

Dev's eyes shot up to meet hers. "Me?" His gaze wavered. "No, I'm not dating anyone."

Joymarie nodded. "May I have a coconut bread and corailee tea to go, please?"

I packaged her order as Dev counted her change. She left the bakery without another word or look.

"What's wrong with you?" I kept my voice down, confronting Dev once we'd cleared the customer counter. "Joymarie's doing everything short of a song and dance to show you she's interested in you. I know you're interested in her. Why are you acting like a blockhead?"

Dev scanned the bakery as though trying to determine if anyone was listening to us. "Yes, I like Joymarie." His voice was so low, I had to strain to hear him. "But we're too different. She likes to go out, to see and be seen. You know I prefer to spend my evenings at home with a cup of tea and a good book. We just wouldn't work, so why even try?"

My eyes stretched wide. "I can't believe you said that. If you're interested in her and she's obviously interested in you, why shouldn't you at least make an effort? It's not like you to give up without even trying."

"Sometimes, you're better off not taking the risk." Dev started to walk away.

I caught his forearm. "Dev, she may not give you many more chances."

"Maybe that's for the best." He tugged his arm free and disappeared into the kitchen.

"That man's a mess." Granny grumbled her verdict without looking up from her latest crocheting project. The sweater was coming along nicely and starting to take shape. It looked like something she was making for a child, her goddaughter, perhaps.

"Dev'll figure it out. He always does." Then why didn't I feel more confident? I plucked an antiseptic sheet from its container and wiped the counter.

"You'll figure it out, too, Lynds." Granny lowered her crocheting and caught my eyes. "What do you have so far, love?"

My sigh was longer and deeper than I'd intended. I rubbed the counter harder. "Not much, Granny. Like I said, Enzo's already trying to sell the bakery. It's losing a lot more money than it's bringing in. Claudio was borrowing from their real estate business to keep the bakery open. He wasn't paying it back."

"Sounds like motive to me." Granny continued her crocheting. "And you saw Enzo using a serrated knife."

"Motive and means."

Granny gave me a hard look. "Then why are you hesitating?" She set her pattern on the table and shifted on her seat to face me. "What's our next move?"

"I'm going to talk with Alfonso about sharing my suspicions with the detectives. Don't get me wrong. Enzo has a serrated knife and I'm sure Claudio would've opened the door to him. But is his father taking money from their real estate business to keep the bakery open a strong enough motive?"

"It's stronger than yours and that's what matters, remember?" Granny nodded as though emphasizing her point. "We're not solving the case. We're giving the bo-bo other suspects who are stronger than you. They can take it from there."

"You're right, Granny." As always. "I'm also digging into Marisol's connections with Claudio. We just found out she's his new tenant."

"I can help you do that." Her eyes sparkled with enthusi-asm.

The idea of my eighty-one-year-old grandmother investi-gating a homicide made my blood run cold. I returned to my seat behind the cash register before my knees gave out. "You know what, Granny, I've got this. But thank you. I'll tell you whatever I find out."

Granny scowled at me. Her lips tightened in disapproval. "Lynds, you can't do everything yourself. You're running the bakery, investigating a murder. It's too much. You need help."

"But you *are* helping me, Granny. Your handling the cus-tomer counter allows me to do this investigation."

"Why do you have so much trouble accepting help?"

Dev doesn't ask for help. Neither does Reena or my par-ents. There wasn't anything they couldn't accomplish on their own. I wanted to be like them, but I'd feel silly admitting that to Granny. "If I need help, I'll ask. I promise."

Granny gave me a scolding look from under her eyebrows. "That's what you always say. Remember, Lynds, a problem shared is a problem halved."

"I know, Granny. I know." But sharing this problem could put the people I love in danger.

CHAPTER 23

"Enzo's having a hard time finding a buyer for his father's bakery." Jenna seemed to relish that news.

The food blogger was the last customer in line. She'd come into the bakery Saturday during the relative calm after the lunch rush.

I spoke in a stage whisper, conscious of the handful of customers enjoying the bakery's food and atmosphere. "Jenna! Where have you been? I've been trying to reach you for *four* days."

"I had a lot of thinking to do." Jenna gave a sharp, awkward nod. "A lot's happened."

I furrowed my brow. "What was all that you were saying about Claudio and your mother?" And what more could she tell me?

Jenna shrugged her shoulders beneath her purple jersey. Reena would've vetoed the garment. Its vivid shade brought out Jenna's bright blue eyes but drained the color from her cheeks.

"I didn't like the way Claudio treated people." Her voice

was flat and angry. "He pretended to care about them just so he could gain their trust. But he was only using them."

"Your anger feels really personal." I considered the other woman. "Did he hurt you? Or your mother?"

"Claudio was a narcissist." Her eyes darkened as a storm of emotions swirled in their depths. "That's the truth. Don't imagine he managed his family's businesses by hard work and sacrifices. He built them by using people. He took everything from them, and when they didn't have anything left he discarded them like trash. People shouldn't treat each other that way."

"No, they shouldn't." My skin iced over to hear the anger trembling in her voice, but it was the pain in her eyes that made me suspect she was keeping secrets. "What did he do to your family, Jenna?"

"I've told you he didn't do anything to me." Jenna took her purchase. She blinked rapidly as though holding back tears. "I'm not sorry he's dead. But I didn't kill him. If I'd killed Claudio Fabrizi, I'd be shouting it from the rooftop."

She turned and marched across the bakery and out the door.

Granny ended the brief silence. "I can see her killing Claudio." She'd been so quiet during my exchange with Jenna, I'd almost forgotten she'd been there.

"Admit it, Granny, you can see pretty much anyone killing Claudio."

"I suppose that's true. He was a very unpleasant fellow."

"But I can't see Jenna killing him, framing me, then continuing to come to our bakery to talk about how happy she is that he was dead."

Granny stared at our glass front door as though imagining Jenna there. "Why not? If she thinks she got away with framing you, why wouldn't she tell you she was glad Claudio's dead?"

"What's to stop me from taking what she's said to the detectives so they could bring *her* in for questioning?"

Granny gave me the side eye. "I don't know. What's stopping you?"

I shook my head. She'd led me right into that trap. "I want to clear my name. There's so much at stake for us, not just my freedom. But I don't have a motive for her. I think Claudio mistreated her mother, in which case her motive could be revenge. But I don't know."

"All right. What d'you want to do, then?"

I gave that some thought. What could I do? "I need to research Jenna. I like her. I don't want to believe she's capable of killing anyone, but she's obviously hiding something."

"The way you feel about her shouldn't stop you from putting her on that list."

I recalled my first conversation with Jenna. I'd turned to find her standing alone beside our order counter. "You're right, Granny, especially since she was in the bakery when I'd removed my bracelet."

"You're a person of interest in my father's murder. I shouldn't be talking to you." Enzo's dark eyes were cool and distant as he assessed me and Granny, who sat in a guest chair beside mine in his office late Monday morning. With the bakery closed Mondays as well as Tuesdays, Granny had insisted on accompanying me to interview Enzo.

I felt a stirring of irritation. I didn't have time for games. My family's reputation and our bakery were at stake. "You know I didn't kill your father. He wouldn't've opened his door to me in the middle of the night. But he would've opened it for you."

From the corner of my eye, I noticed Granny giving me an approving look. Her dark eyes shone and a smile ghosted her lips. Her support strengthened my resolve.

Enzo's scowl darkened. "Get out of my office."

"Not until you answer our questions." It was a struggle to keep my voice down.

Granny narrowed her eyes and adopted an intimidating expression. "Can anyone verify you were at home sleeping when your father was being murdered?"

I lowered my eyes to mask my dismay. Granny was fond of *Law & Order* reruns, especially since many of the episodes had been filmed in Brooklyn.

Enzo's eyes widened in surprise, then narrowed in anger. "I don't have to answer you."

I looked around Enzo's office.

It reflected his expensive tastes with all the signs of wealth and success, but very little evidence of productivity. Where were his project folders? His mail? There wasn't a single calendar on his desk or his office walls. Was everything electronic?

The room smelled of designer cologne and expensive alcohol. A decanter of what appeared to be bourbon stood on the dark wood credenza across the room. A standard-sized black refrigerator had been positioned beside it. A large leather sofa in a far corner of the room was a perfect match to the guest chairs Granny and I had taken.

I turned back to Enzo. He didn't look like a grieving son who wanted justice for his murdered father. In his bronze Italian suit, black Italian shoes, and black silk tie, he looked like a successful business executive without a care. The cost of his outfit could probably cover one month's payment on my bakery's business loan.

"Aren't you anxious to know who killed your father?" Why wasn't he running around Little Caribbean, asking questions about Claudio's murder? Was it because he already knew who'd done it?

He swung his glower between my grandmother and me. "Get out or I'll call the cops."

"And tell them what?" I shrugged, crossing my right leg over my left. "That you're upset because a senior citizen and a smallish woman are showing concern about your father's untimely passing?"

Granny gave me a sharp look before addressing Enzo. I was going to pay for that senior citizen comment. "The sooner you answer our questions, the sooner we'll leave."

Enzo stewed in silence several moments more. I sensed the moment he realized it would be easier to answer us. He sagged against his seat, shifting his shoulders as though easing his tension. "My father and I didn't always agree, but I loved him. I'd never have killed him."

"Even though, according to you, he was running this business into the ground?" I gave him a speculative look, taking in his silk white shirt and gold Movado wristwatch. That watch was the only indication he gave any consideration to time.

And his phone hadn't rung once while Granny and I had been in his office. Perhaps his secretary was holding his calls since he was in a meeting.

Enzo's frown darkened. "We didn't argue about the business. He was in charge here and I understood that. I was just supposed to handle the day-to-day stuff."

"Then what did you disagree about?" Granny asked.

Disbelief cleared his features. "Why should I answer you?"

Granny settled deeper into the chair. "Because you want us to leave."

Enzo's scowl darkened. His eyes bounced from Granny to me and back before dropping to his desk phone. I stiffened. Was he really going to call the cops? He expelled a harsh breath before raising his eyes to us again. I was weak with relief.

"Pop was always involving himself in my personal life." Enzo waved a hand in a dismissive gesture. "He thought I spent too much money. Well, maybe I do, but that's just because when you're a successful businessman, you gotta look the part and what have you. You know what I mean?"

"Sure." But I didn't agree with him. My West Indian roots meant I tended to be much more frugal.

Enzo continued. "And he was always trying to tell me who I could or couldn't be friends with."

"What?" Granny's eyes widened in shock. "But you're a grown man. Why would he treat you as a child?"

"That's what I said." He gave Granny an approving look.

I noted his agitation. "Did that include your love life?"

Enzo turned to me. His lips twisted in a sour smile. "Let's just say Pop thought the only thing women were attracted to was my money."

"That must've made you mad." It was hard not to feel sorry for him. His father seemed to have been an insensitive jerk.

"Not enough to kill him." Enzo glared at me. "Are you kidding me? Listen, I didn't kill my father. And if you didn't kill him, then it must've been one of the tenants, you know? That Marisol Beauvais is a spiteful person. She's been trying to get a tenant association against us. I'm sure that's payback for my father getting that restraining order against her."

Marisol Beauvais? I looked at Granny. Marisol hadn't mentioned she was putting together a tenant association to counter Claudio's corrupt business practices. She was a lot more involved with the Fabrizis than she'd led us to believe. Why would she be so secretive unless she was hiding a motive for murder?

CHAPTER 24

"Enzo Fabrizi and Marisol Beauvais benefit from Claudio's death." I made the pronouncement to Alfonso during an impromptu conference call with him and my grandmother late Monday morning. "The police should look into them and stop wasting their time with me."

There was a pause. Granny and I exchanged a look. We were seated on either side of the desk in our bakery's small office. We'd contacted Alfonso to update him on our investigation prior to my next baking lesson with Granny.

The office was chilly and a little stuffy. The scents of fresh pastries—sugars, fruits, cinnamon, nutmeg, ginger, and butter—were baked into the space. Breathing in those aromas filled me with pride. The thought of what this homicide investigation could do to our goals and dreams for our business was like a cold wave breaking against me.

Granny frowned. "Are you there, Alfonso?"

"Yes, Ms. Bain." His voice sounded hesitant and confused as it carried through the speaker. "I just wasn't expecting an update on Claudio Fabrizi's homicide investigation from *you*."

Baffled, I stared at the landline, picturing Alfonso in a bow tie seated behind his desk. "Who were you expecting it from, the detectives?" He had to be kidding.

He expelled a breath. "I wasn't expecting any updates, not at this stage of the case."

"We thought it was important to keep you in the loop." Granny leaned into the desk, speaking right on top of the phone.

"I appreciate that, Ms. Bain." He didn't sound grateful.

In fact, I heard tension in his tone and had the impression Dev's mentee was thinking of a tactful way to remind his mentor's little sister to stop investigating Claudio's murder. Well, this little sister wasn't going to sit quietly in the corner while the wheels of justice drew her relentlessly into its system.

"Lynds, tell Alfonso what we've learned." Granny's request pulled me from my musings.

I took a moment to collect my thoughts. "I spoke with Enzo—"

"You spoke with the victim's family member?" His question came fast and sharp like an attack. "Does Dev know about this?"

Startled, I shifted my attention from the telephone to Granny. My eyes widened. My muscles tensed. "Well, no. I mean, he knows I'm researching other possible suspects, but I didn't tell him I was going to speak with Enzo."

Alfonso's sigh was short and sharp. I sensed his frustration from the other side of the phone. "Lyndsay, you can't do things like that, at least not without a lawyer present."

I threw up my hands. "Would you have come if we'd asked you?"

"Why can't we talk to Enzo?" Granny asked. "The bo-bo won't do it."

"Whatever you tell Enzo, he could turn around, twist it, and give it to the detectives to use against you in court." Alfonso spoke slowly and carefully as though this conversation was straining his patience.

It was straining mine, too. "OK, that sounds bad. But someone's already twisting this situation against me, as I've been trying to tell you. There are other people with much stronger motives."

Frustration was driving me to the brink of tears. I was losing sleep. Stress and fatigue were fraying my nerves. I needed someone on my side.

Granny reached across the cluttered surface of the desk to cup my fisted hand. "Tell him again now, love."

Taking a deep breath, I turned my hand to hold my grandmother's. "Enzo's the sole beneficiary of Claudio's estate. He profits directly from his father's death. With Claudio gone, he's assumed complete control of his family's real estate business. He's been trying to sell his father's bakery since the day after Claudio's death."

"All right." Alfonso's response was more subdued. "But why murder Claudio? He would've inherited his father's shares in the business and the bakery eventually. What was the urgency?"

I folded my hands on the desk and leaned closer to the phone. Granny and I sat with our heads inches apart over the speaker. "Enzo seemed put out that Claudio was taking money from the real estate business to keep the bakery solvent. His father was hurting their company. The money he was taking prevented Enzo from spending money on their properties' maintenance and upgrades."

"This is good information." Alfonso sounded approving.

"We know." Granny gave me a smug smile.

"I don't like the way you got it, though." Alfonso continued to fret. "This could give Enzo the upper hand."

"Or it could help Lynds." Granny glanced at me. "Tell him what else you've got."

"You have more?" He seemed surprised. "You've been very busy. Dev doesn't know anything about this?"

"Not yet." Granny's tone was dry. "But I have a feeling you're going to tell him, aren't you?"

Alfonso cleared his throat. I pictured him adjusting his tie. "Someone has to, Ms. Bain. He needs to know, and I don't want him to think I'm withholding information from him."

"I can tell Dev myself." I rolled my eyes at the phone as I stood to pace the cramped room. "Marisol Beauvais has a temper and Claudio had a restraining order against her."

"You'd mentioned that the other night." His response was like a verbal nod.

Yes, the night he'd told me to sit tight until the police finished their investigation. I folded my arms across my chest. I might as well get fitted for an orange jumper.

I turned toward the desk. The office really was a very tiny space. If I kept pacing, I'd make myself dizzy.

"What I learned today is that Marisol also is one of the Fabrizis' tenants." I reclaimed my seat. "She's upset that Claudio was violating tenant contracts. In fact, she's so concerned, she's forming a tenant association to prevent his questionable business practices."

Alfonso hummed. "Interesting, but I don't really see that as a motive for murder. Even if she removed Claudio from the picture, wouldn't Enzo continue his father's practices?"

I shrugged. "Maybe Marisol thinks she could negotiate with Enzo but not with Claudio."

Granny nodded slowly. "The son does seem more reasonable than the father."

"This is good information, too. Thank you for sharing it with me." Alfonso's words were stiff and unnatural. It sounded as though he was reading a script. "But you must stop investigating this case. It's a *murder*. You're not only putting yourself in danger, looking for a killer. You also could be strengthening any case against you."

Granny glared at the phone with suspicion. "Have you been texting with my grandson? Are you reading from a text he sent you?"

"What?" He squeaked his interjection. "I'm not . . . No!"

I unclenched my teeth. "Alfonso, I'm not going to sit quietly while the men around me decide my fate."

He rushed to explain. "That's not what we're—"

I cut him off. "Do you think I'm guilty? Is that why you're so hesitant to help me prove my innocence?"

Across the table, Granny's jaw dropped. Her eyes stretched wide with shock.

"I know you're innocent." Alfonso's denouncement was strong. "That's why I'm confident the police will find the real killer and *we* won't have to clear your name."

"You have more faith than I do." Sitting back against my chair, I crossed my arms again. "I want you to get that information in front of the detectives so they can do a real, meaningful investigation. I don't want my name to be the last one associated with the news reports about a murder. It's not just about my name. It also affects my family's livelihood."

Alfonso's sigh was so heavy it seemed to blow through the speaker and fill the room. "I'll speak with the detectives."

"Thank you, Alfonso." I disconnected the call.

Granny looked at me. "Do you think he'll be able to convince them?"

"I don't think I was able to convince *him*." I braced my elbows on the desk and held my head in the palms of my hands. "I thought about bringing this information to the detectives myself, but it's obvious Bryce and Stan see me as some histrionic female. Their eyes glaze over every time I open my mouth."

"It's best to leave this to Alfonso. As a criminal defense attorney, he has experience presenting evidence to the police. And he has more credibility with them."

I raised my head. "But do I carry any credibility with him?"

Jab! Jab! Jab! Cross! Hook! Uppercut! Body blow! Front right kick! Squat! Front left kick! Squat! Repeat!

My workout with the six-foot, foam-filled black vinyl punching bag early Tuesday morning was more vicious than usual. I still carried a lot of frustration and disappointment from Granny's and my conference call with Alfonso yesterday.

When would he speak with the detectives?

How persuasive would he be in conveying the information I gave him?

Jab! Jab! Jab! Kick! Kick! Repeat!

"You're really abusing that bag, girlfriend."

Startled out of my exercise zone, I spun to find Rocky approaching me with a wide grin. "Good morning."

She stopped an arm's length from me and gestured toward the high-density bag behind me with her left hand. It was still rocking forward and back on its round sand-filled base. "Who're you pretending that is?"

There were a lot of candidates: Alfonso. Bryce. Stan. Enzo.

All of the above? "Nobody. I'm just trying to up my workout today."

Rocky lifted her chin and her thinly shaped left eyebrow. Her expression was skeptical. "We've all been there, girl. There's no shame in it. I've kicked the stuffing out of bosses, exes, backstabbing friends. Straight up. You're allowed."

I laughed. It felt even better than the workout. "I'm good, but thanks." I stepped back, giving her access to the bag.

"I know I sound like a broken record, but have you given any more thought to entering the exhibition?" Rocky stepped back to warm up and stretch out. Like me, she started with a series of lateral hops.

I widened my stance to stretch out my hips and legs. "I don't think I can participate this year. There's just too much going on. But I'll think about it next year."

Rocky lay on the floor, balancing herself on her extended arms, and continued with plank jacks, which were basically jumping jacks in a horizontal position. "I read about Claudio Fabrizi's murder last week. The paper listed you as a person of interest. That's pretty hard to believe."

"I appreciate your saying that." Although I was highly uncomfortable discussing my situation with a virtual stranger. I straightened my arms above my head and leaned right, then left to stretch out my spine.

"Is that the reason you don't think you'll have time for the exhibition? Because you think the cops'll charge you?" Rocky didn't seem to have a lot of boundaries. Her voice was breathless as she continued her plank jacks.

"It's a concern." I ignored my unease as I lifted my left knee to my chest and balanced it on my arm to stretch my lower back.

"Then don't think about it."

"What?" I lost my balance, letting my left leg drop to the ground.

"No one in this neighborhood believes you killed Claudio. I believe the cops'll find the real killer in plenty of time for you to participate in the exhibition."

I gave her a side look. "You're really persistent about getting other women to register for this event, aren't you? How many have you recruited?"

Rocky chuckled, lowering herself to do elbow plank jacks. "None. I've only asked you. You're strong, self-motivated, and you're committed to training. You're in here every morning at five a.m. With that kind of discipline, you could go the distance in the exhibition. I don't want to sign up bodies. I want to sign up contenders."

"Look, I'm sorry—"

"Lyndsay, just register." Rocky stood, dusting off her legs and hands. "You need this exhibition as much as I need you to participate. I saw you beating up on that bag. It's a good outlet for you."

I chuckled. "I just don't think this is a good time for me. Perhaps if things were different—"

She stepped closer to me, lowering her voice. "Look, don't act as though you're going to be charged with murder. Act as though you won't be."

Her words eased an invisible weight from my shoulder. "You've set very high expectations for me. Suppose I get eliminated in the first round?"

Rocky shook her head. "Don't act as though you're going to be defeated. Act as though you're going to take the title."

"I like your attitude." I needed to be more like her.

"So are you going to register for the exhibition?" Rocky's eyes twinkled with pleasure.

Her advice made a lot of sense. How often had I psyched myself out of trying things because I thought I wouldn't be welcomed in that space or I wouldn't be successful? Half the battle was in my head. If this was something I wanted to do, then I should visualize myself succeeding.

But was this something I wanted to do?

"Yes. Yes, all right. I'll do it. And I'm going to prepare for success." With the exhibition and the investigation.

CHAPTER 25

"I'm afraid the company that hired me to plan their event passed on your bakery for the catering." Robin's announcement was more deflating than I'd imagined it might be.

We were seated at one of the tables for two in the bakery's dining area Tuesday morning. The shop was closed, so we had the entire space to ourselves. Mommy and Daddy were having a well-deserved rest day. Dev was back at his law firm, and Granny was out with friends.

Robin's news was disappointing, but was there something I could learn from it? Something positive that I could take away? I hadn't expected to have an opportunity to bid on a catering job this soon, so even feedback from a rejection would put me ahead of schedule.

I straightened on the blond wood chair. "Was it the price? Did they think it was too expensive? Was the menu too spicy?"

"No, no." She sat back with a sigh.

I waited a beat. "Then what was it?"

Her eyes were guarded. Her expression was unreadable. Was she afraid of hurting my feelings?

Robin sighed again. "They don't want to be associated with your business because of Claudio's murder."

That kind of stung. I fisted my hands on my lap. Nodding, I took a moment to collect my thoughts and regain my power of speech. I should've been ready for that, but I wasn't. The company's reaction was one I'd been afraid of right from the start of this homicide investigation. First those canceled lunches, now this. How many more times would we hear this before the police caught the real killer and closed this case?

I held Robin's eyes. "Claudio's murder doesn't have anything to do with my shop."

She extended her hands toward me. "That's what I told them. I know you didn't kill Claudio, but they don't want even a whisper of scandal to be attached to their event or their company."

"Scandal? That makes it sound as though there's a manhunt on for Claudio's killer. Did they have business dealings with the Fabrizis?" I wasn't trying to downplay someone's murder, but the company seemed overly cautious. New York's annual homicide rate was pretty high. The city averaged a murder per day. What made this one so personal to them?

Robin sat sideways on her seat and crossed her legs. "I don't think they were any fonder of Claudio than anyone else. I think they're trying to be respectful of Enzo's feelings."

I frowned. There was something in Robin's voice when she talked about Enzo. And I remembered the smile they exchanged the first day of my soft launch. My grandmother had reenacted the moment. "You'd mentioned you and Enzo were friends, but I thought at one point you two had dated."

She looked startled. "How did you know that?"

"I've heard things." I smiled, thinking of Granny.

Robin looked away. This time her silence seemed even

more reluctant than before. When she spoke, her voice was rough. "You heard correctly. Enzo and I had dated for a while." She broke off with a laugh that sounded much more angry than amused. "A while. I'm still trying to downplay it. We were together for seven months. Our relationship was serious enough to start talking about getting married."

My eyebrows took flight. "What happened?"

"Claudio." Her tone was almost a sneer. I'd never heard her express so much hostility toward him. "He convinced Enzo that I was after his money. His father pressured him into breaking up with me."

"I'm so sorry, Robin." If she'd really loved him, that would've hurt.

Was Robin one of the women Enzo had been thinking of when he told Granny and me his father had told him women were only interested in him because of his family's wealth? Were he and Robin still in love?

If so, that could be a motive for murder. I needed to re-search Robin.

"Forget it. Claudio did me a favor." Robin shrugged. "I could never be with someone who'd cave like that. If he loved me, he would've fought for me. It tells me a lot that he didn't even try to go against his father."

"But Claudio's no longer able to stop you."

Robin blew out a hissing breath. "That ship's sailed. I could never trust Enzo again. He'd never put me first. His breaking up with me proved that."

"I'm sorry." I couldn't think of anything else to say, in part because my mind was racing with the possibility of Robin as a suspect. I was pretty sure she'd been in a position to see me take off my bracelet.

"Are you sure you and Enzo are over?" Nerves powered

my pulse like a jackhammer as I tried to navigate this line of questioning.

Robin's eyebrows drew together in suspicion. "Why are you asking? Are you interested in him?"

"No." I raised both hands, palms out. "But you seemed so upset when you talked about Claudio being the reason you and Enzo broke up."

Her lips curved in a humorless smile. "Are you wondering if I have an alibi for the night Claudio was murdered? I was with someone."

I angled my head. "How do you know his time of death? It wasn't in the paper."

Her chuckle sounded genuine. "Between ten and midnight, right? Enzo told me." Her smile faded. "As I said, I've moved on. Enzo didn't care enough to fight for our relationship, and I didn't want Claudio as a father-in-law."

Who would? I nodded. "I understand."

"You know what really gets me, though?" She didn't wait for me to ask. "Claudio's hypocrisy. He had some nerve accusing me of being after his son for their money when he'd swindled women out of theirs."

Hold on. What now? "Are you saying Claudio's stolen money from people? How do you know that?"

"Enzo told me." Robin shifted back around on her seat to face me. "How do you think he got the money to open his bakery?"

My head was spinning. "He stole it?"

"Enzo told me his father told him he'd been wining and dining some widow in Connecticut he'd found on a dating app. Her husband had left her a ton of money. He'd convinced her to let him invest the money—then he'd disappeared."

Claudio had been even worse than I'd thought. "That's

horrible." And it was yet another motive for murder to share with Bryce and Stan.

"I know." She threw herself back against the chair. "And he has the nerve to say stuff about me."

That wasn't my first concern. "Do you know the woman's name?"

Robin shook her head. "No, but Enzo told me a couple of weeks ago, he'd stopped by the bakery in the middle of the day. This is before yours opened. He said it was closed so he let himself in. That's when he heard Claudio arguing with someone in the office. He thought it was the woman's daughter."

I froze, thinking of Jenna. My research online hadn't turned up much about the blogger. For an internet influencer, it was odd she wasn't on any social media platforms. "What made him think that?"

"She kept saying things like 'Mom's money' and 'what you did to my mom.' She was screaming so loudly, he banged on the office door and threatened to call the cops if the woman didn't leave. But Claudio told him that everything was fine."

I was shaking with impatience. "Did Enzo tell the police about this woman? It sounds like she has a strong motive for killing Claudio. He stole her mother's inheritance."

Robin snorted. "Claudio did more than that. She said he'd promised to marry her mother."

I was screaming in my mind. "Did Enzo tell the police about her?"

Robin shook her head. "He doesn't know her name. He doesn't know what she looks like. All he knows is that she might be a blogger."

I went ice-cold. It was like an ocean wave hit me in the face. "A blogger?" *Jenna?* "What makes him think that?"

Robin shrugged again under her gold sweaterdress. "He thought he heard her say something like, 'I'll make you pay. I can do more than blog about it.' But do you know how many bloggers there are in the city? There must be hundreds. Everyone has a blog."

But we were just looking for one. Could it be *The Frost Forum* with Jenna Frost?

"When you didn't come home for dinner, I knew something was wrong." Granny stood in the bakery office's doorway early Tuesday evening.

I'd been startled when I heard the key turn in the lock, then someone disarm the alarm code. I was getting ready to call the police when my grandmother had appeared.

"I'm sorry, Granny. I lost track of time."

She entered the room and came around my desk. She gestured toward the screen on which I'd uploaded Jenna's blog, *The Frost Forum*. "Did Jenna post another review of the bakery?" Her voice lilted with excitement.

"No." The word came out on a frustrated sigh. "I'm researching her. I think I need to put her on our suspect list after all."

"Jenna?" She nodded knowingly. "Told you I could see her killing Claudio."

"I don't know, Granny. I have to clear my name, but I don't know what I'm doing. I feel like I'm going in circles." I dropped my forehead into my palms and clutched a fistful of braids.

"That's why you need to ask for help—and accept it." Granny's words were short. Her voice was heavy with exasperation. "You can't do everything yourself, and you don't have to."

I straightened but kept my eyes on the desk. I bounced the end of my pen against the blank notepad beside me. "Who would I ask for help, though? Dev's gone back to work. Reena's busy with her job. I need you to cover the bakery while I'm out, and Mommy and Daddy don't want me to investigate. So who would I ask?"

"All of us." Granny circled the desk to face me. "Family comes first. We don't want you to put yourself in danger. We're not stupid. But we don't want you on trial for murder, either."

I shook my head. "I asked them for help, and they brought in Alfonso. He's a nice guy, but even he's told me to wait for the police to charge me. How's that helpful?"

"Then make them see how important this is for you, the same way you convinced them to help launch this bakery." Granny folded her hands in front of her hips. "It takes courage to ask for help, but you need it, so find the courage."

I heard her call to action and accepted the challenge. Pushing away from the desk, I stood. "All right. I'll call a family meeting."

"I already did." Granny turned to leave the office. "We're waiting for you in the dining area."

CHAPTER 26

"I really appreciate that you're all here." On Tuesday evening, I sat at one end of the two tables my family had moved together to accommodate all of us: Mommy, Daddy, Granny, Dev, Reena, me, and our unexpected but welcome guest, Alfonso. "It means a lot that you're willing to hear me out."

"We're family." Daddy sat to my left. "Where else would we be?"

We'd cleared away the wonderful dinner of red beans, rice, and curried chicken he, Mommy, and Granny had packed for us. The scent of the curry and the seasonings used with the red beans and rice lingered around the table, keeping the delicious memory of the meal alive.

"How can we help, Sis?" Dev sat on the other side of the table between Granny and Reena.

I drew a breath and glanced at Granny across the table from me. "I met with Robin this morning. She'd presented our catering bid to her client yesterday."

"You told us she was coming today. What did she say?"

Mommy's response was hesitant. She must have sensed it wasn't good news.

My stomach muscles clenched with shame. I took a breath, then exhaled before forcing my eyes to meet hers. "Her client doesn't want to do business with us because of the bakery's connection with Claudio's murder."

A cloud of concern moved over Mommy's face. "That's not good, but we hadn't planned to start catering now. I thought you wanted to wait a while before expanding our services."

"I know, but it's not just about the catering." I struggled between wanting to appear capable and needing to express my uncertainty. Those feelings were still a thing. "Remember those canceled lunches Wednesday?" I waited for them to nod, then looked at Alfonso seated on my right. "We—I—have a lot invested in this bakery. The fact my name was included in the story about Claudio's death has hurt not only my name but our business. With every day that passes, I'm concerned the damage is getting worse."

Alfonso nodded. "I understand your concern—"

"Do you?" Reena interrupted him. "Because this is my family's livelihood that's being attacked. It's my cousin's life-long dream, and you've told her to wait."

Alfonso leaned into the table. "I know waiting's hard."

Granny interrupted. "Lynds's name is our name. We're a family. When one of us is hurting, it hurts us all."

I turned back to Dev seated diagonally across the table from me. "You asked how you could help me. I need your help to clear my name."

Dev rubbed the back of his neck. Tension wafted from him like cologne. "I feel like we're stuck between two bad choices. Do nothing and you could be charged. Investigate and you could be hurt—or worse."

Subdued murmurs of agreement looped around the tables. Their growing fear reached out to me.

I raised both hands, palms out. "I'm not trying to catch a killer. I just want to identify better suspects so the detectives will stop looking at me. I don't want my name or our bakery in the news anymore, at least not in connection with a homicide."

This time, the cacophony of responses had a much more relieved tenor.

Granny turned to Alfonso. "What did the detectives say about the information Lynds and I gave you?"

Alfonso shook his head. "They haven't returned my call yet."

I gritted my teeth. He didn't seem as anxious as I was to hear back from them, but I kept those thoughts to myself.

"What information is that?" Daddy looked between Granny and me. "Tell us what you've learned so far."

"Writing things down helps me process the information." I flipped open my binder to refer to the notes I'd been taking. "Let's start with Enzo, although I don't like thinking Claudio's own son killed him."

Granny pointed at me. "All those true-crime shows on television say people are more likely to be killed by family or someone they know."

I nodded. "So, for Enzo under 'Means,' I wrote that I'd seen him using a serrated bread knife, which is the type of weapon the police said was used to kill Claudio." I glanced around the tables. "Let's all agree anyone could purchase a serrated knife." I returned to my notes. "Under 'Opportunity,' Claudio would probably let Enzo in regardless of the time of day or night. He might even have a key to Claudio's home just like Dev has a key to our house."

"What do you have for motive?" Mommy asked.

"Money. Claudio was taking money from their family real estate business to keep the bakery open. Enzo wasn't happy about that. He said their properties needed repairs and upgrades, but Claudio was taking money he'd set aside for that."

"Enzo sounds like a strong suspect." Daddy nodded, looking at Alfonso. "What do you think?"

Alfonso inclined his head. "I agree. But it doesn't matter what I think. We have to convince the detectives."

"If they ever call you back." Reena's voice was dry as she cut Alfonso a look.

Reena was disgusted. Alfonso's expression was tight with irritation. I understood my cousin's impatience. I was impatient, too. But I had faith that if Dev was his mentor, Alfonso was a very worthy legal representative. I hoped Reena's open hostility wouldn't dissuade him from working with us.

Daddy nodded toward me. "Who else do you have?" I glanced at my notes again. "Robin Jones, Jenna Frost, and Marisol Beauvais."

Reena frowned. "What're their motives?"

I glanced at Alfonso beside me. He seemed to be typing every word I said into his iPad. Hadn't he taken notes the day Granny and I had called him? "Robin and Enzo had talked about getting married. Claudio had convinced Enzo to break up with her. But now Claudio's out of the way."

Alfonso glanced up from his device. "She must've been to Claudio's home at least once. And since they knew each other, he'd probably let her into his home late at night." He seemed to be getting into the spirit of things. I wanted to jump with joy.

"Now why did you change your mind about adding Jenna to the list?" Granny asked.

"Her motive could be revenge." I tightened my lips with concern. "Claudio may have stolen money from her mother. I have to do more checking. I also need to research Marisol. I want to know why she didn't tell me Claudio had bought the building her employer's renting. I heard that from José. And Enzo told me she was forming a tenant association with other Fabrizi property renters."

"You've been very busy." Concern dimmed Mommy's approving smile. "What's next?"

I first looked to Alfonso's iPad, then raised my eyes to his. "Before I do any more research, we need the detectives to take this list seriously. I want them to leave me and my family alone."

Alfonso tapped some keys on his device. "I'll put this information together and take it to the precinct first thing in the morning."

Reena glared at him. "Could you be a bit more enthusiastic about it? Show some passion. We're trying to sell them on this."

Alfonso's lips parted in surprise. The octave of his voice rose with offense. "I've got plenty of passion." His cheeks darkened and his eyes shifted with embarrassment.

Reena raised her eyebrows.

Alfonso turned to me. "I'll call you tomorrow after I speak with them."

I nodded my gratitude before shifting my attention back to my family. "All I ask is that everyone stay alert in case we come across additional information about our four suspects."

They all nodded, murmuring their agreement and support.

I exchanged a look with Granny. She'd been right. I should've asked for help right away. With luck, this nightmare would be over soon.

CHAPTER 27

"Close up the shop. It's time to get your dance on, Cuz." Reena burst into the bakery Friday night before I could put the Closed sign on our door.

Her sudden appearance startled me. "I'm almost done, but I can't go out tonight, Reena. I've got so much paperwork to do. I've been behind all week."

"Urgh!" Reena rolled her eyes. "You've been working too hard for too many years. Tonight, you need to unwind and relax."

Our definitions of relaxing were very different. Hers involved crowds, loud music, and lots of movement. Mine called for a good book and hot ginger tea.

She moved farther into the bakery, swinging her hips as though she was already at the club. Her dress with its black V-neck bodice and tie-dye skirt in blue, gold, green, and white swirled around her, picking up the music in her mind.

"How can I relax, Reena?" I finished wiping down the dining tables and turned to carry the cleaners and cloths back to the kitchen. "It's been three days since Alfonso met with Bryce and Stan. They claim they're looking into other suspects, but there haven't been any updates in the papers. That means my name and the bakery are still the public's last connection to Claudio's murder."

"So what're you going to do, go home and brood?" Reena locked the bakery door before following me into the kitchen.

I cut her a look as I put away my cleaning materials, and collected my coat and purse. "No, I told you I'm going to catch up on paperwork."

"I have a better idea." She linked her arm with mine as we walked together out the back door. "Come to the club with me tonight. Clear your mind. Leave your stress behind. You'll be refreshed and able to think more clearly in the morning."

Sighing, I climbed into her car. "All right, you may have a point."

Less than an hour later, we were walking into the soca club a few blocks from my family's home. It was hot, packed, and loud. Couples on the dance floor were elbow-to-elbow. The air smelled of sweaty bodies and mixed drinks. Reena and I squeezed our way through the crowd to the bar and ordered two Bird of Paradise cocktails. The mixed drink contained pineapple juice, lime juice, and rum.

"Ladies!" An unfamiliar male voice closed in on us. The speaker wore a nature-patterned short-sleeved shirt and a toothy grin. Thick braids collected his hair back from his forehead. A moustache and goatee framed his full lips and square jaw. "Can I buy you both a drink?"

"Too late." Reena sipped her beverage, then looked away from him.

But I couldn't. My attention was stuck to his face like a mouse caught in a trap. I recognized him from the neighborhood— and from school. He was one of the classmates who'd bullied me from elementary through high school, one of the reasons

I didn't go out much. A lot of those bullies still lived in the area. How many more of them would I encounter tonight? Was I replacing one cause of anxiety with another?

"Don't I know you?" He gestured toward me with a two-ounce shot glass filled with a dark beverage.

He and his friends had taunted and mocked me. I was small, awkward, nervous, and studious. An easy target for them, and they encouraged other students to ridicule me as well. They made my childhood a waking nightmare. But I wasn't in school anymore, the shy kid being victimized by mean girls and boys.

"We went to school together." I tightened my hand around the cold, wet glass.

His confusion cleared and a smile spread across his face. It actually made him look friendly. "That's right. You were that shrimpy girl who always had her head in a book."

Reena grabbed my free arm. The act broke my stare. "Let's dance."

I let her pull me away from the bar. "What about my drink?"

"Bring it with you." She pulled me through the crowd.

I didn't see how that could end well in that mass of gyrating bodies. We danced together to Billy Ocean's "Caribbean Queen," Benjai's "Phenomenal," and Patrice Roberts's "A Little Wine." The songs rushed through me. Knots of tension that had been tightening all week broke free and blew away.

The music took over me, moving my feet, lifting my arms, and shaking my hips. I felt joyous, carefree. As one song mixed into another and another and another, I forgot the investigation, the canceled lunches, the rejected catering proposal, and the bank loan.

Two men made their way to us and asked us to dance. I didn't have any reservations since I didn't recognize either from school. My new partner was handsome and polite, and moved well to the music. We exchanged a few smiles but were more involved in the music than getting to know each other. We were enjoying Machel Montano's "Play Harder" when we were interrupted.

"Mind if I cut in?" José didn't give my dance partner a choice. He used his bearing and stature to force the other man from the dance floor before turning to me.

"Are you following me?" I leaned toward him, raising my voice to be heard above Machel Montano's lyrics and beats. Could José be the presence I kept sensing whenever I was out investigating?

His face was covered with a thin coating of perspiration. He must've been dancing in the club for a while. He stepped closer. His deep voice carried to me. "I should ask you that. I've never seen you here before. I come pretty regularly. It's a great place to unwind."

"That's what I thought before you showed up." Some of the joy leached from me. I gave him a pointed look, then glanced at Reena.

She raised her eyebrows, giving José a nod of approval. I rolled my eyes. Returning my attention to José, I decided to focus on the music and do my best to ignore the thorn in my side.

"I took your advice." He leaned forward and raised his voice. "I've been looking at other possible suspects in Fabrizi's murder. The detectives haven't been exactly generous with their information. Maybe we should compare notes."

I considered him. He seemed sincere. And I'd benefit from advancing his investigation as well. Besides, I was out of ideas. "Whatever I tell you is off the record. You can't quote me in your article."

He hesitated. I tightened my jaw, raised my chin, and gave him my best obstinate expression.

José sighed. "Deal."

I caught Reena's eyes and, using hand signals, let her know I was going to speak with the reporter in a space near the bar. Once she nodded her understanding, I led José from the dance floor.

Finding a relatively secluded spot that could accommodate us, I turned to him. "Have the detectives given you any updates on Claudio's case?"

"Like I said, they aren't giving up any info. But I've found out a few things on my own."

"Such as?" I sipped what was left of my drink, which had survived the dance floor, much to my amazement.

He shifted to face me, leaning his shoulder against the wall. "Before I give you my info, I want to make sure this is a fair trade. I tell you what I have and you share what you've learned."

"Agreed." I nodded without hesitation. "So what have you found out?"

"Fabrizi Commercial Property Management's been in the red for almost two years."

"Really." I stared at him. "How do you know that?"

He gave me a half smile. "I know someone who knows someone who knows the person who handles the Fabrizis' books."

This was getting more and more interesting. "Did this acquaintance several times removed tell you what the drain on their finances was? Was it the bakery?"

"The bakery's part of it, but the bigger drain is Enzo's debts. He has a gambling problem."

I frowned. "How bad is it?"

"Pretty bad. My source says he's indebted to to some pretty bad people." José's voice was somber. "At first, it was a couple of pro ball games. Now it's all sports. I think his addiction could have something to do with Claudio's murder."

I didn't see the connection. "How do you mean?"

"Suppose Claudio was killed because of who Enzo owes money to? He was killed in his home and his body was left for Enzo to find as a message."

That didn't make any sense to me. José might be even worse at this investigation thing than I was. "If Claudio's death was a message to Enzo from these bad people, why would they frame me? How would that serve as a deterrent to Enzo for going into debt? Wouldn't they want Enzo to know they were involved to scare him?"

José sighed, sipping his rum punch. "I'll give you that."

"You don't have to *give* me anything. It's mine." I snorted.

"All right. All right, now. You've made your point."

"But the gambling debt gives Enzo an even greater motive to kill his father." A disturbing thought.

"Right." José jabbed a finger at me. "Claudio's bakery's draining money from their real estate business, but so was Enzo's gambling. One of those things had to be removed, so Enzo removed it by killing his father."

"That's what I think."

He turned back to me. "Your turn. What've you learned?"

I filled him in on my family's possible suspects, Enzo, Jenna, Marisol, and Robin. "They all seem to have stronger motives than my ten-minute argument with Claudio."

"I'm impressed." His dark eyes glinted with admiration.

"I'd rather the detectives were impressed. They were quick to name me a person of interest, but they won't discuss other suspects." They also weren't shy about their fondness for our currant rolls. Did purchasing food and beverages from a murder suspect represent a conflict of interest?

José crossed his arms over his chest. "Just because they won't confirm whether they're looking into those people doesn't mean they're not. Don't lose hope."

"You're right." I looked at him again. "Listen, could you see if any of your connections have additional insight on Robin, Marisol, and Jenna? Anything that could either clear them or support an argument for their being suspects?"

"Sure, I've got it."

"Thanks." I checked my watch. It was almost midnight. "I'd better get my cousin so we can leave. Thanks for reviewing the investigation with me."

"Good luck. I'll let you know if I learn anything more and I'd appreciate it if you'd do the same."

"I will." I straightened from the wall and went in search of Reena. Minutes and much cajoling later, I led her out of the club.

"Two hours. Who stays at a club for only two hours? Who?" Reena threw her arms up as she led us to her car.

"Someone who has to get up early in the morning for work." I adjusted my purse with the strap across my chest.

"Two hours. I'm so embarrassed." She met my eyes over her shoulder even as she kept walking forward. "I have a rep to protect. How can I ever show my face in that club again? Are you sure you have to get up at the butt crack of dawn?"

I returned her smile. "It's not just work. I've got to train if I want to do well in the kickboxing exhibition this fall."

Reena stopped in her tracks. "So you're going to do it? You're going to enter the competition? That's fantastic! I'm so excited for you."

I laughed. "You know, even though I'm making you leave early, I'm glad you pressured me to go out tonight. You were right."

"What was that?" She cupped her ear, leaning toward me. "I don't think I heard you."

"Seriously?" I rolled my eyes. "Fine. I said you were right. I feel more relaxed than I've felt in weeks."

Reena started walking again. "Now who was that attractive guy you were talking with all night?"

I scowled as I kept pace beside her. "He's that reporter with the *Beacon*."

"OMG." She stopped again. "The one who named you as a person of interest in the paper that everyone reads? *Why* were you talking with *the enemy*?"

"Because, as I said Tuesday, I need help clearing my name. He had some good information on the investigation." I filled her in on what José had told me about Enzo.

"He did give you good intel." She arched an eyebrow. "But his idea about Claudio's death being a message for Enzo is cray."

"Agreed." I checked the traffic before stepping into the street.

High-beam headlights sliced across the darkness, blinding me. Spinning toward its source, I raised my hand to block the brightness.

Pop! Pop! Pop!

Good Lord! Someone was shooting at us!

"Run!" I grabbed Reena, pulling her with me back onto the sidewalk. I yanked her down with me behind the dumpster in

the alley beside the club. I'd never moved that fast in my life. My heart thundered in my ears. My breathing stopped. My body shook as though I was naked in the middle of a New York snowstorm.

Screaming tires penetrated the deafening roar of my pulse.

"Was that gunfire?" Reena's teeth chattered as she quaked beside me.

I forced myself to look around the dumpster, checking to make sure the car was gone. Still shaking, I collapsed back against the container. "Yes. Someone just tried to kill us."

CHAPTER 28

"*Someone tried to kill you?*" Mommy and Daddy shouted in near unison late Friday night.

Blood drained from their faces. Their lips parted and their eyes stretched wide. Fortunately, I'd convinced them to sit before telling them what had happened. If I hadn't, they would've collapsed onto the hardwood flooring.

Reena and I had made it back to my home after a twenty-minute drive that should've only taken five. We would have driven faster if we hadn't still been shaking. I'd wakened my parents and asked them to meet us in the dining room. Wrapped in light robes, they were seated on one side of the oak dining table. Reena and I were on the other.

We could've died tonight.

Holding each other's hands, we tried hard to stop trembling.

My parents had known right away something was wrong. Their sleepy, puzzled features had stiffened with wary concern. Then I told them: Someone shot at us. Their expressions transformed into wide-eyed horror.

Silence. Absolute stillness. The air left the room. Then in

a flurry of movement, they sprang from their seats. Circling the table, each pulled one of us up from our chairs and into their arms.

"Are you all right?" Daddy's eyes shifted between Reena and me.

"Are you hurt?" Mommy's eyes filled with tears.

She held me so tightly, I couldn't respond. I could barely breathe. I couldn't move. Her whispered, disjointed words gave voice to her fears as she rocked me side to side. She pressed my head into her shoulder. She smelled of vanilla and powder, scents that had been comforting me my entire life. I hugged her back.

"What happened?" Daddy held Reena at arm's length, searching her face with dark, concerned eyes.

Mommy and Daddy switched places, and Daddy enveloped me in a bone-crushing yet comforting embrace.

"What's all this commotion?" Granny's querulous question preceded her down the narrow staircase that led to the upstairs bedrooms.

Mommy's voice was unsteady. "Someone shot at Lynds and Reena as they left the club."

"Oh, Lord." Granny rushed toward us with the speed of someone fifty years younger. Her bedroom slippers made shushing noises as they slid across the hardwood floor. She squeezed her way in front of my parents and gathered Reena and me in a loving, vicelike embrace.

Mommy wiped her eyes with the backs of her hands. "Who would try to kill you?"

"I don't know." I gasped the words past the semi–choke hold Granny had on me. I didn't want her to let go.

"I'm calling the police." Daddy jogged upstairs.

The police. I tightened my hold on Granny. Maybe we

should've called them before leaving the club. At the time, all I could think about was getting out of there, getting away, and going home. I'd fallen into a fight-or-flight mode and chosen to flee. Reena must've felt the same way, because she'd never brought up the police. But Daddy was right. We had to report this. Someone had shot at us.

"It must've been mistaken identity." Reena kissed Granny's cheek before wiggling free of her hold. Her voice was stronger, but her movements were as slow and unsure as mine. She dropped back onto her chair at the table. "Like you said, Aunty, who'd want to kill us?" Her voice sped up and her eyes glittered. Was she trying to convince us or herself that the attack hadn't been personal? "It must've been some scrub whose girlfriend had dumped him. He saw Lynds and me coming from the club and thought we were her and a friend."

"A 'scrub'?" Granny asked.

"A *bababooy*." It wasn't an exact translation, but it was close enough. I sank onto the seat beside Reena, wrapping my arms around myself.

Daddy returned to the dining room, rummaging through his black cloth wallet. He pulled a business card from it, then grabbed the black phone mounted on the warm sandy wall beside the staircase. We all had cell phones, but my parents insisted on keeping the landline for emergencies and spam calls.

I caught Reena's eyes. "We were near the streetlights when the shooting started. The driver would've seen us." And they'd fired anyway? Why?

Daddy spoke into the phone. "Hello? . . . May I speak with Detective Bryce Jackson, please? It's Jacob Murray calling."

My brow furrowed. *Why was Daddy calling Bryce?* I wasn't the only one who found this puzzling.

"Jake, why're you calling the homicide detective?" Mommy asked.

Daddy covered the receiver's mouthpiece. "I want to speak with someone directly about the fact that my daughter and niece were almost killed tonight. I need action. I want to get to the bottom of this *now*."

"I should call Dev." Mommy sounded fretful and distracted. She went upstairs, presumably to get her cell phone and call my older brother.

I could only imagine his reaction to this latest development. First there was Claudio's unwarranted verbal attack. Then we learned Claudio was killed and the police considered me a person of interest. Now Reena and I were the targets of a random drive-by. He'll probably be halfway to our home before he and Mommy ended their conversation.

Granny stood beside Reena's chair, rubbing her shoulder. Her voice was gentle. "You're staying here tonight, love. Call your parents to let them know."

Nodding, Reena took her cell from her purse, then rose unsteadily from her seat. Granny wrapped her left arm around Reena's narrow waist and with her right hand cupped her elbow. Together they managed the few steps to cross the threshold into the kitchen. Seconds later, Granny returned alone.

I turned my attention back to my father. He was still on hold. "Bryce is a homicide detective. He's investigating Claudio's murder. This isn't a homicide and it's not connected to Claudio."

"Are you sure about that?" Granny's voice was skeptical.

I turned to her. "Why would it have anything to do with his murder?"

"Because you're trying to find the killer." Mommy returned to the table and sat across from me.

I stared at her. Could she be right? "No, I'm not. I'm trying to clear my name."

Daddy grunted. "It's the same thing. The killer doesn't see a difference—" He stopped as his call was finally answered. "Yes, Detective. This is Jacob Murray, Lyndsay's father. Someone shot at my daughter and niece tonight. We think it's connected to Claudio Fabrizi's murder." He gave Bryce the club's name and address. "You know it?" A pause. "All right." Daddy cradled the phone. "He's going to search the scene and wants us to meet him there. I'll get dressed."

Mommy and Granny followed him. What had started as a plan to unwind and relax had turned into a nightmare. I went to check on Reena. She looked up as I entered the kitchen. Her eyes were damp and red. She'd crumpled a paper towel in her right hand. "I had to talk Mommy and Daddy out of coming here."

I sat beside her. "If anything had happened to you . . ."

"If anything had happened to *you* . . ."

We held each other close once again. After a few more moments of silence, we reviewed the events in fits and starts as though talking about it would help exorcise our fear. It wasn't working.

"Daddy thinks the shooting could be connected to my investigating Claudio's murder."

She sighed. "Honestly, Lynds, so do I."

"Me, too." Dev's voice made me jump.

He strode into the kitchen, past the dark blue speckled countertop and honey wood cabinets, and didn't stop until he'd reached Reena and me. He hugged us each in turn, looking us over to reassure himself we were fine. At his request, we told him what had happened outside the club.

"I was afraid of this." He shook his head. "Lynds, whoever killed Claudio's coming after you."

My eyes widened in disbelief. I looked from Dev to Reena and back. "But why? They're already framing me for the murder they committed. Who would they frame for my murder?"

Dev shrugged. "They're probably counting on your murder going unsolved." He stepped back. "Come on. I told Mom and Dad I'd go with you to meet with the detective."

CHAPTER 29

"You look great." Bryce gave me a crooked smile Friday night. It was a little after midnight. "I wouldn't have recognized you from high school if I'd first seen you tonight."

That was deflating. I would've recognized him anywhere. I'd recognized him on the other side of the bakery's checkout counter despite his shorter hair and business suit.

Reena's response was testy and protective. "Listen, Detective Smooth, you wanna focus? Someone tried to kill us." Maybe she could've been more diplomatic, but allowances should be made for the hour and our near-death experience.

The faint smile curving Bryce's lips blinked out. "Could you walk me through what happened?" He looked up and down the street as though trying to avoid eye contact.

Dev had parked his car in the lot across the street from the soca club. It was the same spot Reena had used. We'd waited while Bryce and a trio of uniformed officers had prowled the street and sidewalk in front of the club. After speaking with Bryce, the officers had climbed back into their cruisers. The sound of the three patrol car doors slamming in chorus had made Reena and me jump.

I wrapped my arms more tightly around my waist. "Reena and I had left the club. It was almost midnight. We were walking back to her car." I nodded up the block in the direction from which we'd come.

Bryce interrupted. "Were there other people on the street?"

"No." Reena's voice wobbled. Being back on the scene must be having the same chilling effect on her as it was having on me. "No one. It would've felt spooky if I'd been on my own."

Dev moved to stand between us and wrapped his strong arms around our shoulders. Grateful, I leaned into him.

Bryce looked at us, before turning his attention back to the scene. "So there wasn't anyone around. Did you notice the car before the shooting started?"

"Not really." *But I should have.* "I mean, I knew there was a car there. I saw it parked at the corner, but I didn't pay it much attention. I didn't know there was anyone in it."

Reena sounded annoyed with herself. "I was too busy talking with Lynds."

Bryce nodded as though our responses didn't surprise him. He turned to me. "Could you give me any kind of a description? Color? Type? Anything?"

I closed my eyes, bringing back impressions from the swift glance I'd given the vehicle. "Black or very dark blue. Maybe very dark gray. Four-door mid-sized sedan. Older."

He pulled a notepad from his jacket pocket and wrote quickly. "How many shots did you hear?"

Frustrated, I shook my head. "I don't know. I was too busy trying to find a place to hide. I didn't think to count the shots coming at me."

"Lots," Reena grumbled.

Bryce pulled an evidence bag from his pocket. "The officers found three shell casings, but they were recovered on the other side of the street. Whoever shot at you had horrible aim. Or maybe they weren't shooting at you."

"You say that like it's a bad thing." Reena seemed dazed.

I was yanked back into the fear of the moment. Jumping back onto the sidewalk. Grabbing Reena. Racing for the dumpster. Crouching behind it. Afraid for Reena as the shots kept coming. Afraid for myself. A cold shiver raced up and down my spine. The chill spread across my back and settled in my chest.

But now Bryce was saying the shots weren't aimed at us. If they weren't trying to kill us, what were they hoping to do?

I drew a breath before speaking. The air carried car fumes from the street on one side and garbage from the alley on the other. "I can assure you, from where I was hiding, it sounded like those shots were coming for us."

"Do either of you own a gun?" He divided a look between us.

Reena frowned. "No."

I blinked. "Why're you asking?"

Bryce didn't answer. Instead he looked up at the streetlight. "Could you show me about where on the sidewalk you were when you heard the first shot?"

Reena and I exchanged glances before I led the way up the block. We started walking together back down the sidewalk toward Dev and Bryce. Reena reached for my hand. I held hers tightly. Pushing past my fear, I called up the memory of the attack.

Reena grousing about leaving the club after only two hours.

Reena congratulating me on deciding to participate in the kickboxing exhibition.

Reena congratulating herself on suggesting we go out to night.

My lips curved at those memories. I squeezed her hand Reena did a lot of talking.

I hesitated. My back stiffened. "This is where we stopped. I called to Dev and Bryce. "I checked the traffic. Ther weren't any cars coming, so I stepped into the street."

"That's right." Reena released my hand and pointed acros the street. "I saw the car parked there at the curb across th street, but I didn't think anything of it."

Bryce pointed between us. "Were you standing in the sam positions as you are now? Were you under the light?"

We nodded, looking at each other before answering in uni son. "Yes."

He nodded again. "So, Lyndsay, you were standing unde the light and closest to the curb. The shooter must have see you."

Dev turned to him. His voice was gruff. "What're yo saying?"

"If the shooter could see your sister, why did the bullet land away from her?" He glanced at my brother before turn ing back to me. "Did you tell anyone you were coming to th club tonight?"

I shook my head. "No, it was a spur-of-the-moment deci sion."

Bryce cocked his head. "You're not usually at the club Fri day night?"

Reena snorted. "You really don't have a clue, do you Lynds never goes clubbing. She never goes anywhere."

This wasn't true, but I'd save that disagreement for anothe time.

Bryce paused, frowning. "Have you noticed anyone following you?"

The question chilled me to the bone. I swayed.

Reena braced me. "What is it?"

Recent memories of an itching sensation on the back of my neck returned. I recalled the frequent feeling of someone staring at me. But when I turned, no one was there. We lived in a borough with a population of almost three million, though. Someone was always staring at someone else, whether consciously or not. You couldn't help it.

I swallowed to ease the sudden dryness of my throat. "You think this car followed Reena and me to the club to shoot at us?" That seemed farfetched.

Wasn't it?

Beside me, Reena shivered. "You think the driver waited two hours to kill us?"

Dev's eyebrows met in a threatening scowl that darkened his features. The skin around his mouth and eyes tightened. "The only person who'd have any reason to try to kill my sister is the person who murdered Claudio Fabrizi."

Bryce met Dev's eyes. "Or someone who wants revenge for your sister killing Fabrizi."

I gasped. "I didn't kill Claudio."

"My sister's not a murderer." Dev's words were thick with anger and outrage.

"That's the stupidest thing I've ever heard." Reena's response drowned out Dev's. "It makes more sense that the killer would try to shoot Lynds because her investigation's getting too close to them."

Bryce stiffened. "Her what?" He turned to me. "Are you interfering with a police investigation?"

"What investigation?" Dev interrupted, drawing Bryce's attention back to him. "You're focused on my sister and trying to force the evidence to fit her."

Reena settled her hands on her slim hips covered in the multicolored material of her skirt. "Someone tried to kill my cousin—and me!—tonight. It was clearly the killer. What're you going to do about it?"

Bryce pinned me with a look. "If you're investigating Fabrizi's murder, stop." He turned to Dev. "We're not forcing anything. Fabrizi was stabbed. Someone shot at your sister and cousin. Doesn't it seem likely two different weapons, two different people?"

"No, it doesn't. Not to me." I answered for my brother, forcing my numb lips to form words. "Someone's working very hard to frame me."

Bryce expelled a short, sharp breath. "And why would the killer frame you only to try to kill you later? They'd need you alive to take the fall."

I started shaking my head even before he finished speaking. "Because they don't expect the NYPD to put much effort into the homicide investigation of a Black woman who'd been suspected of murder."

Bryce started to respond but appeared to change his mind. "The bullets landed in the opposite direction from where you were standing. No one tried to kill you tonight. They only wanted it to seem that way."

I gave him a level look as fear shifted toward anger. Tonight wasn't about avenging Claudio's death. It wasn't about killing me. It was about intimidation. Having someone mistake my shyness for weakness made me mad.

No one was going to scare me into silence.

* * *

The sweet scents of cocoa, cinnamon, vanilla, and nutmeg drew Reena, Dev, and me into my family's kitchen. It was just after midnight Saturday. Dev had had to drive a couple of blocks before he'd found a spot to park his car on the street. The parking situation in Brooklyn's residential neighborhoods was cray.

Dev carried an overnight bag/gym bag into my parents' house. It wasn't surprising he'd planned to spend the night. It would take a while for my family to feel at ease again after this attempt on our lives.

In the kitchen, we found Granny at the stove and my parents seated together at the table.

Granny spoke without turning around. She was boiling the cocoa balls and water in a midsized saucepan. She added a can of condensed milk. "I thought we could all use some cocoa—the good stuff—to help us get at least a few hours of sleep."

She liked to use the cocoa balls friends and relatives sent fresh from Grenada rather than the prepackaged ones she could find in the local stores.

As we waited for Granny to finish making the cocoa, Reena, Dev, and I filled everyone in on what happened at the scene, what we learned, and our impressions of how Bryce and the police were handling the case. No one seemed impressed.

"They thought someone was trying to shoot Lynds for revenge." Granny kissed her teeth. "Foolishness."

Daddy grunted his agreement. "If someone's trying to harm you, the only way to put a stop to it is to find the person responsible. If the police aren't going to do it, we're going to have to do it ourselves."

Mommy rubbed her arms as though trying to get warm.

"I don't like this. I don't like putting my family in danger, but your father's right. We have to protect ourselves."

I lifted one hand, palm out, as I leaned against the counter beside Dev. Steam from the mug of cocoa Granny gave me drifted up from my other hand to soothe me. "I won't give up my inquiry, but I'm not going to put you all in danger, either. No, I'm continuing this on my own."

Five very passionate, very angry voices rose to challenge me.

"No, you are not." Daddy looked at me as though I'd lost my mind.

"It's too dangerous," Mommy fretted.

"We're going to help, so accept it." Dev crossed his arms.

"Are you nuts?" Reena's voice could've shattered glass.

"Foolishness," Granny added with another kiss of her teeth.

I faced their stubborn expressions. "Reena was almost killed because she was helping me. I can't risk that happening ever again."

Reena blew an angry breath. "Was I scared? Heck, yeah. Thank God you were with me. When I heard those shots, I froze. I never want to experience anything like that ever again, but I sure don't want you to go through anything like that alone."

Why couldn't I make them understand? My hands tightened around the mug of hot cocoa. Its warmth seeped into my palms. "Your safety is too important to me. I won't put you in danger."

Daddy leaned into the table, holding my eyes. "And we won't let you face danger alone."

My breath caught in my throat. I stared into my mug. "I'd never forgive myself if anything happened to you."

Dev put his hand on my shoulder. "If anything happened, it wouldn't be your fault. The murderer would be responsible."

I shook my head. Everything they were saying made sense. I knew I couldn't do this on my own. I knew this wasn't a danger of my own making. But I was more afraid for them than I could ever be for myself. "I can't let you help me."

"We are family." Granny straightened on her chair. Her stern expression pinned me in place. "We are family."

The wealth of meaning behind those three words defeated me. "Yes, ma'am."

CHAPTER 30

"Doesn't my getting up at four a.m. on a *Saturday* prove how important this investigation is to me?" Reena spoke as she drove us to Claudio's bakery late Saturday morning.

She continuously scanned the late-morning traffic. It looked a lot like the traffic I'd navigated as a pedestrian on my way to the gym minutes before five this morning.

"You woke up at four to tell me to have a good workout. Then you rolled over and went back to sleep." I wasn't going to let her rewrite history. I was the one still shaking off fatigue after getting only three hours of sleep, but she was the one complaining.

"If I'm driving you to Claudio's, how are you getting home tonight? Dev's back at work." Reena inched past a stop sign, making sure the intersection was safe.

I shrugged. "It's just a few blocks from the bakery to my house. I've been walking it all week."

Reena shot a quick look at me as she guided her car across the intersection. "Um, hello? Someone tried to *kill* you last night."

"In a commercial area. The shop's off a residential neighborhood. My neighborhood. I must've walked home along those streets long after dark a million times. I'll be fine."

Reena tsked, a sound close to but not exactly like Granny's *strups*. "Just be careful. And don't leave too late."

"I promise."

She turned onto the street where Claudio's Baked Goods was located and slowed to search for a parking spot. "What makes you think Enzo's going to be at his father's shop? I thought he hated that place?"

"Since it's Saturday, we have a better chance of finding him there than in his office." I scanned the opposite side of the street, helping Reena find space for her car. "Besides, he'll have to spend some time in the shop if he wants to get it ready to sell."

Reena maneuvered her compact red hatchback into a parking space so small it looked like it was meant for a skateboard. "Now what're we supposed to be asking Enzo about again?"

"I need to find a way to ask him about his gambling." I climbed out of her car and circled it to join her on the sidewalk.

"Shouldn't we have come up with a plan before coming here?" Reena fell into step beside me.

"I think I work best under pressure. Something will come to me." I shrugged. "Besides, I'm more interested in his reaction when he sees you and I are still alive and looking into Claudio's murder."

I stopped when I realized Reena was no longer with me. Looking over my shoulder, I found her frozen to the sidewalk two strides behind me. Her eyes tracked me until I returned to her side.

"You think Enzo's the one who tried to kill us?" Her words were a harsh whisper.

She planted her fists on the hips of her raspberry skinny pants. I glanced at my relaxed-fit tan khakis, part of my Spice Isle Bakery uniform. My cousin always looked stylish, even in casual clothes.

I spread my arms. "He's the one with the most to gain from Claudio's death."

Reena's eyes grew even wider. "Then why are we walking into his bakery?"

I hooked my arm with hers and continued up the block. "Come on, Reena. You've always been the brave one. I really need you with me now."

She closed her eyes and expelled a heavy breath. "All right. I'm with you."

Claudio's bakery was even emptier than it had been the first day it had reopened. But again, I reminded myself our customer traffic slowed at ten o'clock. That's the reason this was the most convenient time for me to leave the store in Granny's capable hands while I questioned Enzo.

We found him behind the counter. He was opening cupboards and drawers as though he was looking for something or doing an inventory of the store's supplies. Was he planning to stock up or preparing for a sale? More than likely, it was the latter. He'd made it clear he didn't want anything to do with the shop.

The bell chimed as I pushed open the door. "Good morning, Enzo."

He looked up from behind the counter. "What're you two doing here?"

His expression was shuttered as though he didn't want me to read his reaction. Was he surprised to see Reena and me up and around?

"Someone tried to kill us last night." I sensed Reena stiffen with shock beside me. I'd startled myself. I wasn't normally so direct. But then, no one had ever tried to kill me before. Unusual times forced unusual actions.

"There seems to be a lot of that going around." He sent a brief look toward his kitchen before meeting my eyes. His response was taut with controlled grief and anger. Very believable.

"I think the person—or people—targeted us because we're asking questions about your father's murder." I moved closer to the counter.

He raised his eyebrows. "Then stop asking them. Problem solved."

Reena's lips parted in surprise. "Don't you want justice for your father? I know if it was me, I'd be working day and night, night and day to find my father's killer."

Enzo's eyebrows lowered. "You don't know anything about my father or my relationship with him."

"But we want to." I jumped at the opening he gave us.

He turned his glower on me. "And what? You expect me to just spill my personal business and what have you?" He pointed at us. "You're not cops."

Marisol stepped out of the kitchen. "Enzo's right. Let the police find Claudio's killer."

I looked from her to Enzo, then Reena. My cousin looked as stunned as I felt. What was going on?

"Marisol?" I frowned. "What're you doing here?"

"Enzo and I were discussing business, specifically the tenant association. I was waiting for him in the kitchen." She waved a dismissive hand to encompass Reena, Enzo, and me as she crossed to the bakery's front door. "But this is taking too long. I have to get back to work. Leave Claudio's case to the police, Lyndsay. Someone's already tried to kill you once. Who's to say they won't try again?"

I watched Marisol walk through the shop's entrance, then turned back to Reena. Was Marisol's parting comment a threat?

"You tired, love?" Granny walked into the store's office Saturday afternoon. I loved breathing in the aromas of the spices, sweets, and sauces from the baking and cooking.

Mommy and Daddy followed her in. Their eyes were dark with concern as they searched my features.

The lunch rush was over. I was overwhelmed with gratitude for the community's support of my family's bakery. But it was a lot to keep up with especially after a late-night drive-by and three hours of sleep. The four of us had developed an efficient process for providing fresh, delicious, hot meals promptly to our customers.

Thank goodness for Granny's help. Despite her retirement, she'd invested not just her money but her time to help make sure my dream of opening a bakery came true.

Looking up from the computer screen, I offered them a smile. "A little, but Granny, your dress has given me a boost of energy."

I wasn't lying. There was a lot of drama in her cap-sleeved, chiffon dress. The material swirled with ocean blues and seafoam whites. Its full skirt swayed around her ankles. The V neckline showcased her pink-quartz-and-white-gold necklace with matching earrings. She struck a pose, drawing chuckles from all of us.

"Very little sleep with a lot on your mind." She took the seat on the other side of the desk. "We've been thinking about the talk you and Reena had with Enzo and Marisol this morning."

Reena and I had given a summary report to Granny, Mommy, and Daddy after returning from Claudio's bakery. They were as surprised as we'd been that Marisol had been meeting with Enzo. She'd said they'd been discussing the tenant association. Was that all they'd been talking about?

"We think there are even more people we should be questioning as suspects in Claudio's murder." Mommy leaned against the file cabinet that stood on the opposite wall. "We know that would be extra work, but we're willing to help."

The horror of that imagery—my parents "questioning" murder suspects—would keep me up again tonight.

"Why do you think that?" I studied each of them closely, trying to read their minds. I couldn't get anything past a collective wall of concern. I hated being the cause of it.

"You'd told us Claudio had made a lot of people angry with him over his business practices." Daddy's voice was tight with anger. "If the police won't check into them, we should."

My thoughts bobbed like a boat tossed at sea. I couldn't have my parents and grandmother on this case, not after someone had shot at Reena and me. How do I talk them out of this without seeming like a hypocrite? "I agree with your point, but I keep getting hung up on my bracelet. The killer—or killers—placed it at the scene to frame me. We have to concentrate only on those guests who were here the morning of our Saturday soft launch and who'd been close enough to notice me taking off my bracelet. That's why Marisol Beauvais makes so much sense as a suspect. She was here Saturday, close enough in the line to see me taking off my bracelet, and she's a tenant."

I rubbed my bare right wrist. My heart was broken that

the police were keeping it with their crime scene evidence. The sooner the killer was identified and convicted, the sooner I'd get it back.

Daddy waved a hand. "The shop was packed, but a lot of them were friends and neighbors who don't have any dealings with Claudio's business."

Memories of my conversations with Jenna and the news I'd found about her mother came to mind. "Maybe their motivation wasn't *their* dealings with Claudio. Maybe they were motivated by something he'd done to a loved one."

"That's a good point." Mommy nodded; her eyes were soft with affection. "You know, Lynds, I'm very proud of you."

I shook my head in confusion. "Why? Because of my stupid argument with Claudio, I've been labeled a person of interest in his murder. I've brought a cloud over our family and jeopardized our business."

Daddy scoffed. "Claudio came in here looking to start an argument. You told him to leave. That the police consider you a person of anything in his murder is foolishness."

Granny crossed her arms over her chest. "Your father's right. And I'm proud of you, too."

Mommy glanced at Daddy over the top of the file cabinet. They were standing on either side of it. "You've been doing an excellent job handling this crisis and keeping the bakery moving forward."

"You've been calm, logical, and assertive under pressure," Daddy added.

Granny lowered her hands to the arms of the chair. "And best of all, your baking skills have vastly improved."

Mommy and Daddy laughed.

"Maybe that's all I needed, to increase my stress to better focus on my baking." My eyes stung. I lowered my gaze to the cluttered surface of the desk, blinking rapidly to hold back tears. "Thank you. I appreciate your saying that. I know at first, you didn't agree with the idea of my trying to clear my name." Or open the bakery.

Granny interrupted. "I didn't have a problem with it."

Mommy frowned at the back of her mother's head. "That's enough, Mommy."

I continued. "But I felt I had to do something. I couldn't sit and wait for the police to gather more trumped-up evidence against me. I appreciate your help and support."

"That's what families are for." Daddy straightened from the wall. "We'd better get back to work. The evening crowd will be coming in soon."

Granny watched them leave before turning to me. "It's not the stress that's helped you become a better baker, you know. You've gained confidence, Lynds. I see it in the way you're carrying yourself. I hear it in the way you speak. Very assertive. All along, your lack of confidence has been the problem with your baking. Now you've got it, girl."

"Thanks, Granny." I stood with her. "It's amazing how much courage you can find when you're facing murder charges. And how much more you have when you lean on family."

CHAPTER 31

"Finally, home to bed." Looking around the bakery Saturday night, I said the words out loud like a pep talk to hold off my fatigue. After setting the security alarm, I locked up the store and turned toward home.

Parish Avenue was ablaze with lights from the lamps that lined the block. Store signs washed the street in a rainbow of colors: blue, purple, orange, red, and gold. Soca music rolled and bounced up the sidewalk, though not with as much bass as it had played in the mornings. The scents of fried fish and curried beef lingered on the cool night air. I could almost taste the beef patties. I dodged racing teenagers, weaved through strolling seniors, and slipped past meandering couples.

When I rounded the corner of Parish Avenue and turned onto Samuel Avenue, the music faded. The lights dimmed and the lingering aromas disappeared. It was like walking through a curtain into a different world. My home was only three blocks away. Here the streetlamps were much more muted. Strong but aging maple trees rose in defiance of the narrow concrete sidewalks. Buds dotted the branches way above my head. In my mind's eye, I could see them growing and unfurling into leaves.

There was something comforting in the centuries-old brick family homes that stood almost shoulder to shoulder. The scattering of windows lit from inside gave their facades gap-toothed grins. I'd gotten to know these homes well over the decades. Each one had a personality and a story to share.

Across the street, the owners of the house in the middle of the block had painted their formerly redbrick home a startling shade of yellow. It had taken their neighbors months to stop grumbling about them for creating the eyesore.

I was strides away from the house with the always-alert guard dog. During the day, locals knew to move closer to the curb once the silver metal fence came into sight or risk having raucous barking scare years from their lives. Thankfully, the dog's humans brought her inside around dinnertime.

The narrow brown brick house toward the bottom of the block was home to three generations of family members, just like ours. A U.S. flag and a Bajan flag flew from their porch's overhang.

The hairs on the back of my neck tingled. It was the same sensation I'd been having for the past few days. I looked around. I was the only pedestrian on the sidewalk, but a dark mid-sized four-door sedan had entered the street. The driver who'd shot at Reena and me last night had been in a dark sedan, too.

Fear built a case of ice around my spine and settled in my heart. I faced forward and lengthened my strides. My muscles were stiff, my movements jerky. In all of Brooklyn, there must be hundreds of dark mid-sized four-door sedans.

There were several of them parked on both sides of this street alone.

The car drove so slowly. Was the driver looking for an address—or following me?

"Good night!" A singsong greeting caught me on the edge of panic.

I turned toward the chorus of voices and saw a group of children seated together on their porch. I was alone, but I wasn't on my own. Other people were nearby. A little of my fear and tension eased. Just a little.

"Good night!" I called back with a smile and a wave.

The car drove past at normal speed for a residential area. My knees went weak. I almost stumbled with relief. Perhaps this wasn't the car from last night. As I glanced at its license plate, my throat went dry. The car itself was clean, but mud masked the plate. I couldn't read any of its identifying characters. Wasn't it illegal to obstruct a license plate's visibility? What was going on?

I pulled my cell phone from my pants pocket. I needed help. But who should I call? Not my parents or grandmother. If I was being followed, I didn't want to put them in danger. The memory of last night's shooting was still frighteningly fresh in my mind. I also didn't want to lead the stalker to my home and expose my family to them. I'd rather lead them to the police. If I was going to face Bryce and Stan again, I wanted my defense attorney with me. Let them see my family and I were taking this situation seriously and it was time they did the same.

Quickening my steps, I launched my contacts list and tapped Alfonso's number. He answered on the third ring.

"It's Lyndsay Murray. I need your help."

* * *

I stood in front of the cooler in the back of the all-night bodega a block from my home. It seemed like a safe place to
wait for Alfonso late Saturday night. I stood away from the
door and windows, which meant a stalker couldn't see me.
It also meant I couldn't see them.

But the bodega's clerk could see me clearly. His eyes had
been scalding the back of my neck since I'd entered the shop.
I checked my cell phone again. How much longer would Alfonso be?

I made a second tour of the tiny store to give myself more
time.

"You gonna buy something or not?" The testy shopkeep-
er's voice struggled with a heavy Brooklyn accent. A worn
and tattered red jersey set off the middle-aged man's florid
features. His graying hair was thinning down the middle.

I'd been coming to his store several times a week since
the day it had opened more than ten years ago. Still he acted
like he didn't know me and, therefore, couldn't trust me. So
annoying.

"You have so many tempting things here." *Alfonso, where
are you?*

Untidy coolers of sodas, juices, flavored waters, and alcohol ringed the bodega. Dusty gray metal shelves full of overpriced chocolates, chips, and cookies stood in rows down
the center of the stained dark wood flooring. Messy cases of
gum and hard and soft candies framed the cash register.

"Well, I ain't got all night." His exasperation escalated.

"But . . . aren't you an all-night store?" I always felt sticky
when I left. The shop smelled like dirty sanitizing liquid.

"You aren't my only customer."

I glanced over my shoulder, surveying the surroundings.
"I'm literally the only customer you have right now."

A low grumbling noise seemed to come from his throat. I took that as my cue to leave. Swallowing a sigh, I dug my wallet from my burnt umber purse. Now what do I do? Where should I go?

"Can I get that for you?" Alfonso materialized beside me. His features were tight with concern.

A smile of relief curved my lips. "No, thank you. I've got it."

Ignoring me, he pulled several bills from his wallet. He gave them to the grouchy clerk, collected his change and the bottle of diet soda. With his hand on the small of my back, he guided me from the bodega to his car. "Sorry I took so long. I had to change clothes."

I took the soda from him and gave his black lightweight sweater and jeans a quick look. "Please don't apologize. I appreciate your coming to my rescue."

He held the door as I settled into the passenger seat of his compact pale silver hatchback. He circled the hood, then climbed in behind the wheel.

"Are you OK?" He scanned my features through the shadows in his car.

"I'm fine."

"You're sure?"

"I promise."

With a faint sigh, he relaxed back onto his seat. "Do you see the car?"

Feeling bolder now that I wasn't alone, I looked around, checking up and down the street, and squinting into the deeper shadows.

"No-o-o." I let the single syllable drag out on a sigh of relief.

"OK." Alfonso craned his neck as he also checked both sides of the street. "You said you thought you've seen this car before?"

I shifted to face him. "Last night, as Reena and I were leaving a soca club, someone in a dark car shot at us."

"Dev told me. I'm glad neither of you are hurt." He hesitated. "Is Reena OK?"

"She was badly shaken last night, but she'll be fine."

"And you think the car you saw tonight was the same one?" He looked around the street again. "They're probably hundreds of dark four-door sedans in Brooklyn."

"True, but this one seemed suspicious. The body of the car was clean, but its license plate was covered in mud as though the driver wanted to obstruct their identity."

The dim light of the streetlamp feet from the car revealed his pensive frown. "What made you think the car was trailing you?"

"Because it was driving so slowly as though it was keeping pace with me for half a block." A shiver of unease rolled down my spine just thinking about it.

"Could you see anything about the driver? Was it a man or a woman?"

"I couldn't tell." Frustration settled in my gut. "But if it was the same car, then someone's definitely out to get me."

Alfonso was silent for several long moments as he stared through his windshield. I felt my tension rising, or was it his? I kept watch for the dark sedan.

He broke his silence, maintaining his attention on our surroundings. "Dev thinks Claudio's killer could be stalking you. We have to go to the precinct and report this to the detectives. I'll call them."

As he pulled out his cell phone, I got mine. "And I'll call my family."

They needed to know what happened and that I'd be delayed coming home. I wasn't looking forward to the call, though. I'd caused them enough worry.

CHAPTER 32

"So you think this was the same car that shot at you last night?" Bryce took a neutral tone from his seat across from me at the gray metal table Saturday night.

He and Stan had returned to the police precinct to meet with us after receiving Alfonso's call. Both were dressed in much more casual clothes. Stan wore an olive lightweight sweater. Bryce's black collared jersey displayed the Brooklyn Nets logo below the left shoulder. He looked much more approachable in these clothes, more like the kid I'd gone to school with. The high school heartthrob with the kind eyes. Too bad he'd grown into NYPD's Most Unwanted.

Minutes ago, he and Stan had led Alfonso and me into one of the interrogation rooms. I felt some kind of way about that. There were two perfectly good visitor's chairs beside their desks. So why was I here, being questioned as though I'd committed a crime when I'd come to report one? This whole situation was putting me in a mood. Thankfully, I wasn't here alone.

My cell phone vibrated. Granny had sent another text: *What's happening now?*

No, I most definitely wasn't alone.

I responded: *Alfonso and I are still talking with the detectives.*

Although looking at Alfonso, I felt a brush of unease. Either he wasn't paying attention or he had one of the best poker faces in East Flatbush.

I returned my attention to Bryce, my *ex*-crush. If he could believe I was capable of plotting to kill someone and staging last night's shooting to remove myself from suspicion, then odds were he wasn't The One.

"I said it *could've* been the same car." I shifted my attention to Stan. "I didn't get a clear look at it either time. But I had the impression of a dark blue, gray, or black midsized four-door sedan. I was suspicious of it because the license plate was covered with mud, but the rest of the car was clean. As you know, it's against the law to obstruct a license plate."

Beside me, Alfonso broke his silence. Finally. "That makes this a deliberate attempt by whoever was driving the car to prevent witnesses from identifying them."

What he said.

Neither detective seemed impressed.

I stabbed a finger toward the blank notepads on the table in front of them. "Why aren't you writing any of this down?"

Stan spread his hands. His manner was almost apologetic. "Put yourself in our position, Ms. Murray. A person of interest in a homicide investigation comes to you claiming she's being stalked by a mysterious car with a driver out to get her. It seems a little convenient, like she's trying to distract us from the evidence against her."

Sort of like his fake friendliness was meant to distract me? His routine was wearing thin.

"You think I'm making this up?" I narrowed my eyes, bouncing a look from him to Bryce and back.

Outrage burned me from the inside. My thoughts were jumbled from anger and indignation. I was yanked decades into the past. It was just like school all over again. Classmates taunting and bullying me. I'd complain to the teachers, but because they didn't see it happening, they accused me of making it up.

A large, warm hand squeezed my forearm as it rested on the table. It was Alfonso, rescuing me from memories and anchoring me in the present.

His voice was hard. "Ms. Murray isn't making this up, Detectives. Someone followed her in their car tonight. Someone—possibly the same person—shot at her and her cousin last night. You found the bullets."

Bryce lifted his eyes from Alfonso's hand on my arm and cocked his head. "They were found in the opposite direction from which Lyndsay and her cousin claimed they were walking."

Oh, brother. "I didn't stage that shooting and I'm not lying about that car. The same person who's behind both of these incidents is probably the person trying to frame me for Claudio's murder, and you're letting them get away with it."

Bryce's eyes again dipped toward Alfonso's hand on my arm before meeting mine. "We don't have any proof that someone's trying to kill you."

Impatience made me want to jump out of my skin. I took a deep breath to ease my temper. Bad move. The flood of body odor and burned coffee almost made me gag. Did they ever air out this room? "What about the bullets?"

Bryce shrugged. "They were aimed away from you. You and your cousin weren't harmed."

I could argue that point. Considering the mind-numbing fear that still gripped me almost twenty-four hours later, I'd say Reena and I had been harmed. We'd probably never recover from that near-death experience, but this Idris-Elba-as-Luther wannabee didn't think we'd been harmed.

My phone vibrated again. This time it was Mommy: *What's going on?*

Still with detectives.

Alfonso let his hand fall away from my arm. "Detectives, the fact remains that bullets were recovered at the scene. Neither Ms. Murray nor her cousin own a gun. Now whether those bullets had been found at my client's feet, across the street, or up someone's nose doesn't matter. Shots were fired while my client and her cousin were the only pedestrians at the scene."

I studied Alfonso with new eyes. This tough-guy side of him impressed me. I finally saw the defender who'd impressed my brother. He was calm under attack and quick on his feet. I took back every doubt I'd ever had about him. He could even wear the bow tie to my trial.

Stan shrugged. "Meaning they could've fired those shots themselves."

I caught my breath, but before I could speak, Alfonso did.

He inclined his head. "Good luck trying to argue that about two people who have no experience with guns."

Stan's gaze wavered under Alfonso's point.

"Your lawyer talks a good game, but the evidence is stacked against you, Lyndsay." Bryce turned to me, using his right fingers to tick off his points. "Fabrizi's threats against you and your family give you motive. You have access to a serrated knife, which gives you the means. And your bracelet was found at the murder scene, suggesting you were there."

I glared at Bryce seated diagonally across from me. "Then why haven't you charged me?"

Alfonso answered for him. "Because he knows even an average defense attorney would shred his evidence in court. And I am far above average." He stood to leave.

"Detectives, I insist you take these threats against Ms. Murray's life seriously. They cast doubt on her guilt. More importantly, one of the citizens within your jurisdiction's being threatened and she's come to you for help twice. I don't think this is a situation you'd want to ignore."

Stan looked up at him. "What makes you think these two things—her stalker and Fabrizi's murder—are even connected?"

I stood with Alfonso. "Because the only person I could've ticked off enough to want me dead is the killer."

"We've told the detectives to take these threats against you seriously. You need to take them seriously, too." Seated behind the steering wheel of his car, Alfonso hesitated before starting the engine.

We'd just walked out of the precinct late Saturday night. Even in Alfonso's warm and comfortable car, I was shaking as though I'd gotten lost in a blizzard. The past two days had been an escalation of the nightmare that had started almost two weeks ago when the newspapers reported the police had named me as a person of interest in Claudio's murder. Now someone was threatening me and the police thought I was making it up.

"Believe me, I'm taking this seriously." My teeth were chattering. This obvious weakness embarrassed me.

In my peripheral vision, I saw Alfonso give me a quick look before he started the car's engine and turned on the heat.

I looked away, blinking back tears. His kindness after that horrible scene in the police station undid me.

"Then you and Reena need to stop your investigation. It's too dangerous. The two of you could've gotten killed yesterday." He shook himself. "When Dev called this morning and told me what happened, I was so afraid for Reena—and you."

"I understand." I smiled to myself. Another mere mortal caught by Reena's spell. If he thought this investigation was challenging, wait until he tried to win Reena over. Although, if she'd seen him tonight, she would've changed the impression his bow tie had given her.

Alfonso put the car in gear and pulled out of the precinct's parking lot. "Only God knows what could've happened to you tonight. Let me and the detectives handle it."

"The detectives?" I didn't recognize the bark of fake laughter that came from my throat. I turned my head to look at Alfonso's profile. His attention was glued to the traffic. At this time of night, it was lighter than usual, but still heavy enough to require caution. "They're handling it by trying to fit me to the crime. You heard Bryce. They have motive, means, and opportunity."

"Their motive is weak at best. It's little more than a premise." He tapped his horn to stop a driver from pulling out of a parking space just as we drove up. "More importantly, they don't have the most important evidence they'd need to tie you to the scene: your fingerprints."

I knitted my eyebrows. "But they have my bracelet."

My cell phone vibrated. It was Daddy: *Are you still at the precinct?*

On our way home.

"If they'd found your fingerprints at the crime scene, they would've charged you already, which means they don't have your prints on the murder weapon and they certainly don't have them on the bracelet." He swerved to avoid a driver who opened his car door as we pulled beside them. "Whoever took it must have wiped their prints from it, which means they wiped yours, too."

His points made me feel a little better. Just a little. "Alfonso, I agree the investigation's gotten way too dangerous, but I can't leave this to the detectives. They're going to find a way to bring me to trial. I can feel it. Right now, my customers know me. They believe I'm innocent. That could change if I'm put on trial and the detectives twist their evidence to make me look guilty. They'd damage my business and destroy my family."

I was on the verge of a freak-out. Did he feel it, too?

Alfonso shook his head. "Suppose this stalker escalates? Last night and tonight, they seemed to want to scare you. Suppose tomorrow or the next night, they try to do more than that? A trial would exonerate you. I can promise you that. On the other hand, the stalker could kill you."

I felt pinpricks as blood leached from my face. "What about a private investigator? Dev's firm has several on retainer. Do you know of any?"

He was shaking his head again before I finished speaking. "I'm taking your case pro bono. If it wasn't for Dev, I wouldn't have made it into law school, much less have graduated, passed the bar, and gotten this job. He's been there for me every step of the way. He's more than a friend. He's like an older brother."

I warmed with pride. "Yes, he's the best brother."

"He's proud of you, too." Alfonso's smile faded. He slammed on the brake as a young woman stepped into the street in front of us. "But an investigator's another thing altogether. He'd cost real money."

"How much?"

He gave a daily rate that almost caused my budget-conscious West Indian heart to stop. "And that's not including expenses."

Dead. "All right, then I'm on my own." With my family's help or Granny would kill me.

"Lyndsay, it's too dangerous."

I held Alfonso's gaze. "I can't go to trial."

His sigh raised his shoulders and expanded his chest. "Then I'll help you."

"Thank you. And thank you for meeting me tonight. It's so late on a Saturday night and you dropped everything to help me."

His half smile eased the tension that stiffened his features. "You're Dev's sister. I guess that makes you my honorary sister."

I tilted my head. "Does that make Reena your honorary cousin?"

His eyes widened with surprise. "I—"

I laughed at his confusion. "I'm teasing. I'm sorry I underestimated you the first time we met. You were great back there." I jerked my head behind us in the general direction of the police station.

"It's the bow tie." A self-deprecating smile curved his full lips. "People tend to underestimate me because of it. I bet people underestimate you, too. You're a lot tougher than you look."

His comment at first startled me. Then I thought about the

shooter outside the club. The car stalking me on the street. The detectives who seemed determined to fit me for an orange jumpsuit. Maybe I was tougher than even I thought. Heaven knows I needed to be.

CHAPTER 33

"All you must think we're going to run out of food before you get to the counter." Granny laughed at her own joke as she stood back to let in our guests. She wasn't wrong, though. The bakery's entrance was packed with people, squeezing through the doorway to get into the customer order line late Sunday morning. Tanya Nevis was first in line, accompanied by her new gentleman friend, Benny Parsons.

"Good morning, Ms. Nevis. Mr. Parsons." I offered her and Benny a professional yet warm greeting. "What can I get for you today?"

She graced Dev and me with her cherubic smile as she worked to pull something from her oversized mauve hand-bag. "Everybody's nervous. Spice Isle's closed Mondays and Tuesdays. We want to make sure we have enough sweets to get us to Wednesday. Have you seen today's news?"

She offered me today's copy of the *Brooklyn Daily Beacon*. Mine was untouched in the kitchen. I'd planned to read it after the morning rush. She'd folded it open to one of the inside pages.

The headline read: "Baker's Killer Confesses, Commits

Suicide." Stunned, I skimmed the brief story. Dev read over my shoulder. Granny joined us behind the counter. According to the article, written under José's byline, Jenna Frost had murdered Claudio Fabrizi as revenge for swindling her deceased mother out of hundreds of thousands of dollars. In her typed confession, she admitted to framing me. Jenna was found dead of an apparent overdose late Saturday night. A call from a neighbor had alerted police.

Dev turned to the pass-through window behind the counter and called into the kitchen, "Mom. Dad. Come out here, please. We have news."

"Oh, my goodness. Suicide." Granny's words came on a sigh. She made the sign of the cross, touching the fingers of her right hand to her forehead, chest, and left and right shoulders. "May God have mercy on her soul, but I'm so glad this is over."

Dazed, I looked up. It seemed as though every other customer was waving their copy of the *Beacon* and grinning.

"You've been cleared," José called from the middle of the line. "Congratulations."

"José." I gestured toward the paper. "When did you find out?"

He flashed a cocky grin. "I got the tip late last night and filed my story just in time to get it into the paper. I was coming to tell you this morning, but your regulars beat me to it. How d'you feel?"

"Always the reporter." I found a smile. "I feel relieved."

The cheers and shouts of congratulations were almost deafening. I laughed, feeling warmed by the support and encouragement of these friends and neighbors.

Daddy stepped out of the kitchen, looking around the shop in confusion. He gave Dev and me a quizzical smile as he held the door open for Mommy to precede him into the main bakery. "What is it?"

Dev offered them the paper. A relieved smile brightened his spare features. "Jenna Frost confessed to killing Claudio."

"The blogger who gave us the great review?" Mommy took the newspaper from Dev. "She seemed so nice. Oh, oh. She killed herself?" My parents made the sign of the cross.

I was having trouble processing this turn of events. Jenna had typed a note confessing to the murder, then took a fatal dose of pills? I didn't know her well, but that didn't seem right.

Turning back to the line, I shared a smile with Tanya and Benny, who both looked pleased to have been the ones to reveal the good news. "Thank you so much for letting me know. You've put my mind and soul at ease."

Tanya jabbed a finger at me. "When the investigation was on, those detectives never left this place. Now that you've been cleared, where are they?" She gave a grunt of disdain before placing her order.

The older woman raised a good point. Was Bryce's attention solely due to the case? Now that it was over, would I ever see him again? Or would I have to go back to cyberstalking him?

Straightening my shoulders, I put on a happy face to get through the morning rush. I lost count of the number of people who congratulated me and assured me they'd never had a moment's doubt of my innocence. But part of me feared I was missing an important piece of this puzzle. The investigation had been filled with confrontations and danger. For it to end with a suicide and typed confession seemed almost too convenient.

And I couldn't forget one of the last things Jenna had said to me. *If I'd killed Claudio Fabrizi, I'd be shouting it from the rooftop.*

Then why commit suicide, Jenna?

CHAPTER 34

"I'm confused, Lynds. Jenna confessed to killing Claudio. Why don't you believe it?" Mommy approached me before leaving the bakery late Sunday afternoon. This was the first time we were able to return to our conversation about the investigation. We'd been interrupted earlier by the lunch rush.

She continued. "Suicide is a sad thing. You never want someone to take their life, but you don't have to worry about going to trial anymore. Doesn't that make you feel better?"

"No, Mommy, it doesn't." I wrapped my arms around my waist. "I'm not convinced Jenna was the killer."

"What?" Daddy moved to stand behind Mommy.

"What makes you say that?" Granny turned on her chair to face me.

"Why not?" Dev asked.

My family reacted all at once. I was used to that. It wasn't the reason I felt as though my thoughts were all over the place.

I massaged the back of my neck as I paced the empty dining area. The dine-in customers had all gone home. A few carryout customers were trickling in. We still had three hours before Dev and I closed the bakery.

Even though he'd arrived early today to help Mommy, Daddy, and Granny with the baking, he was adamant about staying with me to close the shop. It was left unspoken, but I knew he was unsettled by Friday night's shooting and Saturday night's stalking. The killer may have been caught, but it would be a while before my family and I recovered from those events.

"Jenna had told me she wanted to thank whoever had killed Claudio." I raised a hand, palm out. "I know that sounds horrible. I don't think she should've said something like that even if it was the way she felt. But that's my point. She didn't make any secret about her feelings toward him. So if she was so open about her dislike of Claudio, why would she try to frame someone else?"

Daddy spread his arms. "She didn't want to go to jail for murder."

Granny hummed her agreement. "She wanted to do the crime, but she didn't want to do the time."

I stopped pacing and turned to them. "If she didn't want to go to jail, why was she so open about her happiness that Claudio was dead? She could've stayed quiet."

Dev shrugged. "Maybe she only told you that because she didn't think you'd tell the police what she said."

I put my hands on my hips. "She was taking a big risk. And in the end, I did put her name on the suspect list Alfonso gave the police."

Doubt clouded Dev's dark eyes. "That's true."

"And another thing." Words came faster as I gained confidence in my train of thought. "Framing me was working. The detectives weren't even trying to look at other suspects. So why would she confess?"

Mommy looked around the room. I sensed her certainty

wavering. "Maybe she was afraid you were getting too close with your investigation."

That made sense except for one thing. "If she was the driver of the car that had been following me, why didn't she kill me? Why did she kill herself?"

Mommy, Daddy, Dev, and Granny all looked at each other.

Granny turned back to me. "Let the detectives worry about that. All I care about is that they're not looking at you."

"For the moment." I started pacing again, lowering my voice. "But suppose I'm right and the detectives realize Jenna didn't commit suicide? They'll be looking at me again. And this time, they may even suspect me of killing Jenna."

The silence in the bakery was thick with dread.

Daddy broke it. "It sounds to me like you're borrowing trouble."

Fear wrapped around me like a blanket. I looked to Mommy, Granny, and Dev before turning back to my father. "I'm not so sure I am."

"I agree with Granny. Let the detectives figure it out." Reena waved a dismissive hand as she walked beside me along Parish Avenue.

We'd met for lunch Monday afternoon at a small indie restaurant not too far from the bakery. She'd read about Jenna's suicide in the *Beacon* and had heard the police's statement that they'd closed the case based on her confession. Our families had discussed the investigation yesterday. There was very little for me to add, just the part about my not believing Jenna had killed Claudio and then committed suicide, leaving behind a typed confession.

"Don't you think it's a little suspicious that she'd try to

frame me for something she claimed she would've shouted from the rooftop?" Leading Reena to the bakery, I pitched my voice above the soca music blaring from the produce market on the corner.

The shop was closed today, but there was still a lot of paperwork and preparation to do for the coming week. Usually, I'd bring the paperwork home, but I was more productive in the office. It kept me away from distractions like Granny's pleas for me to accompany her to a concert in the park or Ziggy Cat's displays of cuteness.

Reena turned to point at me with a crimson-tipped fingernail. "No, because that's what I'd say to get you to think I wasn't the killer. Or I'd say something like that."

I expelled a breath, shaking my head. "You're overthinking this."

"And you're not thinking this through." She strode beside me. How could she walk so effortlessly along broken, uneven sidewalks in four-inch heels? But credit where credit was due: The black stilettos looked great with her crimson ruffle-backed blazer and skinny pearl gray slacks. "You based your entire investigation on the goal of getting the police to look at other suspects. Well, now they have no choice. Someone else confessed."

"But if I'm right and Jenna didn't kill Claudio, then the killer is still out there up to who knows what and I'm back on the suspect list."

"What do you want to do, Lynds?" Her question was breathless with frustration. "Call up Detective I-Know-I'm-Fine and tell him Jenna didn't kill Claudio? Then what's going to happen? They'll be back to looking at you even sooner."

"I agree." I led Reena to the entrance at the back of the

shop. If we entered from the front, people might get the mistaken impression we were open for business. "But knowing how and when Jenna died could tell us whether her death was suicide or suspicious."

She held up one hand. "Lynds, you know I love you. Let the police worry about that."

"This whole situation won't—" I froze feet from the bakery as a young man in dark sweats and a black ski mask slunk out of the bakery's back door.

"What the—" Reena stiffened beside me.

Spotting us, he took off in the opposite direction. I didn't think. I didn't hesitate. I just took off after him. Reena squeaked my name. I didn't respond. My vision was overlaid with a red wash of rage. My feet were powered by anger, outrage, and a thirst for justice. Who was this person and what made him think he could break into my bakery and help himself to my belongings?

My target made a sudden and swift turn down Tailor Avenue. His steps were tentative, making me realize he wasn't familiar with this neighborhood. He kept glancing over his shoulder as though hoping I'd give up. Not a chance.

I ticked off a list in my mind. We deposited all cash in the bank every evening as stated in prominent signs posted in our front store window and on the wall behind the register. We didn't accept checks, and credit card receipts were secured in a large safe bolted to the floor in the office. So what had he been after? Would someone break in on the off chance of finding cash lying around?

I was gaining on him. He sped up each time he turned to check the distance between us. I did the same, grateful for my white cross-trainers. Suddenly, he swerved to scramble over a metal fence leading into someone's driveway. With an extra push, I stretched forward. Grabbing his ski mask, I jerked it backward. My nails scraped his neck and I heard a scream. Not a high-pitched shout. A very feminine scream.

The young man was a young woman.

Gloved hands came up to snatch the knitted item from me. She vaulted over the fence and disappeared. Watching her get away, I was tempted to hop the fence to continue the chase, but I was pretty sure this house had a dog. A territorial one. I was satisfied letting the would-be burglar handle that situation on her own. I turned and jogged back to the bakery.

CHAPTER 35

"What were you thinking?" Reena's question was sharp with fear when I returned to the bakery's rear parking lot. Anger brought her Grenadian accent to the forefront. "Suppose he had a gun or a knife or some such thing? How're you just gonna run after some criminal? You don't have a badge, you know."

I rubbed her upper arm. "I'm fine."

"I'm not." She glowered at me. "Don't ever do that again."

I wasn't going to make promises I wasn't sure I could keep. "Did you go inside?"

"No, I didn't go inside. Suppose someone else was in there?" She raised her cell phone. "But I called Detective I-Know-I'm-Fine."

My eyes stretched wide. "You called Bryce? This isn't a homicide. It's a robbery." And I didn't want to see Bryce Jackson. Ever. Again.

She shrugged. "He said he's on his way. I also called Aunty Della, Uncle Jacob, and Granny. Where're you going?"

I paused with my hand on the doorknob. "I want to see what she did to my bakery."

"You can't tamper with the crime scene."

"Your cousin's right." A deep voice interrupted our conversation and sent shivers down my spine. Or maybe that was fatigue. "Let me take a look first."

I braced myself before turning to Bryce. I hadn't heard his car. He must have parked on the street, then walked through the alleyway. "That was quick. Were you in the neighborhood?"

"You know the station's not that far away." His words reminded me of our chats in the inhospitable police interrogation rooms. Not my fondest memories. He gestured toward the door. "Do you have an alarm system for your bakery?"

"Yes." I folded my arms over my chest. I was still shaking with anger. "And we always set it before leaving. Always."

Even before our launch, my parents, Granny, Dev, and I had gotten into the habit of setting and double-checking the alarm system before leaving the building. We'd invested too much into the business to be careless.

Bryce frowned. "Does anyone outside of your parents, grandmother, and brother have the code?"

I shook my head. "No. I'm certain of that."

Bryce held up a hand, palm out. "All right. Let me take a look around to make sure the store's secure before you come in."

Reena nodded vigorously. "That's smart."

He returned in mere minutes, holding the door open for us. "All clear."

Crossing the threshold before Reena, I looked around, searching for anything out of place. The anteroom and kitchen were still as spotless as Dev and I had left them Sunday night. Before meeting Reena for lunch, I'd turned off the bakery's lights. Again, I didn't want to give anyone the impression we were open today. But had I signaled an invitation for someone to break in?

I strode forward to the office where I'd been working that morning. "That's strange."

"What is?" Bryce asked from too close behind me.

I walked farther into the office. "Nothing. It's just that the chair's turned toward the door. I'd turned it toward the desk when I left."

"Maybe it swung back," Reena suggested.

"It never does." The small hairs on the back of my neck ruffled a warning.

I shoved the chair out of the way and opened the top left-hand drawer. It was the smallest one on that side of the cherrywood desk. I paused, spotting something that should not be there, and that had never been there before: A small, clear brown-tinted pill bottle.

Pointing to it, I stepped back before I could give in to the urge to pick it up. "That does not belong here. I've never seen it before."

Bryce pulled a kerchief from inside his gunmetal gray jacket pocket and used it to pick up the bottle. The label had been torn from its surface. Figures. Now the unfamiliar bottle couldn't provide any information on the medication, pharmacy, or person to whom the prescription had been given.

Bryce studied it. "Who else uses your office?"

"We all use it. It's not *my* office. It's the bakery office." Fortunately, we were all tidy and always trying to outdo each other with our organizational skills. Otherwise, there could be problems.

"Are your parents or grandmother on prescription medication?" Bryce placed the bottle in an evidence bag.

"No, and neither am I." I looked around the room. "Do you think she came here just to plant an empty medicine bottle in my desk? Why would she do that?"

Reena frowned. "Why do you keep saying 'she'? That thief looked like a guy."

"It was definitely a woman." I lifted my right hand. "Before she got away, I grabbed her ski mask. She screamed when my nails scratched her."

Reena pointed at me while addressing Bryce. "You should clean her nails to collect any DNA."

I studied my hand. That was a disgusting thought, but Reena had a point. I squeezed past her and Bryce to survey the rest of the shop. They followed me into the customer service area. I checked the register, the display case, and the cupboard behind the desk while Reena surveyed the waiting and dining areas.

Sighing, I settled my hands on my hips above my sage green slacks. "It doesn't look like she tossed the place, but why would she plant an empty drug bottle in our desk?"

Bryce stopped in front of the counter. "Jenna Frost died of an overdose. The medical examiner is running tests to identify the drug."

Wide-eyed, Reena and I exchanged a look. I drew a breath, catching the scents of the confectioners' sugar and fresh bread that had baked themselves into the walls of our little shop. "You think the killer broke into our bakery and planted that bottle to make you think I'd killed Jenna?"

Reena's voice was thin. Blood drained from her face. "That means the person Lynds chased after was the killer."

I really had to work on my impulse control.

* * *

Maybe Reena was right. Maybe I should leave well enoug alone. But I was too angry to walk away.

And maybe Mommy and Daddy were right. I had to ex ercise greater control over my temper. But someone was try ing to frame me for two murders. Even if I never got a answer to the question of why they'd picked me to take th fall for their crimes, I at least wanted to know who was tar geting me.

I checked my cell phone again as I paced the lobby c Enzo's office. It hadn't even been a minute since his recep tionist had gone to get him. I forced my shoulders to rela and drew a deep breath. The smell of lemon polish, leathe furniture, and aspirational wealth struck me. The waitin, area was small but tastefully designed in dark wood an leather furniture meant to impress. Vibrantly patterned are rugs scattered across the dark hardwood flooring adde much-needed color to the room.

"Mr. Fabrizi will see you now." The thin blonde had re turned on silent feet to make her announcement.

Startled, I spun to face her. "Thank you."

I followed her back to Enzo's office. My black pump echoed her stilettos across the flooring as we advanced dow the short hallway late Tuesday morning. Instead of my usua slacks, jersey, and chef's hat, I'd worn a black pantsuit. Th receptionist's sleeveless pink A-line dress was a splash o brilliant color in the dark hallway.

She knocked on the half-open door. "Mr. Fabrizi, Ms Murray is here." She stepped back with a final smile befor leaving.

Enzo sat back behind his sturdy dark wood desk. "Why are you back, Lyndsay? The police closed the case."

Across the room, Enzo's navy suit coat hung on a black

metal coatrack in a corner behind a glass-and-silver-metal conference table. The red-and-gold-and-blue-patterned area rug beneath the table provided a burst of colorful relief to the dark wood flooring.

Ignoring that he hadn't invited me to sit, I settled onto one of the two silver-metal-and-black-faux-leather chairs in front of his desk. "Do you really think Jenna Frost killed your father, then killed herself?"

His eyebrows rose in a brief expression of surprise. He sat straighter on his chair, pulling it farther under his desk. "I take it you don't."

I considered his attempt at a poker face. It was pretty good. "Are you satisfied with the police's investigation into your father's homicide or not?"

He returned my stare for several silent moments. What was he looking for as his eyes searched mine? I held his gaze, refusing to give away my impatience.

Finally, he responded. "Yes, I am. Is there any reason I shouldn't be?"

I shrugged as casually as I could. "I was just curious."

"Well, since Jenna's confession gets you off the hook, I'd think you'd be satisfied with the police, too. So why're you still asking questions?"

I'd expected that. Enzo had been irritated by my investigation from the beginning. That was one of the reasons he was so high on my list of suspects. "I'm relieved to have my name cleared. I'm just surprised Jenna and your father knew each other. I suppose she must've reviewed your father's bakery at some point. Is that how they met?"

Another hesitation. "I can't answer that." He balanced his forearms on his desk. The sterling silver cuff links on his pearl gray shirt looked expensive. "But the first time I learned of her existence, I heard them arguing in my father bakery. When I asked him about it, he said Jenna'd accuse him of ripping off her mother."

I shook my head in regret and disgust. "You didn't kno he'd done that?"

Enzo's hesitation spoke volumes. How horrible would be to have a father so dishonorable? It made me wonder eve more about Enzo's mother. What had she been like? An what had attracted her to Claudio?

"My father had told me Jenna's mother had invested in hi bakery." His voice was devoid of inflection, leaving me t guess whether he'd believed Claudio or not.

I guessed not. "Did he repay her investment?"

He studied his watch as though trying to subtly end thi unscheduled meeting. "I don't know."

That meant no. How could he? The bakery was losin money.

The thin lines bracketing his mouth deepened. There wa pain in his eyes as though the harm his father had cause Jenna's family hurt him, too.

I crossed my right leg over my left and leaned back again my seat. "Do you think Jenna's belief that your father stol so much money from her mother gave her a motive to kil him?"

"Isn't that what she wrote in her note?"

"Why didn't you tell the police about this argument? Wh didn't you tell me?"

Enzo's features hardened. His voice was even harshe "Would you tell the police your father faked some woma out of her life savings? Would you tell anyone?"

"Are you still playing amateur investigator, Lyndsay? Robin's voice carried from the doorway.

I turned on my seat to look at her. Why hadn't Enzo's receptionist announced her the way she'd announced me? Did the receptionist have a reason to believe Robin and Enzo had the kind of relationship that didn't require an announcement when she visited? How often did she visit?

And how much longer would I feel compelled to question everything I saw and heard? It was exhausting.

Enzo circled his desk to greet her in the doorway. He lowered his head to kiss her cheek.

What was going on there?

Robin's comments about the possibility of rekindling their failed relationship came back to me: *That ship's sailed. I could never trust Enzo again.*

He straightened. "Lyndsay was asking about Jenna Frost."

"I heard." Robin lowered herself onto the chair beside mine and shifted to face me. "Don't you think it's insensitive of you to continually ask Enzo to relive his father's death?"

"I—" My attention dropped to her scarf. It had sagged away from her neck, settling onto her shoulder. The shift bared her throat, revealing three deep scratches on its left side. I lost my breath.

My eyes shot to hers before I caught myself and looked away. Standing, I adjusted my burnt umber purse strap on my shoulder. "You know, you're right." I stepped away from the chair and backed toward the door. "I'm so sorry, Enzo. Thank you for answering my questions. After speaking with you, I'm sure the police have the right person. Thank you. Bye, Robin. Good to see you again."

Spinning on my heels, I strode from the office and out of the building, barely pausing to wave goodbye to the receptionist.

I exited into the office building's rear parking lot and

jumped into my car. Recovering my cell phone from my purse, I got Bryce's voicemail: "I think Robin Jones killed Claudio Fabrizi and Jenna Frost. Please meet me at the bakery as fast as you can."

CHAPTER 36

Bryce, where are you?

I checked my cell phone again as I paced the length of the cooking island in the bakery's kitchen late Tuesday morning. I'd only been waiting a short while, less than twenty minutes. But it felt like two hours. I thought Bryce would've been here by now. I'd already left a second message. *Should I leave a third—*

"I knew the moment you realized I was the one who'd broken into your bakery." Robin's voice came from behind me.

Startled and scared almost out of my mind, I spun to face her. "How do you keep doing that? I know I set the alarm."

The thin smile curving her lips sent a chill rolling down my spine. "I used my cell phone to make a video of you entering the code that day I met with you about your catering bid."

That was last Tuesday. She'd come in that morning to tell me the company that had hired her for their event had passed on my proposal because I was a person of interest in Claudio's murder. The murder she'd committed. I thought she'd been texting when she'd pulled out her phone. I'd been wrong.

She'd been scheming against me since the day we'd met. That ticked me off.

I pressed my damp palms against the sides of my pants and dug deep for courage. My arm brushed against my car keys in my pocket. "Were you also lying when you said you didn't have feelings for Enzo anymore? The two of you seemed very close in his office."

Robin shoved her hands deeper into the pockets of her navy blazer. She'd coupled the outfit with a pale gray skirt and an off-white blouse. "I've wanted to marry Enzo since the first time I'd read about how successful his family's real estate business was. The article's headline had read: 'The Fabrizi Fortune.' It swept me off my feet."

Her words made me nauseous. "So you never had feelings for Enzo. It was always about his money."

She didn't deny what I'd said. "The Fabrizis have more than enough money to keep me happy. And Enzo would make the perfect spouse: rich and easily manipulated."

"But Claudio didn't approve of you."

"No, he didn't." Her tone was ugly. "No matter what I did or said, he refused to believe I loved Enzo and that we should get married."

"And he was right." My voice rose to incredulous octaves. "What family member wants their loved one to marry a gold digger?"

Her face flushed with angry strokes of red. "I'm not a gold digger."

Confused, I drew my eyebrows together. "What would you call someone who'd marry for money?"

Robin drew a gun from her right-hand pocket. This was why one shouldn't challenge a homicidal maniac. It also was the reason I hadn't gone straight home to my family when I'd realized she was the killer. The bakery was about half-way between Enzo's office and my home. I'd chosen to stop at the bakery. I thought I'd be safe once I'd activated our security alarm while I waited for Bryce. I was afraid if I'd gone home, Robin would follow me, bringing a dangerous situation to our doorstep. I didn't want to put my family in jeopardy. I'd been right about Robin following me, but I'd been wrong about being safe with our security alarm. Robin had had the code all along.

Now she was waving a gun around our kitchen. I felt angry, violated, and helpless, just as I'd felt in school when the bullies would tease and taunt me and there was nothing I could do to defend myself against all of them. At least my family was safe.

She covered the scratches on the left side of her neck with her palm as she kept her gun pointed at me. "You didn't need to scratch my neck. You really hurt me."

"Good." I pushed the word through my teeth. My skin burned with anger. She must be crazy. That was the most obvious explanation for her behavior.

"Such a temper." Robin tsked, shaking her head. Her blue eyes glittered with amusement. "You really should work harder to control it. That's what got you into this mess in the first place."

"No, Robin. *You're* what got me into this."

She gave a careless shrug that stoked my anger. "I had to kill Claudio. He was an obstacle to my goal of marrying his son so I could access their money. And I had to frame you. What good would it do to get rid of Claudio if I ended up going to jail?"

Nutty as a fruitcake.

"The truth will out." My parents' words gave me strength. "You're not going to get away with killing three people."

"You don't think so?" She grinned, rubbing the scratches again. I hoped they were infected. "I do. You see, the police were focused on *you*. You were the *only* one looking for other suspects." Her smile faded and her lips tightened at the memory. "You were running all over Brooklyn, trying to find the real killer."

I narrowed my eyes as the memory of being watched on the streets as I met with people about the investigation came back to me. "You followed me."

"And I could tell by the way you started looking at me that you'd added me to your suspects list, even though I tried to get you that catering job."

"Did you really?"

"Well, I said I was going to try, but my event-planning projects dried up after Claudio convinced Enzo to break up with me." Her words were clipped and tight. "The Fabrizi name had opened a lot of doors for me. With Enzo out of the picture, all those doors closed."

"I bet that made you even more anxious to become Mrs. Enzo Fabrizi."

Robin screwed up her face as though she'd just breathed in a bad odor. "I would've made that sacrifice to achieve the lifestyle I wanted."

"It was you outside the club, wasn't it?"

She smiled as though pleased I'd asked. "So you know I'm not afraid to use this gun."

"I also know you can't hit the side of a barn. Or do you expect me to believe you deliberately missed us?" I wanted to push her, but not too far.

"Of course I did." She rolled her eyes. "Besides, I couldn't kill you because you were never alone. You were always surrounded by either family or friends. Like that night you were walking home alone."

"That was you, too." I'd thought as much.

"Yes. I was hoping to get you alone, but those neighbors waved to you from across the street and then you called your friend."

"Why did you kill Jenna?"

"You were getting too close."

I was? I thought I'd been moving in circles. "What made you think that?"

"I could tell by the people you were meeting with and the way you were looking at me. You'd stopped going to Marisol Beauvais's office." Her laugh was dry. "I'd tried really hard to make you suspicious of her. Marisol's even easier to anger than you are."

Every word out of her mouth made her seem even crazier. "You were sloppy with Marisol. You didn't take into consideration that her motive was ancient history. Claudio's theft of her recipe and her threats occurred almost a year ago."

Robin scowled. "She's not over that. How could she be? Claudio stole from her."

"Despite that, everything's worked out for her. She's built a new career and is in line for a great promotion. If you'd done your homework, you'd have realized that."

Robin was shaking her head vigorously as I spoke. "I'm right. She's not over it. And you'd stopped investigating Jenna, too. That really irritated me." She stepped to the side and waved her gun toward the back door. "Enough talking. You ask too many questions. We have places to go."

I gave her a skeptical look. "Like where?"

And why hadn't Bryce called me back? It felt like hours since I'd left those urgent messages for him. Maybe I should've called Dev. But he was at work in midtown, which was more than an hour from East Flatbush.

"Just move," she barked at me.

I was tempted to refuse, but something about the way her eyes gleamed at me told me she wouldn't hesitate to shoot me in the kitchen and let the police figure it out. I didn't want my parents to find my body here.

I hadn't moved this slowly since I was a child on my way to school. Every step I took late Tuesday morning brought me closer to my final expiration date. I couldn't allow that. Holding Robin's eyes, I slid my car key from my pocket and palmed it. My heart was in my throat. My hands were damp and sweaty. *Please, God, don't let me drop these keys.*

Why hadn't Bryce called me back? Was he out somewhere? Had he even gotten my messages? What should I do now?

I walked out of the back door with Robin close beside me. Feeling somewhat braver out in the open, I dug in my heels. I needed to buy time. I needed Bryce to get here. "Tell me why you decided to frame me. You didn't know anything about me, but you chose to put me in the middle of your schemes. Why?"

"That was pathetically easy and it was your own fault." She lowered her gun. "You gave yourself motive by confronting Claudio in front of dozens of witnesses. You told him if he returned to your bakery, his son would have to carry him out. That's a threat."

I still regretted those words. "You went further, though.

You stole my bracelet and bought a serrated bread knife to implicate me."

She shrugged, holding the gun close to her side to mask it from anyone who might happen upon us. "I'd call it hedging my bets."

I gritted my teeth. "What do you plan to do now? Kill me and leave another suicide note like you did to Jenna? Won't it be awkward, having two people commit suicide and confess to the same murder?"

Robin laughed as though I'd made a joke. "It won't be two suicides. It'll be one, yours. You'll confess to killing Jenna and planting the suicide note to frame her for killing Claudio so you could clear your own name. But then the guilt of killing that innocent young woman was too much for you."

I shook my head. "My family would never believe I'd commit suicide, especially since they know I'm innocent."

"Who cares what your family thinks? The police will believe it. They already think you're guilty and that's all that matters."

I folded my arms. "I'm not writing that note."

"I already wrote it for you."

I glanced at the gun at her side, masked by the folds of her skirt, before meeting her eyes again. "You're going to shoot me anyway."

Robin blew a breath. "I know what you're trying to do. You're trying to buy yourself time. Get moving. Move! My car's over there next to yours."

I stepped back an arm's length from her. "I'm not trying to buy myself time. If you're going to shoot me, then shoot me. But then how will you make it look like a suicide?"

"I'm going to—"

I used the cover of her latest tirade to press down hard on my automatic car door lock, initiating the panic siren. The horn blared. Sirens sounded. Headlights and brake lights flashed.

Shocked, Robin's jaw dropped. She spun toward our cars, then turned back to me, wide-eyed. "What have you—"

I landed two quick punches to her face with my right fist, followed by a cross blow with my left, and a cuff to the side of her head with my right. A kick from my left leg knocked the gun from her grip. The pattern followed the familiar routine of my gym workouts.

Jab! Jab! Cross! Hook! Front kick!

Robin collapsed onto the pavement and lay there stunned. I kicked her gun aside.

"Lyndsay!"

"Ms. Murray!"

A chorus of voices shouting my name in its various forms carried down the alleyway before the speakers appeared, Bryce and Stan.

Relief made me weak. I staggered toward Bryce on rubbery legs. He met me halfway. His crushing embrace kept me from crumbling onto the ground. He was speaking. Was he asking me something or telling me something? I couldn't understand a word of it.

"Thank God," I sighed against his shoulder. And then the tears came.

CHAPTER 37

"Is it finally over?" I looked at my family seated in the dining area early Tuesday afternoon.

Granny wrapped me in her arms. She was warm, and smelled like powder and cinnamon. Her bronze cotton blouse was soft beneath my palms as I squeezed her back. "Oh, my poor love. I'm so sorry this happened to you and so glad it's finally over."

We held each other for several long moments, rocking side to side, before Mommy, Daddy, and Dev encircled us for a family hug. Their collective relief was strong and showed in their embrace. Underneath was the same lingering fear and anger I felt.

Separating, we gathered around the two tables we'd pushed together for our family meeting. Dev had brewed ginger tea. The warm, sweet, spicy scent brought comfort. He'd placed a platter of fresh currant rolls to the center of the combined tables.

Mommy and Daddy had come with me when I'd given my statement to Bryce and Stan at the police precinct. They looked as tired as I felt.

"So many times during this investigation, I've been more afraid than I'd ever been before." I looked at my parents. "I you hadn't enrolled me in those kickboxing classes years ago, I wouldn't've been able to defend myself."

Granny squeezed my hand. "But you did defend yourself and you brought a killer to justice."

"Thank you, Granny." I inclined my head, acknowledging her praise. "I had a hard time not telling Bryce and Stan *told you so.*"

Dev took a currant roll from the platter. "And Robin told you she killed Claudio because she wanted to marry Enzo? I hadn't realized she was so unhinged."

"Me, neither." Granny shook her head. "She's obviously a good actress. I doubt Enzo realized it, either."

"Enzo arrived as we were leaving the precinct." I watched the steam rise from my mug, picturing Enzo's shattered expression. He'd been pale and badly shaken. "He was so upset. Something about the blank look in his eyes made me think he's blaming himself for his father's murder."

"He shouldn't." Mommy's elegant features tightened. "Robin killed his father. What I don't understand is why she picked you to frame. You and Claudio had just the one argument."

"It had been a very public argument, and she'd needed someone to frame." I heard the remnants of anger in my voice. "Robin'd heard Enzo and Claudio arguing about the money Claudio had stolen from Jenna's mother. First she tried to use that information to blackmail Claudio, but he wasn't having any of it."

Daddy gestured toward me with a currant roll. "Then she realized she could make it seem as though Jenna killed Claudio because he stole her mother's money."

I continued the explanation. "But then Claudio and I got into it at the bakery and she decided to frame me instead."

Dev's eyes shone with pride. "But you refused to let her get away with it even though more than once we tried to talk you out of getting involved in the case."

I stared at him in surprise. He was proud of me? He was always the one making our family proud: graduating from college with honors, getting accepted by a top law school, making partner at his law firm.

I drank some tea to clear the lump of emotion from my throat. "You were afraid for me. I understand that. *I* was afraid for me." I looked around the table. "But when I needed help, you were all there for me. Thank you."

Granny grunted as she swallowed a bite of her currant roll. "You're welcome. And now maybe we can get a good night's sleep."

Mommy hummed her agreement as she reached for a second currant roll. She turned to me with an impish expression in her eyes. "So what did the detectives say when you solved the case for them?"

"Not a thing. Not even a thank-you." I thought of Bryce's sheepish expression and Stan's clueless act. At least I thought it was an act.

"Really?" Granny shifted her attention from me to her tea. "They'll thank you later."

I shrugged. "I doubt it. Now that the investigation's over, we won't see them again." Why didn't that fact make me happier? Shrugging off the sudden sense of disappointment, I considered my family. They were each eating what I thought was their second currant roll, perhaps Dev's third. "What do you think of the currant rolls?"

Dev nodded. "They're delicious, of course."

Mommy's eyes widened. "Lynds, did you make these?"

I nodded. "This morning before I went to speak with Enzo I left them cooling on the counter."

Daddy grinned. "They're wonderful, darling. Good job."

"No, they're not wonderful." Granny gave me a solemn look. "They're exceptional."

"Congratulations on clearing your name, Lyndsay." Alfonso stepped to the bakery's customer counter early Wednesday morning. He was back to wearing his bow tie. Today's was red, which added a spot of color to his tan suit.

"Thank you, Alfonso. And thank you for helping me and my family."

His smile was modest. "I'm glad I didn't need to represent you."

"So am I."

He flashed a grin, then hesitated. "I was wondering if your cousin's dating anyone? Because, if she's not, I was wondering if I could call her?"

My attention dropped to his plain, bright red bow tie. There were many layers to Alfonso Lester. The man who wore that tie? Reena would chew him up and spit him out. But the one who'd worn the black jeans and jersey when he'd driven me to the precinct the night Robin had followed me could hold his own.

I smiled at him. "My parents are arranging a gathering tonight to celebrate the investigation being over. You know how we do; any excuse for a party, right?"

Granny interrupted us, proving again that she was always listening. "Eh, this isn't an excuse, you know. The fact that my granddaughter isn't being charged with murder is a real cause to celebrate."

I couldn't suppress a shiver. "I know, Granny. You're right." I turned back to Alfonso. "Anyway, come by the bakery after hours tonight. Reena will be there. You can ask her yourself. Her parents will be there, too."

His expression relaxed. An air of excitement enveloped him. "Thank you. I'll see you tonight then."

Perhaps something positive, besides my exoneration, had come out of this horrible experience. Alfonso was a great guy. I had a feeling he and Reena would be good influences for each other.

I turned to greet Joymarie at the counter. It was too bad Dev wasn't here this morning. Or maybe it wasn't, considering how he'd behaved toward her in the past.

"Good morning, Joymarie. Would you like your usual?" Her coconut bread and corailee tea had gone from an impetuous request to her standing order.

"Yes, please." She was glowing. "I heard you telling that man that all you are having a party tonight."

I nodded, turning to wrap the bread and pour the hot tea. "It's a small family gathering with a few friends."

"Dev invited me to it. He texted me this morning." She pulled out her cell phone and showed me the text thread. If she hadn't, I wouldn't have believed her.

It started with a message from Dev sent thirty-five minutes earlier, asking awkwardly whether she was free tonight and, if so, if she was interested in attending the family event with him.

My jaw dropped. I handed back her phone. "This is from Dev?"

"I called to make sure." She dropped the instrument bac
into her purse.

Finally! This was a great day. "Then I'll see you tonight
Smiling, I handed her the order bag and change.

I waited on several more customers. The pace was hec
tic without Dev. Granny had offered to help, but Momm
Daddy, and I were keeping up.

My professional smile of welcome froze as Bryce steppe
up in the line. My heart leaped before I chastised it. I didn
think I'd see him again. Stan was with him. My tone coole
several degrees. "Detectives, good morning. What can I g
for you?"

Stan briefly considered the menu on the wall behind me
"I'd like to try your baked banana pudding, please." H
glanced toward Granny before meeting my eyes again. "An
we'd like to thank you for your help with the case."

Granny harrumphed.

"My help with the case?" I glanced at Granny befor
turning back to the detectives. My confusion cleared. "M
grandmother put you up to this." Her silence was confirma
tion. They had to be told to acknowledge my help? *Oh
brother.* "Well, consider your obligation met."

José peeked out from among the other customers in th
line. He drew attention to himself as he leaned into th
counter, raising his voice above the animated conversation
and soca music. A notepad was in his left hand. In his right
he held a pen. "Detectives, do you have a quote for the pres
about Claudio Fabrizi's murder and Lyndsay Murray's rol
in solving the case?"

Silence crashed into the bakery. All eyes turned to Bryc
and Stan. A movement from my peripheral vision claimed
my attention. Mommy and Daddy had left the kitchen to joi

s. Amused, I returned my attention to Bryce and Stan, wait-
ng to see how they'd get themselves out of this one.

Bryce exchanged a look with his partner, then tipped his
ead toward me. "While the NYPD strongly advises civil-
ans *against* putting themselves in danger by involving them-
elves in criminal cases, we acknowledge Lyndsay Murray's
nvestigation was critical to solving Claudio Fabrizi's homi-
ide. Personally, I'd go so far as to say we wouldn't've been
ble to identify the suspect or obtain a confession without her.
Thank you, Lyndsay."

My face burned with embarrassment. His expression of
raise and gratitude was more than I'd ever imagined. The
ilence lengthened as I struggled for a response.

Granny started a slow clap, shattering the quiet. "Well,
ow, that's a proper statement."

The shop exploded with applause, whistles, and cheers
of support. I waved my hands, hoping to gain their atten-
ion. "Thank you, everyone, but that's enough. Really. That's
enough."

The cheers trickled down.

José once again shouted to be heard. "Lyndsay, do you
ave a comment for us?"

I looked at my parents and grandmother, then shifted my
attention to the friends and soon-to-be-friends gathered in
he customer service area. "Yes, I do, and you can quote me.
Spice Isle Bakery is open for business. I encourage one and
all to stop by for a taste of the Caribbean."

RECEPES

Currant Rolls

2½ tablespoons brown sugar
½ teaspoon ground cinnamon
1 egg
1 tablespoon milk (optional)
1 9¾" × 10½" × ³⁄₁₆" puff pastry sheet, thawed but
   cold to the touch
4 tablespoons butter (melted)
1½ cups dried currants
Parchment paper
Baking tray

Mix together the brown sugar and cinnamon in a medium-sized bowl. Set the bowl aside.

Make an egg wash by mixing together the egg and milk in a small-sized bowl. Set the bowl aside.

Ensure there is a rack positioned in the middle of your oven. Preheat oven to 375 degrees Fahrenheit.

Allow the puff pastry to thaw in the fridge for approximately

four hours, until it's soft enough to work with but still co
to the touch.

On a flour-dusted surface, use a rolling pin to roll the pu
pastry into a rectangular shape about 1/5 of an inch thick.

Brush half of the melted butter over the surface of th
dough.

Sprinkle the currants evenly all the way across the su
face of the dough to the edges.

Following the long side of the rectangle of dough, ro
everything tightly into a log shape. Cut the log into two even
sized pieces. Place both pieces onto a parchment-lined bakin
tray, seam side down to keep the log closed as it bakes.

Brush the egg-and-milk wash over the surface of each o
the two halves of dough.

With a fork, poke a few holes in the surface of each log.

Put the tray on the middle rack. Bake for 25 minutes.

Remove the logs. Brush the remaining melted butter ove
both logs. Place the logs back into the oven for 5 more mir
utes.

Place the logs on a cooling rack for approximately one hou
or until cool. Cut the logs diagonally into serving-size piece
using a serrated knife. Use a gentle motion to cut through th
logs without destroying the pastry.

Coconut Bread

1 teaspoon butter, softened
1¾ cups all-purpose wheat flour
1½ cups brown sugar

1 cup shredded coconut
1 teaspoon baking powder
¾ teaspoon salt
2 eggs
⅓ cup coconut milk
¼ cup water
¼ cup canola oil
1¼ teaspoons coconut extract (optional)
1 teaspoon vanilla extract
½ teaspoon ground cinnamon

Preheat oven to 350 degrees Fahrenheit.

Grease a 9" × 5" loaf pan thoroughly with butter.

Combine the flour, brown sugar, shredded coconut, baking powder, and salt in a large bowl. Mix thoroughly with a spoon. Add the eggs, coconut milk, water, canola oil, coconut extract (if using), vanilla extract, and ground cinnamon. Mix well until the batter is blended.

Pour batter into the greased loaf pan.

Bake in the preheated oven for 1 hour. Leave in the pan to cool for 15 minutes. Then place the loaf on a cooling rack for approximately one hour or until cool.

Don't miss the next
Spice Isle Bakery Mystery
by Olivia Matthews!

A
SPICE ISLE BAKERY
MYSTERY

HARD DOUGH
Homicide

OLIVIA MATTHEWS

Solving this murder
is the yeast she can do.

ON SALE 5/23/23

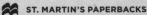